Milo Ryder

AND THE T BAR RANCH

Lowell F. Volk

Milo Ryder and the T Bar Ranch

Copyright © 2023 Lowell F. Volk. All rights reserved. No part of this book may be reproduced or retransmitted in any form or by any means without the written permission of the publisher.

Published by Wheatmark®
2030 East Speedway Boulevard, Suite 106
Tucson, Arizona 85719 USA
www.wheatmark.com

ISBN: 979-8-88747-042-9 (paperback)
ISBN: 979-8-88747-043-6 (ebook)
LCCN: 2023901434

Bulk ordering discounts are available through Wheatmark, Inc. For more information, email orders@wheatmark.com or call 1-888-934-0888.

To my wife, Mary Lou,
and to my fans, who keep asking for more books

Other books by Lowell F. Volk

Milo Ryder US Marshal Series
Purgatoire Valley
Milo Ryder: Return of the Lawman

Luke Taylor and Trevor Lane Series
The Taylors' Civil War
Luke Taylor Westward Bound
Trevor Lane and the Civil War
Trevor Lane and Independence
Luke Taylor and Trevor Lane
A New Beginning

Lukas Yates and the Roses
Trouble in the Mancos Valley
Mystery on Benchmark

CHAPTER 1

Milo Ryder lived in the Purgatoire Valley with his wife, Hannah. Milo had retired as US marshal from New Mexico but became reinstated after Marshal Sieke of Stonewall requested that he be reinstated by the New Mexico US Marshal's headquarters. After being reinstated, Milo tracked down the men who robbed the Stonewall bank and recovered the money with the help of three of his men who worked on the ranch. They recovered the money outside Willow Springs, New Mexico, where Gentry Soyer lived. Milo and Hannah saved Gentry's life after being attacked while taking his new Aberdeen Angus bull home. Gentry offered Milo and his men to stay at his ranch, and in return for saving his life, he gave Milo two of his bulls from his Aberdeen Angus bull.

Hannah, Milo's wife, hired Maria Sanchez to help feed the men on the ranch and help with the house. After Maria lost her family, she lived alone on her father's land. It was there that Hannah first met Maria and asked her to move to the Rocking R Ranch. Before the Stonewall bank robbery, the men who robbed the bank stayed on Maria's land in her cabin. Not wanting to return to the cabin, she decided to sell the ranch and remain at the Ryder ranch.

The Rocking R Ranch foreman was Burton (Burt) Ware, along with six hired hands: Nate Mayfield, Billy Jenkins, Cord Martin, Hick Thompson,

Porter Reeves, and Emmett Dunn. Milo would deputize them as US marshals when Milo needed them to help him go after outlaws.

Milo now had two ranches. Due to a sick wife, the Lazy S Ranch became available, and Milo purchased it. His main ranch was the Rocking R, where he and Hannah lived. The Lazy S was where his friend and former foreman Cody Paxton, also reinstated as a US marshal, lived with his wife, Rosie.

Cody, a retired US marshal and friend of Milo's, moved to Colorado after retiring. After Milo purchased the Lazy S Ranch, Cody moved into the house after taking over the ranch's operation. After becoming the overseer of the Lazy S Ranch, he became involved with Rosie and married her. Rosie was one of the people who stayed and did the cooking and cared for the house. After they were married, Rosie hired Sadie Ruggles to help with the house. After Sadie and her husband's divorce, Sadie's ex-husband tried to kill her, so she went into hiding. Working with Rosie at the Lazy S Ranch gave her comfort and protection.

Cody took over the Lazy S Ranch operation with his foreman, Luke Porter, and hired hands James Small, Sam Jones, Rufus Barnham, and Jose Cortez, who lived on the ranch.

With Maria's help in the house at the Rocking R Ranch, Hannah could spend more time with her horse, Buttercup, that she had raised from a colt. In addition, she could go with Milo when he left on ranch business. Hannah took to Maria like she was her daughter, since she'd had no children of her own. So when Maria decided to sell her property, she helped Maria work with Clyde Anderson to sell her property like a mother would help her child.

While Hannah and Milo were with Maria closing the sale of her property, Clyde Anderson told Milo about a ranch for sale with four sections of land called the T Bar Ranch. The T Bar Ranch was located west of Stonewall in the San Luis Valley near the Rio Culebra River. He thought Milo might be interested in it. The nearest town to the property was San Luis de la Culebra, established in 1851. Milo decided that he would like to look at it. He would buy it if it turned out to be a good purchase. Research showed that the Old Spanish Trail ran near the area, where he could drive cattle, and there could be a market with the Ute or Comanche Indians.

When Milo asked why the ranch was for sale, Clyde said, "The Tilghman family, who owned the ranch, were killed in a raid believed to be committed by Comanches. Bass, the father, Adaline, his wife, and their four children, Harvey, Ameillia, William, and Nora, were killed at the house. The maid and most of the hands at the ranch had escaped. The bank now owned the property and was to sell it for the money it was owed.

"How many of the hands who worked at the ranch were killed?" asked Milo.

"There are men still several men at the ranch running it for the bank," replied Clyde. "The foreman, Richard Fleming, was not at the ranch when the attack came. He was out with some of the hired hands rounding up cattle. They were preparing to drive them closer to the ranch to brand. When they heard gunfire, they tried to get back to help the family, but the Indians cut them off."

"Do you know what they are asking for the ranch?" asked Milo.

"No, you will have to talk to Seth Brewer at the San Luis de la Culebra bank," said Clyde. "If you decide that you want to make an offer, I can do it for you and process the paperwork."

"I will let you know what I decide," said Milo.

Two weeks after Maria had sold her property, Milo prepared to look at the T Bar Ranch. Calling Burt into the house, he said, "In two days, I would like to go look at that property Clyde told me about. I want Nate to go with me. If you want to go to El More, you can take some time to see Shellie while we are gone. I will need you to go there with me if I decide to buy it."

"Do you want me to get Nate?" asked Burt.

"Have him come in," said Milo.

"I can have Billy watch the ranch while I am gone, if that is all right with you," said Burt.

"Billy will do a good job here while you and I are gone. He can always call Cody for help if needed," said Milo.

Burt left and found Nate and told him that Milo wanted to talk to him. When Nate got to Milo's office, he asked, "You wanted to see me?"

"Yes, I got a lead on some property for sale in San Luis de la Culebra, and I want you to go there with me," said Milo.

"How long do you think it will take us to look over the property?" asked Nate.

"We will have to go into San Luis de la Culebra and talk to Seth Brewer at the bank before looking at the property," said Milo.

"Why the bank?" asked Nate.

"From what Clyde told me, the bank owns the property, as the owner Bass Tilghman and his family were killed in an Indian raid," said Milo. "With no relatives, the bank took over the property by foreclosing on the loan against it. Clyde thinks they are willing to sell it for what the loan is."

"If you buy it, who will you have run it?" asked Nate.

"I don't know," said Milo. "Let's see what it is like and if I decide to purchase it."

Two days later, Milo and Nate rode out to San Luis de la Culebra. They arrived as it was starting to get dark. Finding the San Luis Hotel, they got rooms before stabling their horses. While checking in, Milo noticed the Rocky Café across the street from the hotel was still open.

Leaving the hotel, they took their horses to the livery. There they put up their horses before going to the café.

Entering the Rocky Café, they found only a few people still eating. Taking a table by the window, they ordered their supper. While waiting for their meal, Milo noticed that there weren't many people on the street. When the waitress came with their meal, Milo was saying to Nate, "The town doesn't look like it has a lot of activity at night."

The waitress overheard Milo, and after setting down their meals, she said, "You two are new here. Not too long ago, we were having a lot of trouble with the Indians in the area. Now, most ranchers stay close to home and keep guard."

"What is your name?" asked Milo.

"Nora McNab," said Nora. "May I ask who you are?"

"I am Milo Ryder, and this is Nate Mayfield," said Milo.

"Did you know the Tilghman's?" asked Milo.

"Yeah, they used to come in here," said Nora.

"What kind of people were they?" asked Nate.

"What is your interest in them?" asked Nora.

"We came out to look at their ranch," said Milo. "I heard that it was for sale and that the family had died."

"They were killed in an Indian attack," said Nora. "If you are interested in their ranch, you will have to talk to the bank. It was a terrible thing, the way their four children were killed. The talk was that they had been tortured before they died."

"It is terrible," said Milo. "In the past, I have seen how some of the Indians have tortured their victims."

After Nora left, Nate said, "With a ranch that big, I would think there would be a lot of hands around to help protect it."

"Tomorrow, we should be able to get a lot of information from Mr. Brewer at the bank," said Milo.

When they finished their supper, Milo and Nate returned to the hotel. Milo was up early in the morning. As he was coming out of his room, Nate opened his door. "Let's get some breakfast," said Milo. "The bank should be open by the time we finish."

After breakfast, Milo and Nate walked over to the bank. The cashier asked, "What can I do for you?"

"We would like to see Mr. Seth Brewer. Is he available?" asked Milo.

"Who should I tell him wants to see him?" asked the cashier.

"Milo Ryder," said Milo.

"Let me check," said the cashier, going to a door at the back of the room. He said, "Mr. Brewer will see you," when he returned.

Mr. Brewer stood five feet eight inches tall with brown hair and a beard that matched his hair. He wore glasses with round gold rims. His eyes were brown, and he wore a blue suit with a matching vest. His desk sat in the middle of the room with two chairs in front of it. On the desk was a green pad with an ink bottle and pen. A filing cabinet and safe sat off to the right side of the desk against the wall, and a coat tree was on the left side. Mr. Brewer stood when Milo and Nate walked in, and he shook their hands.

"Mr. Ryder, what can I do for you?" asked Mr. Brewer.

"I go by Milo, and this is one of my men Nate Mayfield," said Milo. "I heard that you have a ranch called the T Bar for sale."

"Yes, the bank does own the T Bar Ranch," said Mr. Brewer. "What do you want to know about it?"

"How did the bank come into possession of the ranch?" asked Milo.

"The owners were killed in an Indian attack," said Mr. Brewer. "They didn't have any family to take it over, so the bank had to foreclose on the property. It is run by some men who forcibly took it over after Tilghman's death. You will find that there are still some men there who were there before the attack."

"Don't you have a sheriff here that could look into it?" asked Nate.

"He said it is out of his hands," said Mr. Brewer. "I want to sell it before they get rid of everything. I have heard that they are getting rid of some of the cattle. There is a rumor that they use the ranch as their hideout where outlaws come and stay for a time."

"How many men are out there?" asked Milo.

"As many as six to eight men come and go from the ranch," said Mr. Brewer.

"What are you asking for it?" asked Milo.

"The bank is holding a loan of ten thousand dollars. That includes the buildings, land, and livestock," said Mr. Brewer. "Have you been out to look at the ranch?"

"No, we just got here last night and wanted to talk to you first," said Milo. "I am surprised you haven't sold the ranch at your asking price."

"The outlaws on the ranch control it," said Mr. Brewer. "Those men have run off everyone who has asked about it."

"Do you think the men out there need to be run off?" asked Nate.

"Whoever buys it will have to run them off because the sheriff has refused to do it," said Mr. Brewer.

"Is the ranch isolated?" asked Nate.

"The nearest neighbor is three miles away," said Mr. Brewer. "The ranch covers four sections of land, but some of it is mountains."

"How many cows are on the place?" asked Milo.

"At one time, Bass was running two thousand head," said Mr. Brewer. "From what I understand, the herd has been reduced to fifteen hundred by the hands. It may have been cut even more."

"Why haven't you got the law to get help with getting the men taken off the ranch if they are selling your cattle?" asked Nate.

"The local law is afraid to go out there, and he has refused to bring in any help," said Mr. Brewer. "Ike Evens is the man running the ranch and doesn't like anyone coming out there. So if you go out there, you will have to be careful."

"Where is the ranch located?" asked Milo.

"It is eight miles north of town," said Mr. Brewer.

With the information from Mr. Brewer and directions to the ranch, Milo and Nate left.

"What do you think?" asked Nate.

"If the ranch is as good as Mr. Brewer said and at the price he is asking, it would be hard to turn it down," said Milo.

"What about the men at the ranch now?" asked Nate.

"Let's wait and see what we find," said Milo.

CHAPTER 2

Milo and Nate rode north out of San Luis de la Culebra. The T Bar Ranch was located eight miles from town, where the south entrance to the land began. Milo kept looking at the land as they rode, checking its condition. Once they entered the property, they followed the road to the ranch buildings. Stopping before they reached the buildings, Milo wanted to look the place over to get an idea of what was there. Milo saw several buildings located around the ranch. The main house sat in the middle of all the buildings, and it was a two-story house made of adobe. It looked to be in good shape. The three smaller houses were located to the right of the main house and were also adobe. Located in front of the houses were women working on different tasks. To the left of the main house were a bunkhouse and a barn with a corral. Inside the corral were several horses.

As they rode into the yard, the house's front door opened, and a man standing six feet tall carrying a shotgun came out. Looking at the two men who rode in, Ike asked, "What do you want?"

"Are you Ike Evens?" asked Milo.

"Who is asking?" asked Ike.

"My name is Milo Ryder," said Milo. "We came here to look at the ranch. I heard it was for sale."

"Who said it was for sale?" asked Ike.

"Mr. Brewer at the bank in town," said Milo. "It is my understanding that the bank owns the property."

"Well, it ain't for sale," said Ike. "I suggest you turn them horses around and ride back out if you don't want to be buried here."

Milo looked at Nate and said, "It looks like we are not welcome here; let's go back and talk to Mr. Brewer again."

While Milo was talking to Ike, Nate kept looking around and noticed that four men came out of the barn carrying rifles and stood by the barn, watching them. Even the women who were in front of the houses had disappeared.

Turning their horses around, they started to ride out of the ranch.

While riding away, Milo asked, "Did you think it was strange that the women disappeared?"

"I kept looking around, and as soon as the four men came out of the barn, the women disappeared," said Nate. "If you buy it, we will have to determine how many men Ike control if we have to run them off."

"Remember, Mr. Brewer thought that six to eight men would come and go from the ranch," said Milo.

"It's no wonder he can use it as a safe place for outlaws," said Nate.

"Remember, Mr. Brewer said that the sheriff would not come out to the ranch," said Milo.

Returning to town, they went back to the bank. In Mr. Brewer's office, Milo said, "I will buy it. First, I will have to arrange with my realtor in Stonewall to draw up an offer, and if you accept it, I will transfer the money."

"What are you going to do about Ike and the men he has out there?" asked Mr. Brewer.

"Once we close the deal, I will run them off," said Milo. "If they refuse to go, I will arrest them."

"Under what authority can you arrest them?" asked Mr. Brewer.

Milo pulled out his badge and said, "I am a US marshal."

"As soon as I see your offer and if it is acceptable, I will get the papers drawn up and have them ready for you if that is all right with you," said Mr. Brewer.

It will allow me to look the town over," said Milo. "What is the sheriff's name?"

"His name is Ed Drew," said Mr. Brewer. "You can find him in his office down the street or in the saloon."

"Thanks," said Milo. "I will contact my man in Stonewall, and he should have the offer to you this afternoon or in the morning.

Milo and Nate went to the telegraph office and sent a wire to Clyde Anderson, telling him to put an offer to Seth Brewer for the ten thousand dollars for the T Bar Ranch. He told him to have the offer telegraphed to the bank that afternoon or first thing in the morning. They waited while the telegraph was sent before leaving.

Leaving the telegraph office, Milo and Nate walked down the street to the sheriff's office. Opening the door, they found Sheriff Ed Drew sitting at his desk.

Ed looked up at them and said, "Is there something I can do for you?"

"I am US Marshal Milo Ryder," said Milo. "I am in the process of purchasing the T Bar Ranch. We were just out there, and a man named Ike Evens lives on the property and thinks he owns it. Once I close the deal, I intend to run him off. There could be a few dead men."

"What do you want me to do?" asked Ed. "I want you to know what could happen," said Milo. "If I find that he is selling the cattle, I will arrest him for rustling."

"He has brought in several men since Bass Tilghman was killed, and I don't believe they are honest men," said Ed. "I believe that there are posters on some of them."

"Are all the men out there new to the ranch since the attack?" asked Nate.

"A few have been with Bass for several years and are good men," said Ed. "Since Ike took over, outlaws have moved in."

"Why haven't you gone after them?" asked Nate.

"I don't have enough men to confront them since the Indian attack," said Ed. "How are you going to get him out?"

"I will bring in the men to do it," said Milo.

That evening Milo and Burt went to the café for supper.

Nora met them as they came in and said, "I see that you are still in town."

"Yes, we are," said Nate.

Nora asked, "Did you talk to Mr. Brewer at the bank?"

"We did," said Milo. "We rode out to the ranch to look it over."

"I heard there are outlaws on the ranch now," said Nora.

"We met a man called Ike Evens," said Nate. "He did not want us to look at the place."

"What are you going to do?" asked Nora.

"We are meeting with Mr. Brewer at the bank in the morning," said Milo.

"Are you going to buy the ranch?" asked Nora.

"That is the plan," said Milo.

After Nora brought their meal to them, she said, "If you get the ranch, I will look forward to seeing you in here again."

"We will be back in the morning for breakfast," said Nate.

When they finished supper, they went to the Delta Saloon. Inside, like in the town, there weren't many men. Finding a table, they sat down and waited. It wasn't long before the barkeep came over. "What can I get you?" the barkeep asked.

"We will each have a beer," said Milo.

"You are new in town," said the barkeep. "Are you staying or passing through?"

"We are only here till tomorrow," said Nate.

Shortly after getting their beers, Sheriff Ed Drew came into the saloon. Seeing Milo and Nate, he walked over to their table and asked, "Mind if I sit down?"

"Not at all," said Milo.

"What are your plans?" asked Ed.

"We will meet with Mr. Brewer, at the bank, in the morning," said Milo.

While they were talking, four men walked into the saloon and took a table near the back of the room. Sheriff Drew said, "Those four work at the T Bar Ranch. They are some of the men Ike brought in."

"Have you checked to see if there is a poster on them?" asked Nate.

"No, they have not done anything in my jurisdiction to warrant me to check them," said Sheriff Drew.

Milo looked at them, trying to remember what they looked like. Then, when he got back to Stonewall, he would look at posters and see if there were any warrants for their arrest.

Sheriff Drew finished his beer and left.

Nate continued to watch the four men while they sat there. "I see that one of the men keeps looking at us," said Nate. "I believe that he was one of the men by the barn when we were at the ranch."

"Did you see the other two while we were there?" asked Milo.

"No," said Nate.

"If those four and the other three at the barn, along with Ike, that makes eight men with Ike," said Milo. "I wonder if there are any more."

"The one I recognized near the barn kept his rifle pointing at us while we were there. What do you think we should do?" asked Nate.

"After we talk to Mr. Brewer in the morning, I think I will send a telegram to Cody," said Milo. "I may have him get some men together and come here to help run Ike and his men out."

When Milo and Nate finished their beers, they returned to the hotel.

After Milo and Nate had visited the T Bar Ranch, Ike called in Ben Daniels. "I don't like the looks of those men that were just here."

"Who were they, and what did they want?" asked Ben.

"The one man said his name was Milo Ryder and that he was looking for a ranch for sale," said Ike.

"What did you tell them?" asked Ben.

"I told them it wasn't for sale," said Ike. "I believe he will go back to the bank, and there may be trouble."

"While they were here, I noticed that the one not doing the talking kept looking around like he was trying to figure out how many men we have," said Ben.

"I need you to keep watch that they don't come back," said Ike.

"Do you want me to take some of the men and go after them?" asked Ben.

"No, not yet," said Ike. "I need you to tell the men to keep a lookout for any strangers that come around here."

Later that day, Ben Daniels, Carter Lay, and Frank Logan rode into town and stopped at the Delta Saloon. Frank said, "See the two men sitting with the sheriff? They were the ones that were at the ranch earlier today. I wonder why they are talking to the sheriff."

They found a table further toward the back of the saloon and sat down. When the barkeep came over, they ordered a bottle. After what Frank had said about the men with the sheriff, he kept watching them.

"What were they doing at the ranch?" asked Carter.

"Ike told me that they were interested in the ranch; the guy who did all the talking asking about the sale of the ranch," said Ben. "Ike told him it wasn't for sale, and they left."

"Do you know their names?" asked Carter.

"Ike said that the one fella said his name was Milo Ryder," said Ben.

"Why do you think they are talking with Sheriff Drew?" asked Richard.

"Maybe they are trying to get the sheriff involved," said Frank.

"We know the sheriff won't do anything," said Carter. "He only came to the ranch once, and we ran him off."

"That name, Milo Ryder, sounds familiar," said Frank. "I remember a US marshal from New Mexico by that name. Do you think it could be the same man?"

"I don't know, but when we get back to the ranch, I will let Ike know," said Ben. "If he is a US marshal, that could be why he talked to Sheriff Drew."

When they got back to the ranch, Ben went to the house looking for Ike. He found Ike in the den. "What do you need?" asked Ike.

"Carter, Frank, and I were in the Delta Saloon and saw those two men that were here earlier today talking with the sheriff," said Ben. "When I told Frank the name, you told me he remembered a US marshal by that name from New Mexico."

"That is interesting," said Ike. "I wonder if the sheriff has contacted the US Marshal's office asking for help. If he has, we may have more trouble than just someone interested in the ranch. Make sure you let all the men know who he is. I want you to kill him if he shows up."

"Do you want me to send a man into town to watch him?" asked Ben.

"If Frank thinks he knows him, have Frank go and watch him," said Ike.

Ben found Frank at the bunkhouse and sent Frank to town to watch what Milo was doing.

When Frank got to town, he wasn't sure where to find Milo. So Frank went to the hotel and asked the clerk if they had a man named Milo Ryder.

The clerk asked, "Do you need to talk to him? Unfortunately, he is not here, but you can leave a note for him."

"Thanks, I will look around town for him," said Frank.

Frank went back to the saloon and looked but did not see him there; he went back to the front of the hotel and sat down in the shadows to wait to see if Milo had returned to the hotel. It wasn't much longer when Milo and Nate walked up the street, returning to the hotel. Once they had gone in, Frank rode back to the ranch. Finding Ike, he said, "I found them still in town. They are staying at the Hotel San Luis. What do you want to do?"

"Tomorrow, I want you to go back and see what they are doing. If they plan to stay, we may have a problem," said Ike. "If they leave, we don't have to worry about them."

The following morning Frank rode into town before the sun was up. Arriving in town, he found a place where he could watch the front of the hotel. Frank waited. An hour later, he saw Milo and Nate come out and go to the café. Frank saw them sitting at a table near the window. He kept watching while they ate breakfast.

When they left the café, he watched them walk to the bank. When they went into the bank, Frank went to the café. Sitting where he could watch the bank, he ordered breakfast. He saw Milo and Nate come out of the bank and go into the telegraph office. After leaving the telegraph office, they got their horses and gear and rode out of town.

Frank, seeing them leave, rode back to the ranch.

Ike saw Frank ride in and went to see what he'd found. "What are they up to?" asked Ike.

"They went to the bank this morning and telegraph office before they rode out," said Frank.

"How much time did they spend at the bank?" asked Ike.

"They were in there for about an hour," said Frank.

That got Ike thinking that maybe they were working on a deal to buy the ranch. Now he would have to wait and see what they did next.

CHAPTER 3

Milo was up early and waited for Nate in the lobby. When Nate arrived, they went to the café. Nora came over with coffee when they sat down and said, "I see you are still in town. What will you have this morning?"

"We are here for part of the day," said Milo. "We may be heading home after talking to Mr. Brewer."

"Are you still interested in the T Bar Ranch?" asked Nora.

"Yes, we are," said Milo. "By the way, we will have your breakfast special."

"I will get it going for you," said Nora.

After Nora left, Nate asked, "Have you thought about who you will have run the ranch?"

"What would you think about running the T Bar Ranch?" asked Milo.

"I don't know," said Nate. "Maybe Burt would be better at running the T Bar, and I could be the foreman at the Rocking R. Burt has had the experience running a ranch, where I have only worked on one."

"I see," said Milo. "You are starting to make decisions like a foreman already. I will think about it."

When they finished eating breakfast, they walked over to the bank. Mr. Brewer saw them coming and opened the door when they got there. "Milo, Nate, it is good to see you this morning," said Mr. Brewer.

"How are you this morning, Mr. Brewer?" asked Milo.

"I am fine, but please call me Seth," said Mr. Brewer. "Come into my office. I received your offer and have the papers ready for you to look at. If you agree with what I have written up, you can sign them, and you will have the T Bar Ranch."

Milo read the documents over and agreed to the terms. He would give the bank two thousand dollars and take a loan for eight thousand dollars. In addition, Milo would take possession of the ranch today, relieving the bank of all responsibility. Once Milo signed the papers, he shook Seth's hand and said he would send a telegram to the bank in Stonewall and have the money sent down.

Leaving the bank, they walked to the telegraph office and sent a telegram to Cody and Hannah. After sending the telegrams, they left the telegraph office, and he said to Nate, "We need to go home and get the men together and come back and take over the ranch."

"Will Cody be able to get the men together?" asked Nate.

"In the telegram I sent to Cody, I told him we were taking over a ranch and needed to run the men off who are there now. He should be able to get the men from both ranches who would be able to take over the ranch," said Milo.

Getting their horses, they started their return trip home. It was late when they rode into the ranch. There was still a light on in the house. Seeing Hannah was still up, Nate took Milo's horse and put it in the corral.

Milo went into the house, where Hannah was waiting. "I got your telegram today. I was glad to hear that you would be home tonight," said Hannah. "Maria has food ready for you. Call Nate, and you can tell me what happened while you eat."

When Nate got to the house, they went to the kitchen and sat at the table to eat.

"We own another ranch," said Milo.

"What is it like?" asked Hannah.

Milo explained to her the conditions of the purchase. He then explained that there were people on the ranch that he had to drive off.

"How are you going to do that?" asked Hannah.

"I sent Cody a telegram and told him we needed to gather some men. After that, we should be able to take over the ranch," said Milo.

"When are you going back there?" asked Hannah.

"As soon as Burt gets back," said Milo. "Have you heard from him?"

"No, I haven't," said Hannah.

"I will send him a telegram and ask him to meet us at the ranch," said Milo.

CHAPTER 4

The day Milo and Nate left for San Luis de la Culebra, Burt left for El More to see Shellie. Before he left, he told Billy to watch the ranch for him. He arrived in El More late that night. Not knowing the location of the Marker ranch where Shellie lived with her parents, Burt got a room in the hotel. In the morning, he went to the café. While eating breakfast, he inquired about the Marker ranch.

The waitress said, "You are new. What brings you to our town?"

"I am looking for the Albert Marker ranch," said Burt. "Do you know where it is located?"

"You can get directions to it from Sheriff Parker," said the waitress. "That is him heading this way."

Before the waitress went to get coffee for Burt, she waited for the sheriff to come in. When the sheriff opened the door, she motioned for him to come to Burt's table. When Sheriff Parker got to Burt's table, she said, "This gentleman would like to talk to you."

Burt stood up and said, "Sheriff Parker, my name is Burt Ware."

"That name sounds familiar," said Sheriff Parker. "Were you one of the men who rescued Shellie Marker?"

"Yes, I was," said Burt. "Would you like to join me?"

"Thank you," said Sheriff Parker, sitting down. "Violet, I will have the special."

"How about you, Mr. Ware?" asked Violet.

"I will have the same," said Burt.

"What brings you to El More?" asked Sheriff Parker.

"I came here to see Shellie and see how she is doing since she got home," said Burt. "I don't know where their ranch location is. Could you give me directions?"

"From what I know, she has not ventured far from their ranch," said Sheriff Parker. "I heard that she is afraid of men. Do you think she will see you? Albert has been keeping a close watch over her since she has come home."

"After Milo and I rescued her, we spent a lot of time together," said Burt. "I believe that she will see me. I think Albert will allow me to see her as well."

"Albert has talked a lot about you and Milo Ryder," said Sheriff Parker. "I believe that Mr. Ryder was a former US marshal."

"Milo is currently a US marshal," said Burt. "He has the authority to deputize us when he needs us. After a problem at the ranch a few years back, he was reinstated as a US marshal. He only goes when he needs to. He spends most of his time at his two ranches. He is looking at a third ranch near San Luis de la Culebra."

"It sounds like he is doing well as a US marshal," said Sheriff Parker.

"He has done well with his ranches," said Burt. "We are changing the herd from longhorns to a cross with an Aberdeen Angus."

"What breed is that?" asked Sheriff Parker.

"It is a breed that came down from Candida," said Burt. "He saved a man's life who was ambushed while taking the first bull to his ranch in New Mexico. Last year the man gave Milo two young bulls from his herd that he is using on the current two ranches."

Sheriff Parker gave Burt directions to the Marker ranch when they finished eating and said, "I am glad to have met you. I hope that you find Ms. Marker happy to see you."

"Thank you, Sheriff," said Burt.

Leaving the café, Burt got his horse and rode out to the Marker ranch. As Burt rode up to the ranch, there was no one around. A man came out of the barn carrying a rifle as Burt got close to the house.

When he got close to Burt, he asked, "What can I do for you?"

"Are the Markers home?" asked Burt.

'No," said the man holding the rifle. "Who are you?"

"My name is Burt Ware," said Burt.

"Burt Ware," said the man holding the rifle, thinking about the name. "They are not here. Are you one of the men who recovered Miss Marker?"

"Yes, I was with Milo Ryder when we found her. Is she all right, and is there a chance I could see her?" asked Burt.

"As I said, they are not here; they rode over to their son's place. My name is Ned Davis, the foreman here," said Ned. "Get down, and you can put your horse in the corral. I am sure that the Markers would like to see you, and I know that Shellie has said that you had asked to come to see her."

"Thank you," said Burt. "While we were coming back to Stonewall, Shellie said she had a brother."

Burt shook Ned's hand and said, "It is nice to meet you."

They walked together to the corral, where Burt loosened the cinch and removed the headstall from his horse before turning him loose in the corral.

While Burt turned his horse loose, Ned said, "Shellie has talked a lot about you and how nice you and Mr. Ryder treated her. She mentioned that the lady who helped Mrs. Ryder had loaned her clothes until the folks arrived. I am sure she will be surprised to see you when they get back. She has asked us several times if we thought that you would come to see her."

"I have wondered how she would react to my coming here," said Burt. "Do you or your folks have any concerns about me coming here?"

"No," said Ned. "I know that Wanda and Albert will be happy that you came. Come up to the house, and we can have some dinner. Mabel should have it ready, and I can introduce you to the rest of the men."

While Burt put his horse in the corral and talked with Ned, he noticed men walking to the house. Ned said, "Mabel, we have a guest joining us. I want you to meet Burt Ware."

"Mabel, I hope it is not too much trouble if I join you," said Burt.

"No, you are welcome. I have plenty," said Mabel. "You can take this seat, and I will get you a plate."

Ned went around the table and introduced the men. "Men, I want you to meet Burt Ware. He is one of the men who rescued Shellie. Burt, these are the men who work here: Porter Flores, Crawford Moore, and Boone Jackson."

While each man was being introduced, they said hello to Burt.

While eating, Burt asked Ned, "Do you know when the Markers will be back?"

"Usually, when they go to Josh and Rebecka's place, they would be back by suppertime," said Ned.

"We were all happy and surprised when the word got here that Shellie was safe," said Crawford. "We heard that when someone was kidnapped, most of the time they were never heard from again."

"We got some good leads on where we could find her," said Burt. "How is Shellie doing?"

Mabel joined them at the table and said, "Shellie does not leave the ranch without someone being with her. Most of the time, she stays near the house. She does not trust any strange men, but, health-wise, she is fine."

"She was put through a lot for a woman," said Burt. "She did not know what was going to happen to her. The men who took her had her drugged on laudanum when we found her. It took her a couple of days to get over the effects of that."

"Do you work for Mr. Ryder?" asked Boone.

"Milo has two ranches," said Burt. "I am the foreman at the Rocking R, the first ranch Milo bought. He also owns the Lazy S Ranch, which is connected to the Rocking R. When I left to come here, Milo and one of the other hands were going to San Luis de la Culebra to look at a third ranch."

After eating, Burt spent the rest of the day with Ned. Ned had several questions about the ranch after Burt mentioned the Aberdeen Angus bulls. He wanted to know the differences and how Burt thought it would improve the herd.

Wanda, Albert, and Shellie drove into the yard in the middle of the afternoon. Burt and Ned were in the barn looking at a colt born a few days earlier. Although, at first, they did not hear the buggy come in, when they did, they both went to see who had come.

Driving into the yard, Albert noticed a strange horse in the corral. He wondered whose it was. The horse did look somewhat familiar. It wasn't long after they stopped that Albert saw them coming out of the barn. Wanda and Shellie got out of the buggy and were headed to the house when Albert said, "Well, I'll be if we don't have a guest. Shellie, I think you are going to like this surprise."

Shellie turned to see what her father was talking about. When she saw Burt, she turned and walked toward him. "You did come," said Shellie.

"I wasn't sure if you would welcome me or not," said Burt.

Shellie said as she hugged Burt, "I have been hoping that you would come."

Albert and Wanda waited until Shellie finished hugging Burt before saying, "We are glad to see you. Please come into the house."

"I see you are in good hands," said Ned, returning to the barn and leaving Burt with the family.

Inside, the Markers removed their covers before everyone sat in the living room. Albert and Wanda sat in chairs while Burt sat on the couch. Shellie sat next to Burt. Burt asked, "How have you been, Shellie? I have been thinking about you a lot and hoped you were doing well."

"I have not been going out alone," said Shellie. "Ever since I got home, Mom and Dad have ensured that someone is always with me when I leave the ranch. That helps, but I still worry."

"We worry about her as well," said Wanda. "She is getting better about going around the ranch by herself, but someone is always with her when she leaves."

"How are the Ryders doing?" asked Albert.

"Milo is doing good," said Burt. "He bought a second ranch, and when I left to come here, he went to look at a third ranch."

"Has he been looking for anyone else?" asked Wanda.

"There was a bank robbery in Stonewall a few months back. Milo, Billy, Nate, and I went after them," said Burt. "We caught them in New Mexico with all the money. While we were there, we talked to Gentry Soyer. Gentry gave Milo two Aberdeen Angus bulls. Milo is working at changing the herd to the Angus breed."

"What is so special about that breed?" asked Wanda.

"The calves it produces have more muscle with more marbling in the meat. Even though it is smaller than the longhorns, it produces more meat," said Burt.

"I would be interested in seeing what the offspring look like," said Albert.

"It will be a while before we have any calves," said Burt. "The bulls are young, and we have already bred the mother cows. After that, the bulls will be old enough to be used in the next breeding season."

"Where are you staying?" asked Wanda.

"I stayed in the hotel last night," said Burt.

"Well, you are going to stay here," said Albert. "After the Ryders put us up, I would not feel right if you didn't stay here. Why don't you get your gear and bring it to the house? We have a spare room that Josh grew up in."

"I will go with you," said Shellie. "Then I can show you the room."

Burt and Shellie walked out to the corral to Burt's horse. While they were walking, Shellie took hold of Burt's hand. When she took his hand, Burt looked at Shellie, and she smiled at him.

"I have not thought about another man since I got home," said Shellie. "I don't mean to be forward, but I feel safe with you."

"I enjoyed our walks by the river when you were at the Rocking R," said Burt. "I wanted to come up here right after you left, but I don't want to rush you into anything."

Burt went into the corral while Shellie stayed outside. Ned saw Shellie standing by the corral and went to see if something was wrong. When he got close, he saw that Burt was unsaddling his horse and knew that he would be staying. So he said, "I think you like this man," walking over to Shellie.

Shellie looked at Ned and said, "I got to know him when he rescued me. I felt safe with him and wanted to be near him. If he would ask me to go with him, I would."

"Does he know that?" asked Ned.

"No, but I hope he will before he leaves," said Shellie.

Burt brought his saddle over and placed it on the fence. Ned said, "I will put it in the barn for you. It looks like it could rain tonight."

"Thanks," said Burt.

He grabbed his gear, Shellie took his hand, and they walked back to the house. Inside, Shellie took him to Josh's room, where Burt left his things.

When Shellie and Burt had left to get his gear, Wanda had asked, "Did you see how Shellie is looking at Burt?"

"Yes, I did," said Albert. "She seems to be happier with Burt here."

"What do you think of Burt?" asked Wanda.

"He has proven that he is honest and a good man," said Albert. "I would be proud to have him in the family, if that is what he would want."

"I can't believe how fast she has changed since she saw Burt," said Wanda.

Mabel overheard what Wanda and Albert were talking about and walked into the room. "I met him at dinner," said Mabel. "He is a gentleman. I noticed that Ned and the men seemed to take to him."

"He will be staying in the house," said Wanda. "When they come back, Shellie will set him up in Josh's old room."

"How long will he be staying here?" asked Mabel.

"We don't know," said Wanda. "I guess that is up to Shellie."

"He is the foreman at the Rocking R Ranch," said Albert. "He will have to get back there sometime."

While they were talking, Shellie and Burt came in. Shellie took Burt to Josh's room, not stopping to talk to them. After placing his gear in the room, they went back to the living room.

At supper, no one talked about what had happened to Shellie. Ned had told the men about the bulls, and the conversation was Burt explaining the bulls to Porter, Crawford, and Boone.

After supper, Shellie got up to help Mabel and Wanda clean up. Wanda told Shellie, "You go with Burt. You have been waiting for him to show up, so spend your time with him now."

Shellie saw that her dad was going to take Burt outside, so she got a wrap and joined them.

Albert asked Burt, "What are your plans for the future?"

"I have been saving some money," said Burt. "Someday, I hope to purchase a ranch, but I will work for Milo for now. He treats me good, and I am the foreman of one of his ranches."

"Does he pay enough that you can save enough?" asked Albert.

"We have put a few outlaws away," said Burt. "When there's a reward, Milo shares it with the men who helped him. His former partner as a US marshal now oversees the operation for the Lazy S Ranch. Milo lets him share in the profits that the ranch makes. If he keeps buying ranches, I may get to run one."

"It sounds like you know where you are heading," said Albert. "What do you want to do about Shellie?"

Burt was surprised by the question. He looked at Shellie, and she saw that Burt was unprepared for the question. "Dad, Burt just got here, and we have not even had time to be together to find out how we are doing," said Shellie.

Burt took Shellie's hand and said, "Mr. Marker, I fell in love with Shellie when she was at the Rocking R Ranch. We got to walk down by the river and talk. We had only known each other for a short time, but I saw how strong and beautiful she was. Because of the short time we have known each other, I feel it is not right for me to ask her to come with me."

"That is being honest," said Albert. "Shellie, what do you think?"

"Dad, I have been thinking about Burt ever since we met. He has always looked out for me and kept me safe. Like Burt, I fell in love with him at the Rocking R," said Shellie. "If he asked me, I would go with him."

"Well, that is a lot," said Albert. "Does your mother know how you feel?"

"Mom and I have talked," said Shellie.

"I see," said Albert.

Wanda came outside to find out what they were doing. As she approached them, she heard Shellie say that they had talked. "From what I heard just now, it sounds like the conversation is getting serious," said Wanda.

"Mom, we were just saying that you and I had talked about Burt," said Shellie.

"Oh," said Wanda. "What do you have to say about it, Burt?"

"Ma'am, I fell in love with Shellie when she was at the Rocking R Ranch," said Burt. "But I thought it was too early to say anything to Shellie or you."

"How long do you plan on visiting us?" asked Wanda.

"I hope to be here at least a week," said Burt. "That is, if you will have me."

"We would be happy to have you stay for the week," said Wanda. "I know Shellie would like it to be longer, but I assume you have to get back to the Rocking R Ranch. Come on, Pa, let's leave these two alone."

Albert and Wanda returned to the house, leaving Burt and Shellie alone.

CHAPTER 5

A TELEGRAM ARRIVED FOUR DAYS after Burt arrived at the Marker ranch. When Shellie saw that the telegram was for Burt, she asked, "Is something wrong?"

"Milo bought the ranch near San Luis de la Culebra," said Burt. "He wants me to meet him back at the ranch, and I will need to return."

"I hoped you would be here longer," Shellie said.

"I wanted to stay longer as well," said Burt. "I know this is soon, but will you marry me?"

"Yes, I will marry you," said Shellie, wrapping her arms around Burt and hugging him.

"I have to go back to the ranch," said Burt. "Once I find out what Milo wants, I will send you a telegraph, and we can set a date."

Shellie and Burt entered the house and found Wanda and Albert drinking coffee in the kitchen. Wanda looked up and asked, "What are you smiling about, Shellie?"

"Burt asked me to marry him," said Shellie.

"That is good news," said Albert. "When will the wedding take place?"

"I have to go back to the ranch and see Milo," said Burt. "Once I know what he wants, I will let Shellie know so she can set a date."

"When will you leave?" asked Albert.

"I will leave in the morning," said Burt.

After breakfast the following day, Shellie walked with Burt to the corral. After saddling his horse and putting his gear on, he turned to Shellie and said, "I will let you know as soon as I find out what Milo wants."

"I am going to miss you," said Shellie. "I want to get married as soon as possible. Mom will want the wedding here."

"I am sure that when we plan the wedding, several of the men from the Rocking R, along with Milo and Hannah, will want to be here," said Burt.

Shellie wrapped her arms around Burt's neck and kissed him. "I love you," she said.

Mounting his horse, he rode out. Shellie stood and watched him until he was out of sight.

It was going on suppertime when Burt rode into the ranch. Billy was in the yard finishing with a colt. Seeing Burt, he waited until he got off his horse before asking, "How are the Markers doing?"

"They are doing good," said Burt. "Is Milo back?"

"He got back last evening," said Billy. "He is up at the house."

After Burt put up his horse, he washed up and went to the house. Maria and Hannah had supper ready, and the rest of the men were already at the table. When Billy came in, he told Maria that Burt was back, so she had set a place for him.

Once Burt sat down, he asked, "What did the ranch look like?"

"The ranch looks good," said Milo. "I bought it. However, we have a problem with the men that are on it. The family who owned it was killed in an Indian attack. Some outlaws have moved onto the ranch, who we will remove."

Hannah asked, "How are the Markers doing?"

"They are fine," said Burt.

"How is Shellie?" asked Milo.

"She has recovered but spends most of her time at the ranch. She does not leave unless someone is with her," said Burt.

"Are you going to see her again?" asked Milo.

"I plan on it," said Burt. "First, we have to take care of the new ranch."

"How have things been going here?" asked Burt.

Billy said, "things have been quiet. The new bull is in the pasture with the cows."

Milo said, "Nate, I want you and Burt to come into my office when we finish supper."

Once they were in the office, Milo said, "I have been thinking about what I will do with the new ranch. First, I have to put someone in charge of the operations. Burt, you are the first choice to run the operations of the T Bar Ranch. I have talked to Nate about becoming the foreman here. What do you think?"

"Are there any men left who have been working the ranch before the outlaws moved in?" asked Burt.

"From what we understood, there still are some good men there," said Milo. "We will have to find men once we run the outlaws out."

"If you feel that I am qualified to oversee the operations, there is something I would like to ask you," said Burt.

"What do you want to know?" asked Milo.

"If you feel that I could run the ranch, how would you feel if I went in half as a partner with you?" asked Burt.

"You want to put up half the money for purchasing the ranch?" said Milo. "That is a good thought. If you own half the ranch, I am sure that we could make good money from it. Let me think on it, and I will let you know."

"I have the money to invest in the bank from the rewards we have gotten," said Burt. "I would like to do something with it, and if I am going to get married, I would like to have a permanent home for Shellie."

"Tomorrow, I want to get with Cody and see who he has talked to about going there to get rid of the outlaws," said Milo. "We need to do that as soon as possible. Once they are out, there is a house that you will be staying in."

"Who is the man leading the outlaws?" asked Burt.

"Ike Evens," said Nate. "Milo wants to go into the marshal's office and check posters on the men we saw. We may be able to collect some rewards on them."

"First thing in the morning, send Billy to get Cody," said Milo. "Once we talk to Cody, we will ride into town and look at the posters."

"I will tell Billy when I go to the bunkhouse," said Burt.

Leaving the house, Nate and Burt went to the bunkhouse. "Milo asked me if I wanted to run the T Bar Ranch," said Nate. "I told him I would feel better as foreman here, and you should be the one running the new ranch."

"I know you will do a good job here," said Burt. "I am sure that if you had accepted Milo's offer, you would do a good job there."

Inside the bunkhouse, Burt found Billy sitting with the rest of the men. Billy asked, "How did it go with Shellie at the Markers'?"

"She is doing well," said Burt. "We got a chance to talk and spend some time together."

"What did Abert and Wanda think of you coming there?" asked Nate.

"They were happy to see me," said Burt. "They even had me stay in the house while I was there."

"What did Milo say about the new ranch?" asked Billy.

"Billy, Milo wants you to get Cody in the morning after breakfast. He plans to take men there to run the outlaws out," said Burt.

"Did he say who would stay at the new ranch?" asked Emmett.

"Milo said that he would have Burt oversee the new ranch," said Nate. "First, we have to take it over."

"If Burt goes there, who will become the foreman here?" asked Hick.

"Nate will become the foreman," said Burt. "Does anyone have a problem with that? If you do, say so now."

None of the men thought it was a bad idea. On the contrary, they all said they would be happy working under Nate.

"We will have to find more men," said Burt.

"Will you take any of us with you?" asked Porter.

"I don't know," said Burt. "It will depend on what we find once we take over the T Bar."

After breakfast the next day, Billy rode over to the Lazy S. Cody saw him ride in and waited for him. "Hi, Billy, what's up?" asked Cody.

"Hi, Cody, Milo wants you to come to the Rocking R. He got home yesterday and said that we need to put together a plan to take possession of the T Bar Ranch," said Billy.

"It came about," said Cody. "I received a telegram from him before he came back, asking that I put men together to go there. Let me get my horse, and we can go see Milo."

Milo was waiting for them when they arrived. Burt saw them ride up and got Nate before going to the house. Inside, the five men met in the kitchen.

Milo asked Cody, "What have you been able to do about gathering men?"

"I figured we could use some of the men from each ranch to drive them out," said Cody. "From the Lazy S, it would be me, Luke, and James. From the Rocking R, it would be you, Nate, Billy, and Burt. That would be seven men; if we have to, we could force the San Luis de la Culebra sheriff to join us."

Hannah walked in while they were talking and said, "I will be going there with you."

All the men looked at her, and Milo said, "Why do you want to go?"

"Once you take over the ranch, I will need to see what has to be done and make sure the men are fed and cared for," said Hannah. "I want to see what the ranch looks like."

"We will have to figure out the best place to attack Ike and his men," said Milo.

"How will we know which men are with Ike?" asked Billy.

"I will go into the marshal's office and see if I can find posters on the men I saw with Ike," said Milo. "If I can find posters, it will help us identify them."

"When do you want to head there?" asked Burt.

"I would like to go back there tomorrow," said Milo. "We will have to work fast to get ready to leave."

"I will get Maria to help me, and we will get the food ready to go," said Hannah. "Will we take a wagon, or are we going on horseback?"

"We will be going on horseback," said Milo. "We will be able to move around more."

"With eight of us going, we will need to take at least four packhorses," said Burt.

"I think we can get by with two packhorses," said Milo. "We need to go into San Luis de la Culebra before going to the ranch. I need to let the sheriff know that we are there and tell him what we intend to do. While there, we can get supplies."

"If we are out in the open, we will need to take at least one tent to store our supplies and give Hannah a place to sleep," said Burt.

"I can sleep on the ground," said Hannah. "Milo and I have done that before. I can even handle a rifle."

"We will leave in the morning," said Milo.

Once they finished putting together their plan, Cody went back to the Lazy S while Milo got ready to go to the marshal's office.

Nate rode with Milo to town to help look at the posters. They knew the name of Ike Evens and the faces of some of the others. When they opened the door, they found Tom standing by the stove, getting coffee.

"Milo, Nate, what brings you to town?" asked Tom.

"I purchased the T Bar Ranch near San Luis de la Culebra, and there are men on the ranch we have to run off. We want to look at your posters and see if they are wanted," said Milo.

"Do you know any of their names?" asked Tom.

"The leader is Ike Evens," said Milo. "Have you heard of him?"

"I think I saw a poster with that name," said Tom.

The three men sat down, and Tom took out a stack of posters and handed them to Milo. Milo handed some of them to Nate and said, "You go through those, and then you can go through these. I will go through them after you."

Halfway down the stack, Milo had found the poster on Ike Evens. By the time they had gone through the posters, Nate had set aside two other posters. Milo had set aside three. The names on the posters were Ike Evens, Ben Daniels, Frank Logan, Cullen McCarthy, and Carter Lay.

Milo asked Tom, "Do you mind if we take these with us?"

"No," said Tom. "If you capture those five, you will get a nice reward."

"My first concern is to get them off the ranch," said Milo.

"How are you going to do that?" asked Tom.

"I am taking six of my hands with me," said Milo. "I will deputize them to make any arrests legal."

"Will the local law help you?" asked Tom.

"No, I don't think he will do anything," said Milo. "Nate and I met him when we were there. He has done nothing to get rid of the men after the bank who owned the ranch asked him. I am sure he will not help us."

"If it were closer, I would be happy to lend you a hand," said Tom.

"Thanks, Tom," said Milo.

Leaving the marshal's office, Milo and Nate rode back to the ranch.

Burt saw them ride in and met them. "Were you able to find any information on the men?"

"Get Billy and come to the house," said Milo. "We found posters on five men. I want you two to read them so you will know who we are after. I will show them to Cody, Luke, and James tomorrow."

"From what I saw on the rewards, it could be a nice sum of money," said Billy. "I hope I don't forget who they are."

"I will have them with us to look at again," said Milo.

Hannah came into Milo's office and said, "Supper is ready. Call the other men."

Billy went out and rang the bell. It wasn't long before all the men were in the house. Once seated, Emmet asked, "When will you leave?"

"Cody and his men will be here in the morning, and then we will leave," said Milo. "While we are gone, I want Cord to be in charge of the ranch."

During the day, Hannah and Maria were busy baking and making jerky to take. After baking, they put together canned goods along with the jerky. In addition, they put flour, salt, pork, and coffee. Hannah was preparing to have food for the noon meal.

By morning everyone was ready. Milo made sure that each man had extra ammunition and spare guns.

Cody had instructed his men to get ready when he returned to the Lazy S. Rosie and Sadie were busy getting supplies ready for them. Each man had an extra gun and ammunition. Rosie and Sadie had breakfast ready before the sun was up. Cody, Luke, and James had finished breakfast before the rest of the men were in the house. While they were eating, Sam saddled their horses and got a packhorse ready for them.

When Cody and the others came out of the house, Sam was there holding their horses. James and Luke had the supplies that Rosie had prepared and loaded them along with the extra ammunition on the packhorse while Cody said goodbye to Rosie.

"You take care of yourself," said Rosie to Cody.

"I will be all right," said Cody. "If you have any trouble, Sam is here to help you.

Kissing Rosie goodbye, Cody mounted his horse, and they rode to the Rocking R Ranch.

CHAPTER 6

When Milo and his men left for San Luis de la Culebra, a man rode into Stonewall looking for Sadie Ruggles. The man stopped at Millie's Café and ordered dinner. Betty waited on him and said, "You are new in town. Are you going to be here long?"

The man looked at Betty and said, "I am looking for someone."

"Who are you looking for?" asked Betty.

"I am looking for Sadie Ruggles. Do you know her?" asked the man.

At first, Betty was taken aback by his statement. Finally, she answered, "Is she new around here? Who is asking?"

"Her husband, Ruben Ruggles," said Ruben.

"I don't believe I know her," said Betty. "Do you know how long she has been here?"

"Not too long. If you hear of Sadie, let me know," said Ruben.

"Where can I find you?" asked Betty.

"Leave word at the Red Dog Saloon," said Ruben.

Betty got his food and left him alone. She found Millie in the kitchen and said, "Do you see that man sitting by himself? That is Sadie's husband."

Millie walked out to the dining area so she could get a better look at him. When she returned, she said, "When he leaves, go find Levi and have him go out to the Lazy S Ranch and let Sadie know he is in town."

When Betty went back to the counter, Marshal Tom Sieke came in. After he sat down, she went to get his order. "Hi, Tom, what can I get you?"

"I will have the special," said Tom. "Do you know the man who just left here?"

"He said that his name was Ruben Ruggles," said Betty.

"That name sounds familiar," said Tom. "Is he that ex-husband of Sadie's?"

"Yes, he is looking for her," said Betty. "I need to let her know he is here."

"Do you know where she is?" asked Tom

"She is at the Lazy S Ranch," said Betty. "I was going to find Levi and have him ride out there and warn her."

"When I get done eating, I will find Levi and tell him to go out there," said Tom.

"Thanks," said Betty.

When Tom finished eating, he decided to ride out and tell Sadie that her ex-husband was there. After getting his horse at the livery, Tom noticed that Ruben was watching the café. Tom thought it was strange but figured that he was watching for Betty to warn Sadie.

When Tom rode into the Lazy S Ranch, Sam saw him. He asked, "Hi, Tom, what brings you out here?"

"Hi, Sam, is Sadie here? I need to talk to her," said Tom.

"I believe she is in the house," said Sam. "Get down, and I will take you in."

They found Rosie and Sadie cleaning the kitchen from dinner. Rosie turned when she heard them and said, "Hi, Tom, Cody is not here."

"I came to see Sadie," said Tom.

Sadie said, "What do you want to see me about?"

"I came to warn you that your ex-husband is in Stonewall," said Tom. "Betty in Millie's saw and talked to him today. He told her that he was looking for you. Where is Cody?"

"He went with Milo to kick some men out of the ranch he just bought," said Rosie.

Tom looked at Sam and said, "You need to be on the lookout for any strangers. I think that there is a chance that someone in town might mention to him that Sadie is around Stonewall but may not know where you are."

"We will keep an eye on anyone coming here," said Sam. "I will tell Rufus and Jose to ensure they always have their Colts with them. Rosie, make sure you have a rifle handy for you and Sadie. I will make sure that there is someone near you, Sadie, at all times."

"Tom, would you like some coffee?" asked Sadie.

"Thank you," said Tom, sitting down.

Sam went to find Rufus and Jose to tell them what Tom had said.

After Tom sat down, he said, "Sadie, I heard that your ex, Ruben, has threatened to kill you. Can you tell me what happened?"

Sadie looked at Rosie, and Rosie said, "Go ahead and tell Tom. You can trust him."

Both Rosie and Sadie sat down, and Rosie said, "Ruben used to beat me. After living with it for a year, I divorced him. When the divorce was granted, he went mad. I had to have a guard with me until I could get my things and leave. He yelled out that he would not let me go and that he would kill me. So I ran. He is mean enough of a man that he will kill me if he gets the chance."

"You should be safe here," said Tom. "I know the men that work here will protect you."

When Tom finished his coffee, he got up. "If I were you, I would not venture into town until Rufus is gone," said Tom. "If I find out he is gone, I will let you know."

"Thank you for coming out and letting me know he is around," said Sadie. "I will stay here and do not plan on leaving the ranch."

Tom rode back to Stonewall. He went through the wanted posters in his office, looking for one on a Ruben Ruggles. Not finding one meant Tom could not arrest him. He would have to wait and see what he did.

Sam ensured that someone was always at the ranch with the women when he checked on the cattle. Rufus was usually the one who would stay. Jose would ride with Sam, as Sam decided to have two men together when someone left the ranch. For the following few days, things at the ranch remained calm. Then one day, a man came riding up to the ranch.

Sadie was down by the barn when the man rode in. Before he saw her, Sadie recognized Ruben. She ducked back into the barn before he saw her.

Sam was in the barn and saw her get nervous and asked, "What is the matter?"

"That man who just rode in is my ex-husband," said Sadie.

"Stay here in the barn and hide," said Sam.

He picked up his rifle and started toward the house when Rosie came out carrying a rifle.

Ruben was watching Rosie and did not see Sam.

Rosie asked, "Can I help you?"

"I understand you have a woman here by the name Sadie Ruggles," said Ruben.

"I don't know what you are talking about," said Rosie.

"Who owns this ranch?" asked Ruben.

"US Marshal Milo Ryder," said Rosie.

"Is the marshal here?" asked Ruben.

"No, he is not," said Rosie.

"I want to see inside the house," said Ruben.

"You are not welcome to come in," said Rosie.

Ruben started to get down from his horse when Sam said, "If I were you, I would listen to the lady and stay on that horse."

Ruben turned as soon as he heard Sam and settled back in the saddle. Ruben thought the old cowboy was the only one besides the lady on the ranch. Ruben drew his gun as he settled back down in the saddle and pointed it at Sam, when a bullet hit him in his chest, knocking him from the saddle. On the ground, Sam went over to him and took his gun.

Ruben said, "I didn't think she would shoot."

Sadie was watching from the barn when she saw Rosie shoot Ruben. After he fell off his horse, she walked over to where he lay.

The last thing Ruben saw was Sadie looking at him as he died.

Sadie looked at Sam and then Rosie and said, "That was my ex-husband. Thank you. I am now free from worrying about him."

Sam said, "I will get the wagon to take him to town and tell Tom what happened."

Rosie said before he left, "Let me give you the money to have him buried."

Sam said, "Let me check him and his saddlebags. He may have the money to bury himself."

Going through Ruben's pockets, Sam found enough money to bury him. "You can save your money, and we will keep his horse and guns here," said Sam. "Any extra money he has is yours now."

When Sam got to town, Tom was coming out of his office. Sam drove the wagon to where Tom was and stopped.

Tom looked in the back of the wagon and said, "I see you found Ruben. Do you want to tell me what happened?'

"He came looking for Sadie," said Sam. "When Rosie told him he wasn't welcome, he tried to shoot me."

"Did you kill him?" asked Tom.

"No," said Sam. "Rosie shot him. I guess he didn't think that she would shoot a man."

"I guess that would surprise me as well," said Tom.

"Is there anything she will have to do?" asked Sam.

"No," said Tom. "Let's take him over to the undertaker."

At the undertaker, they unloaded the body, and Sam paid for the burial.

Tom said, "Tell Sadie I will come out and see her. Tell Rosie that she does not have to do anything about this."

Sam drove back to the ranch, informing Sadie and Rosie what Tom had told him.

CHAPTER 7

MILO MET THEM AS SOON as Cody, Luke, and James rode into the yard. The men from the Rocking R Ranch were finishing getting ready. Luke was surprised when Hannah was wearing pants and climbed on her horse. He said, "Do we have the pleasure of your company on this adventure?"

Hannah smiled at Luke and replied, "You most certainly do."

Billy was the last one to get mounted. Maria was standing with Billy as he put his gear on his horse, and before he could mount, Maria kissed him. "You take care of yourself and come back here," said Maria.

Billy hugged her and mounted his horse. With Hannah, there were eight people with three packhorses leaving for San Luis de la Culebra. Hannah rode up front with Milo.

James wondered how Hannah would ride all day and said something to Billy. Billy said, "You don't have to worry about Hannah. She rides a lot. That is her horse, Buttercup, raised from a colt and has been helping us when the calves come in the pasture. She will hold her own."

They stopped and had coffee with a cold dinner at noontime before going on. It was late when Milo and his men rode into San Luis de la Culebra and Milo said, "Let's go to the Rocky Café and get some supper."

Nora was surprised to see Milo with a woman and six other men. She waited until everyone found a seat before she walked over to Milo. "I see you made it back. Did you buy the T Bar Ranch?"

"Hi, Nora," said Milo. "Yes, I did buy the ranch, and I want you to meet my wife, Hannah. Hannah, I want you to meet Nora."

After exchanging pleasantries, Nora asked, "What can I get you? We have beef, potatoes, gravy, and pie as a special today."

The men agreed to have the special, so Nora went away to get their food.

While they were waiting for their food, Sheriff Ed Drew walked in. Seeing Milo, he walked over to him and asked, "Are these your men, Marshal?"

"Yes, they are," said Milo. "This is my wife, Hannah. Hannah, I want you to meet Sheriff Ed Drew."

"Sheriff," said Hannah. "Will you be available to help us?"

"That depends on what you are planning on doing," said Ed.

"I am going to take over my ranch," said Milo. "I have posters on some of the men at the ranch. They are either going to jail or will wind up dead. We will bring those we arrest to your jail, where I expect them to be held for trial."

"Not all the men at the ranch are outlaws," said Ed. "What are you going to do with them?"

"If they are good men and want to stay and work on the ranch, they can stay," said Milo. "This is Burt. Once we take over the ranch, Burt will oversee the operations there, and I expect you to treat him like me."

"Are you going to be here?" asked Ed.

"I have two ranches near Stonewall," said Milo. "My headquarters is at one of them. After taking over the T Bar Ranch, we will be returning to my headquarters."

"When do you intend to start driving those men out?" asked Ed.

"We will start tomorrow," said Milo. "Do you have any problems with that?"

"You being a US marshal and owning the ranch, I don't have any problems with what you do," said Ed. "Once you have arrested or killed any outlaws on which there is a poster, I will see you get the rewards."

Nora brought their food, so Ed excused himself and left them alone. After Nora left, Hannah said, "He doesn't seem like a very nice man."

"For a lawman, I have to agree," said Burt. "Maybe once we get done moving into the ranch, he may become a little more friendly."

Cody asked, "Where do you want to set up camp tonight?"

"I think we will stay in town tonight and look for a place where we can set up camp in the morning," said Milo. "I want to find someplace where we can get to the ranch to see what is going on and get to town if needed."

Milo and Hannah went to the Hotel San Luis when everyone had finished eating. While the men took the horses to the livery, Milo got rooms for everyone.

Everyone met in the lobby and went to the Rocky Café for breakfast in the morning. Nora again met them as they came in. "You keep coming, you will become a regular," said Nora. "It is good to see you this morning, Mrs. Ryder.

"Please call me Hannah."

After breakfast, Hannah said, "While you get the horses, I need to go to the mercantile and get the supplies we did not bring with us."

"We will get the horses and meet you at the mercantile," said Milo.

Burt said, "Why don't you go with her, and we can get the horses."

By the time the men had returned with the horses, Hannah had gathered the added supplies they had needed. After loading them on the packhorses, they rode north out of town.

After going four miles halfway to the ranch, Milo looked for a place hidden from the road to set up camp. Burt spotted a valley that looked like no one was using it just west of the road. After finding a spot with a stream, where there was shelter to protect them from the rain, they set up camp. With camp set up, Milo wanted to go check out the ranch. Leaving Nate with Hannah, he took the rest of the men to show them the ranch's location. They found a spot where they could see the ranch and watch the operations that were going on.

Milo pointed out the layout of the ranch to them before they were able to see it. He said, "The main house sits in the middle of the ranch and is a two-story house made of adobe. Three smaller houses are located to the right of the main house, also made of adobe. Those houses look to have married men living in them. A bunkhouse near a barn with a corral is to the left of the main house. I have shown you the posters that Nate and I found. Watch the ranch to try to spot those men. Watch for any of them to leave the ranch. If we can arrest them while they are away from the ranch, do it. The fewer men we have to deal with at the ranch, the better it will be for us."

"How do you want to work it?" asked Luke.

"I think we need to spend a couple of days getting to know their operations," said Milo. "If we can get Ike away and arrest him, it should make it easier to stop the rest at the ranch."

"How do you want to watch the ranch?" asked Cody.

"Let's set it up into two shifts a day," said Milo. "Cody, I want you to be here with James and Luke. I will be with Burt, Nate, and Billy during the second shift. I want to start watching them today. So, Cody, you stay here with your men now, and we will come to relieve you this afternoon. Find spots where you can see each other and still watch the ranch. Are there any questions?"

"Do you want to meet here, or do you want us to come back to camp first?" asked Cody.

We will ride back here to relieve you," said Milo. "If you see a man or two leave the ranch, try to arrest them and bring them to our camp. Always go after them with more than one man. If need be, all of you go to arrest them. I don't want anyone to take risks."

"Are you going to keep them in our camp?" asked Burt.

"No, I want to question them before taking them to Sheriff Drew," said Milo.

"How long do you want to watch the ranch each day?" asked James.

"If we start early in the morning, I think we can stop watching when it gets dark unless we see some men ride out at night," said Milo. "Once we know their operation, we can make our plan to take the ranch."

With the understanding of what each man had to do, Milo and his men rode back to camp. When they rode into camp, Milo saw that Hannah had been busy getting everything set up.

"You have the camp organized," said Milo.

"Nate was a big help in getting it ready," said Hannah. "We are using the tent to store the supplies. Where are Cody and the rest of the men?"

"Cody is watching the ranch," said Milo. "The rest of us will relieve him this afternoon and watch the ranch until dark. I hope to arrest some of the men away from the ranch. Once we do that, Ike will know that something is up, and it could get hot."

"How do you think you will be able to get some of the men away from the ranch?" asked Hannah.

"If they leave to check the cattle or other jobs in the field, we should be able to arrest them," said Milo. "Even if they head for the town, we can follow them and arrest them in town."

"What if they are not outlaws?" asked Nate.

"If we can find one who is not part of the men Ike brought in, we should be able to find out who worked there before Ike," said Milo. "We might be able to get some inside help in removing Ike."

CHAPTER 8

After Milo left, Cody separated his men, instructing them to stay hidden if anyone came in their direction. He said, "I will ride around the ranch and see where the cattle are. If there are men with the cattle, that might be the easiest place to arrest them."

Leaving, Cody made it to the north side of the ranch. In a valley with grass and water, he found what looked to be between five hundred and six hundred head of cattle. Seeing that the valley contained everything the cows needed, Cody knew they would not wander. Going further north, he found an open pasture with more cattle. These would have to be checked on from time to time. He would mention to Milo that maybe he would need to put a couple of men here to watch for activity.

Riding back to where he left Luke and James, he found they had moved to a new location. When James saw that it was Cody, he came out in the open so Cody would know where he was.

Cody saw James and rode over to him. James asked, "What did you find?"

"There are some good places to hold cattle," said Cody. "One of the places is in a valley with good grass and water that would keep the cattle from roaming. Another is an open pasture that would require men to check on the cattle from time to time. What have you found out here?"

"There has been activity around the ranch. As far as ranch work, it looks like some of the men don't do much. I believe those doing the work are some of the original hands. Those men we might be able to get to help us. I noticed that about four others were pushing them, and they did not like what was going on," said James. "The three smaller houses have families living in them. I have identified three men who seem to be the husbands by how the women act toward them."

"The ones doing the pushing sound like the ones we saw on the posters," said Cody.

"If the rest are original ranch hands, we should be able to isolate them," said James.

"Where is Luke?" asked Cody.

"He made his way to the other side of the ranch," said James. "He wanted to see what was behind the building. Luke wanted to see if there was a way to get into the ranch without being seen. That looks like him coming back now."

Luke rode over to where Cody and James were talking. "What did you find out?" asked Cody.

"Behind the house is a lot of cover. They have a garden attended by the women," said Luke. "We might be able to get the women out of danger when we attack the ranch. If no one is working the garden, we could get to the house before anyone would see us."

"Watching the ranch, I think we can determine who are Ike's men and who are the original ranch hands," said Cody. "If we see one of the original ranch hands get away from the ranch where we can talk to him, maybe we can get a layout of the inside of the house. He might be able to give us additional information on how many men Ike has with him."

"Where do you think we will find them away from the house?" asked Luke.

"I don't think we will find them going to town," said James. "Do you think we will be able to get them with the cows?"

"I will suggest to Milo to have someone watch the cattle," said Cody.

It was early afternoon when Milo, with Burt, Billy, and Nate, relieved Cody and his men. When Milo rode in, Cody told him what they had found. He mentioned the pasture where the cows were located.

Luke said, "We have been watching the ranch house all morning, and

Ike has not been seen. I wonder if he is even in the house. However, according to the posters, a couple of his men were seen going into the house for some time. Because of that, I believe that Ike is in there."

James said, "We have identified three men who have families in those three houses. If we could get one of them alone, I am sure we could get a lot of information."

Before Cody and his men went back to camp, he told Milo the pasture location on the north side of the ranch.

After Cody left, Milo said, "Nate, you and Billy ride out to the pasture and keep watching. If anyone shows up to check the cattle, arrest them and bring them here."

Nate and Billy left, circling the ranch. They found the pasture and located a place to watch the cattle. They waited, not seeing anyone show up during the afternoon, and rode back to where Milo and Burt were waiting in the late afternoon.

Nate told Milo, "We didn't see anyone come check the cattle. Maybe we can move some cattle to another location, and it will draw Ike's men out."

"We don't have to worry about being accused of rustling, seeing that you own the cattle and the ranch," said Billy.

At suppertime, a dozen more men showed up at the ranch.

They set up a table in front of the house and lit a fire. Soon the women brought food out of the house and put it on the table. Once everyone finished eating, some men brought out instruments and started playing.

When Milo determined that the men would remain at the ranch, he took his men and returned to camp.

While eating, Cody asked, "What did you find out?"

"No one left the ranch," said Milo. "I had Burt stay with me and sent Nate and Billy to watch the cattle. Nate suggested moving some of the cattle from the pasture to another location. If Ike thinks someone is taking cattle, it should draw them out."

"When do you want to do that?" asked Cody.

"We will all go to the ranch in the morning," said Milo. "We will split up, and Cody will circle the ranch with Luke and James. When you get to the cattle, take half of them and move them into the other valley. Leave them there and go back to watch the rest to see if someone comes to check them."

Hannah was listening to the men talking. She worried that one of them could be wounded or killed. Knowing that she would be alone in camp the next day, she had to be prepared if someone found her.

That night she said to Milo, "Do you want me to do anything special tomorrow?"

"Just remain safe," said Milo, going to his saddlebag, taking out a .32 Colt, and handing it to Hannah. "I want you to keep this on you all the time. I know you know how to use it if you cannot get to the rifle."

"I will be fine," said Hannah. "I may ride into town and get some added supplies while you are gone."

"If you do, make sure you have the Colt with you," said Milo.

After that, they lay down and went to sleep.

The following morning after breakfast, the seven men rode out of camp. After Hannah had cleaned up, she rode to town.

Before the men reached the ranch, Milo had Cody take his men to move the cattle.

When Milo reached the ranch, he found that the men were finishing breakfast. Two men looked to be ordering three other men around. The three men who were being pushed did not look happy. Milo watched as they got their horses saddled. They mounted, left, and rode toward the pasture.

Seeing where they were headed, Milo said, "Burt, take Billy and follow them. Try and capture them without gunfire."

Burt and Billy rode hard to get around the ranch. Once they were on the north side, they picked up the trail of the three men. When Burt and Billy saw the three men again, the three men had stopped and were watching Cody and his men moving some of the cattle. Seeing an opportunity, Burt and Bill came up behind the three men and said, "Raise your hands. If you go for your guns, you will be dead," said Burt.

The three men raised their hands. "Billy, take their guns," said Burt.

After Billy collected their guns, they moved the three men into the open. Cody saw the men ride out into the open and stopped, seeing Burt and Billy had them under control. Cody waited as Burt and Billy moved the three men to him.

"I see you found some of the ranch hands," said Cody.

"You are rustling our cattle," said Amos.

"No," said Cody. "We are moving some of our cattle."

"Who are you?" asked Amos.

"I am US Marshal Cody Paxton," said Cody. "Who are you?"

"I am Amos Chavez. I work for the T Bar Ranch, and these are T Bar cattle."

"You are right. These are T Bar cattle, and US Marshal Milo Ryder owns them," said Cody. "He also owns the ranch."

"Ike Evens runs the ranch," said Amos.

"Not for long," said Burt. "As soon as we arrest or kill Ike, I will be running the ranch."

"Are you Milo Ryder?" asked Amos.

"No, I am his foreman," said Burt. "I will be the one overseeing this ranch."

"What is your name?" asked Amos.

"Burt Ware," said Burt. "Now, if you want to help us move some of these cattle to draw Ike out of the ranch house, we would be happy for the help. But before we move them, who are the men with you?"

"This is Jasper Arguello and Reeve Cortez," said Amos.

"How many men does Ike have at the ranch that work for him?" asked Cody.

"He has eight men he brought to the ranch when he took it over," said Reeve. "There are twenty men who are at the ranch, counting us."

"Are you saying that twelve are the original ranch hands?" asked Burt.

"Si," said Amos.

"How many of them are good men?" asked Burt.

"Mr. Tilghman hired all of us," said Amos. "Only Ike and his eight men came to the ranch after Comanches killed Mr. Tilghman and his family."

"Who is the foreman Mr. Tilghman used?" asked Burt.

"Richard Fleming is the foreman," said Amos. "He lives with his family in the first house next to the main house. Since Ike came, his man Ben Daniels took over as boss of the men. He is mean to all of the original hands. Ike's men have their way with the women at the ranch, and the men don't like it, but none are gunmen who can stop them."

"What do you three want to do?" asked Burt. "Do you want to help us and remain at the ranch working for me, or do you want to run with Ike?"

Amos talked to the other two men, and when he finished, he said, "We want to stay with the ranch, and we will work for you."

"Let's move these cows to another canyon," said Cody.

"North of here is a canyon where you can hide the ones you want to move," said Amos. "We will show you."

After moving the cattle, they rode back to where Milo was waiting. Milo was surprised to see that the three men rode with their guns in their holsters and were talking to the other men.

Burt said, "Milo, I want you to meet Amos Chavez, Jasper Arguello, and Reeve Cortez. These men now work for you. Men, I want you to meet the new owner of the T Bar Ranch, Milo Ryder."

Milo said, "I understand that the three of you want to keep working at the ranch once we run Ike out."

"Si, Mr. Ryder," said Amos. "What do you want us to do?"

"They helped us hide the cattle we took out of the pasture in another canyon on the ranch," said Cody. "Now, I think we need to take them to our camp and hide them. When they don't return to the ranch, I think Ike will look for them. He will find the cattle missing and will think that these three took them."

"Do you think that the other men who Mr. Tilghman hired will want to stay and would help us?" asked Milo.

"If we can tell them what is going on, they will help," said Reeve. "Maybe when it gets dark, I can go in and tell Richard, and he can let the other men know."

"You need to stay with us," said Milo. "You can help us understand what has been going on at the ranch. We need to figure out how to get Ike and his men out without hurting women and children."

"Maybe we have too many men here now, and some of us should go back to camp," said Cody.

"James, I want you and Billy to stay here and watch the ranch," said Milo. "If you find any of Ike's men leaving the ranch, come and get us."

"Mr. Ryder," said Amos. "Maybe Jasper should stay with James and Billy. He knows all of Ike's men and who is not."

"That is a good idea, Amos," said Milo. "Jasper can stay with Billy and James, and the rest of us will go back to camp."

After the rest of the men left for camp James, Billy, and Jasper found a spot to sit together and watch the house while remaining hidden. As men moved around the yard, Jasper would tell them who they were and whether they came with Ike or were among the original hands. The rest of the day, no one left the ranch.

Close to suppertime, Jasper said, "See that man looking toward the north? That is Richard, the foreman. He is looking for us to return from the pasture."

It wasn't long before Richard shook his head, turned, and went to his house.

CHAPTER 9

Ben Daniels ordered Amos, Jasper, and Reeve to check the cattle in the north pasture that morning. Ben had been riding these three men hard for the past several days, and they were fed up with him constantly on their backs.

They left Ben and got their horses. Once they started riding to the north pasture, Amos said, "Someday, I would like to kill him."

"Do you remember those two men who stopped about two weeks ago wanting to look at the ranch?" asked Reeve. "Maybe someone is looking at buying the ranch."

"I hope someone does," said Amos. "I would like to see Ike and all his men gone. Before Mr. Tilghman died, it was a good ranch to work at. But, with Ike and his men threatening to kill us if we leave, no one likes working there."

After they left the ranch, work continued. Ike was trying to figure out when he would sell some more of the cows. Early that morning, he told Ben to have some men go out and check the herd to ensure nothing had happened to them. Ben forgot about them and looked for a woman after sending Amos, Jasper, and Reeve to check the herd. Finding Yolanda, he forced her into the barn. Once he was satisfied, he let her go and went to the house.

Ike asked, "Who did you send to check the cattle?"

"I sent Amos, Jasper, and Reeve," said Ben.

"Do you trust them?" asked Ike.

"They have gone before," said Ben. "Why, what is up?"

"Ever since those two men came looking at the ranch, I have felt uneasy," said Ike. "They had checked with the bank about it before coming out here. After that, Frank said he saw them talking to the sheriff when he was in town. Then, when he was in the café, he overheard Nora tell one of the other customers that the man looking at the ranch was a US marshal."

"Did you do any additional checking about who they were?" asked Ben.

"No. Wait until the three men return to find out how the cattle are doing," said Ike. "We may have to sell some more."

It was getting late in the day, and Amos, Jasper, and Reeve had not returned. Even after supper, they still had not returned. Ben decided that he would ride out and see what was going on. Getting his horse, he rode to the north pasture. When Ben got there, no one was around. Riding around the herd, he discovered that almost half the herd was missing, and Amos, Jasper, and Reeve were not there. Checking the ground, Ben found tracks of several horses used to push the cows. Riding back to the ranch, he went looking for Ike.

Going into the house, he found Ike and said, "We have a problem. I rode out to check on Amos and the men I sent out there, and they are gone and so is half the herd."

"What do you mean they are gone and so is half the herd?" said Ike. "Those three men could not have driven off half the herd by themselves."

"I found tracks of six or seven horses," said Ben. "Either the men were surprised, or they were working together with the ones who took the cows."

"Who would dare to take our cattle?" asked Ike.

"Do you think those two men who showed up that day had anything to do with it?" asked Ben.

"We need to find out if they came back," said Ike. "Maybe they captured our men or killed them."

"What do you want to do?" asked Ben.

"I think we should send Frank into town and see if he can find out if anyone new has been in town," said Ike. "Frank saw them when they were in town before."

Ben went looking for Frank. When he found him, he said, "Ike wants you to go into town in the morning and see if strangers have come to town or if the ones who came looking at the ranch are back."

The next morning before sunup, Frank rode to town.

While he was gone, Ben sent some men out to see if they could find the missing cattle. Ben sent Cullen with two ranch hands to ensure more men didn't leave.

When Frank got to town, he went to the café. He figured that if there were strangers in town, they would show up there to eat. When Nora waited on him, he asked, "Have you seen any new people in town?"

"A couple of days ago, a man and his wife came through here," said Nora. "They spent the night in the hotel and left the next day. Why are you asking?"

Nora knew that Frank was one of Ike's men, and she knew that Milo and his men were there to take over the T Bar Ranch.

"Some of the men from the ranch are missing," said Frank. "Do you know Amos Chavez?"

"I know Amos. Is he one of the men missing?" asked Nora.

"Have you seen him in the last two days?" asked Frank.

"No, he has not been in here," said Nora.

After she left to get his food, Nora remembered seeing Hannah in town the day before. She would have to watch if she came back, and she would have to warn her that Ike and his men were looking for them.

After eating, Frank went to the saloon. When he saw Milo and Billy bring Cullen in and put him in jail, Frank waited until he saw them ride out of town before he left. Frank returned to the ranch and told Ike that he saw one of the men who had stopped by the ranch with a new man. "They brought Cullen in and put him in jail."

"What about the two men with Cullen?" asked Ike.

"I did not see them, only Cullen," said Frank. "They had his hands tied behind his back, and Sheriff Drew put him in jail."

CHAPTER 10

When Milo and the rest returned to camp, Hannah had coffee brewing. Hannah was surprised to see two new men with Milo. Once they had put up their horses, Milo brought them over to introduce Amos and Reeve to Hannah.

"Hannah, I want you to meet Amos Chavez and Reeve Cortez. These are two men who came from the ranch," said Milo. "Gentlemen, I what you to meet my wife, Hannah."

Both men removed their hats, bowed to Hannah, and said, "We are pleased to meet you."

"Do you want to tell me what happened and where James and Billy are?" asked Hannah.

"James and Billy are watching the ranch with Jasper," said Milo.

"Who is Jasper?" asked Hannah.

"Jasper is a friend of ours from the ranch. We were sent out to check the cattle this morning when we found some of your men moving the cows," said Amos. "We thought they were stealing the cows, and we were waiting to see how many men were there when two men came up behind us and took out guns. Once we found out that Milo had purchased the ranch, we helped them move the cows."

"Why didn't you return to the ranch for more help?" asked Hannah.

"We have been trying to get away from the ranch since Ike took it over," said Reeve. "He has promised to kill us if we tried to leave."

"What have you decided about these men?" asked Hannah.

"They will stay with us, and they will be three of the hands at the ranch who will work for Burt," said Milo.

"Are there more who are not part of Ike's men?" asked Hannah.

"There are twelve of us," said Amos. "Ike brought eight men with him who took over the ranch after the Tilghmans were killed."

"If you had twelve men working the ranch, why didn't you drive Ike and his men out?" asked Hannah.

"We are not gunmen," said Reeve. "Some of us have wives and children who Ike's men threatened."

"Once we get rid of Ike and his men, they will be safe," said Milo.

It was suppertime when James, Billy, and Jasper rode into camp. After putting up their horses, Milo introduced Jasper to Hannah while getting their food. Once they had their food, Milo asked, "What did you find out?"

"One of Ike's men, Ben, left the ranch and returned a couple of hours later and went straight to the house," said Billy.

"Jasper pointed out the original foreman, Richard Fleming, who kept looking for them to come in from the pasture," said James. "He finally went to his house when it was suppertime."

"What do you want to do in the morning?" asked Burt.

"They must know by now that cattle are missing," said Milo. "We need to go back to the herd still in the pasture and see who they send out there in the morning. We will take Amos with us so he can explain to the men from the ranch who we are."

Before sunrise the following day, Milo had his men up and eating. He wanted to get to the cattle and be in place before anyone from the ranch showed up. Not knowing if Ike would send anyone out there, he hoped it would include some of his men if he did.

They rode out, taking Amos, Cody, Burt, Luke, and Billy. They arrived at the pasture and saw that they were there alone. Finding cover in the trees on the hill surrounding the open field, they settled in to wait.

About two hours after sunrise, three men rode into the valley and started circling the cattle, looking for tracks that would lead them to the missing cows. Amos saw Cullen McCarthy was with them. "Milo," said Amos, "see the man on the red horse? That is Cullen McCarthy, one of Ike's men."

Milo said, "He is one that we want to arrest. Are the other men from the ranch?"

"Si," said Amos. "That is Garth Daly and Eugene Alsup. They are both good men."

Milo rode out, pointing his pistol at Cullen when Cullen rode near to where Milo and Amos were waiting. "You are under arrest," said Milo.

When Cullen saw Milo, he started to reach for his gun. But seeing that Milo already had his out, he stopped. "Who are you?" demanded Cullen.

"I am US Marshal Milo Ryder, and you are under arrest for stealing my cattle," said Milo.

"These cattle belong to the T Bar Ranch," said Cullen.

"I own the T Bar Ranch," said Milo. "Take your left hand, unbuckle your gun belt, and let it drop."

While Milo was arresting Cullen, Cody, Billy, and Luke stopped the two hands from the ranch. Seeing they were confused about what was going on, Amos rode over to where they were.

When they saw Amos, Garth asked, "What are you doing?"

Amos said, "Meet the new owners of the T Bar Ranch. Cody, these are two more of the original hands. Garth, you now work for these men and will take orders from them."

Burt went to help Milo with Cullen. Getting off his horse, he tied Cullen's hands behind his back, relieved him of his rifle, and picked up his holster. Then, taking the reins of Cullen's horse, Burt remounted and led his horse. Cody had brought the other two men over to where Milo and Burt were.

"We need to take this one to the sheriff in San Luis de la Culebra and put him in jail," said Milo. "Burt, you need to take these two men back to camp and let Hannah know what is going on. Cody, you, and Luke watch the ranch. Take Amos with you. Billy, I want you to ride into town with me to take Cullen to the sheriff."

Burt, Garth, and Eugene rode with Billy and Milo until they turned to their camp. It was noontime when Milo, Billy, with Cullen rode into town.

Going directly to the sheriff's office, they stopped in front. Hearing someone out front, Sheriff Drew came out of his office in time to see Billy dragging Cullen off his horse. "Marshal, what do you have?" asked Sheriff Drew.

"This is Cullen McCarthy," said Milo. "He is wanted for rustling and murder. You can add that he is part of the gang rustling my cows at the T Bar Ranch. There is a five hundred dollar reward on him as well."

Sheriff Drew did not look happy with a prisoner to care for, but he had no choice, as Milo was a US marshal. Billy escorted Cullen into the sheriff's office behind Sheriff Drew. Inside, Sheriff Drew picked up the keys to the cell and opened the door. Billy put Cullen in the cell and closed the door.

Cullen hollered at the sheriff, "He has no right to what he is doing."

Sheriff Drew looked at Cullen and said, "He has every right. He is a US marshal, and he owns the T Bar Ranch. If I were Ike, I would hightail it out of there."

Milo said, "He is the first of the eight men I plan to arrest. You can hold the reward money until we get them all."

"Who will pay for his keep?" asked Sheriff Drew.

"You can make the bill out to the US marshal's office in New Mexico," said Milo. "I suggest that you have a guard on him at all times. When Ike finds out that he is in jail, I am sure he will try and get him out."

Leaving the sheriff's office, Milo and Billy went to the café. Nora saw them coming and opened the door as they arrived. Showing them to a table, she said, "One of the men who work for Ike has been in here looking for you."

"Does he know who we are?" asked Billy.

"He said he was looking for strangers in town," said Nora. "I saw you come in with a man. Is he one of Ike's men?"

"Yes," said Milo. "Ike should be starting to have some trouble. With one of his men taken out, we have five regular hands working with us and away from the ranch."

"What would you like for dinner?" asked Nora.

"We will have the special," said Milo.

Once they finished eating, they rode back to camp.

Cody, Luke, and Amos rode back to watch the ranch. Because they had missed Frank going into town, they didn't know that one was missing from the ranch. Watching the activities, Amos said, "With the five of us not at the ranch. I would think there would be more activity."

"Do you see any of Ike's men?" asked Luke.

"I see Carter and Ben," said Amos. "I would think that Frank would be out with them unless Ike sent him somewhere."

"Who is the one that keeps looking like he expects someone to show up?" asked Cody.

"That is Richard Fleming," said Amos. "He is the foreman. I think he knows something is up but does not know what."

"Can we depend on him to help us if needed?" asked Cody.

"Yes, he is treated the worst," said Amos. "His wife has been mistreated by Carter, one of Ike's men. I know that he would kill Carter, but then his family would take the punishment for it."

In the middle of the afternoon, a rider came up the road and rode into the ranch. Amos was watching at the time and recognized Frank. He turned to Cody. "That is Frank, another of Ike's men. I wonder if he was in town. He could have seen Milo and Billy take Cullen in."

"Let's see if there is a change in activities," said Luke.

Amos had seen Frank go into the house. It wasn't long before Frank came out, and Ike followed him.

Cody was watching when they found Richard, and from what Cody could see, they were questioning him. When it looked like they didn't get the answer they were looking for, they started to beat him.

CHAPTER 11

When Frank told Ike about Cullen being in jail, Ike wanted to find out what was going on. Ike and Frank went looking for Richard. They found him near the barn talking with Dusty. Ike walked up to Richard and asked, "What is going on?"

Richard looked at him and asked, "What are you talking about?"

"What happened to the five men you sent out to check the cows?" asked Ike.

"I don't know what happened to them," said Richard. "Haven't they come back?"

"No, how many are missing?" asked Ike.

"You sent Cullen out with the last two. Where is he?" asked Richard.

"He is in jail," said Frank. "I want to know how you are working with that marshal."

"I don't know anything about no marshal," said Richard.

With that, Ike hit Richard, knocking him to the ground. Ike kicked him and said, "How are you helping that marshal?"

"I don't know any marshal. I have not been off the ranch for days," said Richard.

Ike beat on Richard some more before leaving him lying in the dirt. When Ike and Frank left, Izar came running to help her husband. She took him back to their house, where she could clean him up and clean the blood off his face.

"Someday, I am going to kill Ike," said Richard.

While walking back to the house, Ike said, "We need to get Cullen out of jail. Get Ben and Carter and come to the house."

It wasn't long before Frank returned with Ben and Carter. "What do you need?" asked Ben.

"It looks like the marshal who was asking about the ranch has returned. Frank saw him bring Cullen into town and put him in jail.

"When did this happen?" asked Ben. "I just saw Cullen this morning."

"Frank saw them taking Cullen to jail this morning. We need to get him out and find this marshal before he arrests anyone else," said Ike. "I want you two to get him out of jail."

Ben and Carter went to the barn and saddled their horses. Ike stood by the house and watched them as they rode away, heading for town. Ike figured the two could get to the sheriff and force him to open the jail.

Cody watched as the two men rode out of the ranch. "We need to follow them and see where they are going. If they head to town, the sheriff may need help."

The two men rode past where Cody and the others were hiding, and Cody started to follow them, staying out of sight as they headed to town. When they got close to the camp, Cody said, "Amos, go to the camp and tell Milo that two of Ike's men are heading for town. Tell him that we will help the sheriff if he needs it."

Right after Ben and Carter had started to ride out, Ike told Frank to follow them. Knowing where they were going, Frank took his time to make sure that no one was following them.

Frank had not gone far when he saw three men following Ben and Carter. Frank was surprised when he recognized Amos riding with the men following Ben and Carter. He continued to follow them until he saw Amos leave them, so instead of following the men going to town, he followed Amos to where Milo had set up camp. Hiding where Frank could see how many men were in the camp, Frank was surprised to find that all the men missing from the ranch were there. His second surprise was when he saw a woman in the camp.

Frank noticed the five men from the ranch were armed and were helping to take care of the camp. Now that Frank knew where the marshal had his camp, he had to let Ike know.

While Ben and Carter rode into town, they kept looking to see who was on the street. They wanted to make sure that no one would interfere with their getting Cullen out of jail. Finally, Ben and Carter stopped in front of the sheriff's office. After getting down, they drew their guns before going in.

Sheriff Drew was sitting behind his desk when they came in. When he looked up, he recognized Ben and Carter before seeing that they had their guns out and pointed at him. He started to reach for his when Ben said, "I wouldn't do that if you want to live. Slowly take it out and drop it on the floor."

"What do you want?" asked Sheriff Ed Drew, after dropping his gun on the floor.

"We came to get Cullen out. Get up, open the cell, and let him out," Ben ordered.

Ed got up and took the keys off the peg on the wall before walking back to the cell.

Cullen had heard what was going on in the office and recognized Ben's voice. He was standing with his hat in hand when Ed unlocked the cell.

"Stand aside and let him out," said Carter.

After Cullen came out of the cell, Ben said, "Now you get in there." Ben hit him as Ed entered the cell with his Colt. Ed fell to the floor and lay there, not moving.

Going to the office, Cullen looked for his gun and holster. Finding it on a peg on the wall, he took it and put it on. "How did Ike know I was in jail?" asked Cullen.

"Frank was in town when that marshal brought you in," said Ben. "Where did he find you to arrest you?"

"When Garth, Eugene, and I went to check on the missing cattle, they were waiting," said Cullen. "They jumped me before I had a chance."

"What happened to Garth and Eugene?" asked Ben.

"They went with a couple of other men the marshal had with him," said Cullen. "Amos was with them, and they were as surprised as I was to see Amos. I take it that Amos, Jasper, and Reeve have to be working with the marshal."

"Let's get out of here," said Carter.

"Maybe we should shoot the sheriff since he has seen all three of us," said Cullen.

"Nah, he won't come to the ranch," said Carter. "When Ike took over the ranch, the sheriff was told, but he has been too afraid to come out there."

Putting up their guns, they opened the door and walked out.

Before Cody and Billy reached the town, Milo, Burt, and Nate joined them. As they rode down the main street, Cody saw the horses of Ike's men tried in front of the jail. "They are already in jail," said Cody. "Let's get on both sides of the jail and get them when they come out."

Cody and Billy went to the far side while Milo, Nate, and Burt waited. It wasn't long before the door opened and Ben came out, followed by the other two men.

The three men went to their horses without expecting anyone to be waiting for them. As the three men reached their horses and started to mount, Milo called out, "You are under arrest!"

Hearing Milo, Cullen drew his gun and started firing. Seeing Cullen draw his gun, Cody opened fire, hitting Cullen before he could fire more than twice. Carter and Ben started to shoot but found themselves caught in a crossfire.

When the shooting ended, Billy and Nate had minor wounds. Cullen was on the ground with a wound to his chest. Ben and Carter had wounds to their legs.

Milo, Nate, and Burt helped take the wounded men back into jail. Inside they found Sheriff Drew locked in the cell, where he was alive but out cold on the floor. Moving the sheriff out of the cell, they brought him to the front of the building and locked the three men in the cells.

Milo looked at Nate and Billy's wounds and found that they were only minor wounds to their arms and would just need to be cleaned and wrapped.

While he was looking at the wound, the sheriff came to. Then, looking around in surprise, he said, "What happened?"

"Your prisoner escaped, but now you have three prisoners," said Milo. "How are you feeling?"

"Outside of my head hurting, I am fine," said Sheriff Drew.

When the door opened, a man saw Cody and Luke holding several guns and stopped, not knowing what was happening.

Sheriff Drew said, "Charlie, what are you doing here?"

"I heard the shooting and came to help," said Charlie.

"Marshal, this is Charlie Aiston. He helps me out as a deputy when I need one," said Sheriff Drew. "Charlie, this is US Marshal Milo Ryder, and these are his deputies. He is the new owner of the T Bar Ranch."

"Nice to meet you, Marshal," said Charlie, holding out his hand to shake Milo's.

"It is nice to meet you," said Milo. "Is there a doctor in town?"

"Charlie, go get Doc Jones," said Sheriff Drew.

Charlie left, and it wasn't long before the doctor arrived. "Who is wounded?" asked Dr. Jones.

"These two have a minor wound in their arms," said Milo. "If you have something for the wounds, we can take care of them while you check on the ones in the cells."

Dr. Jones went with Ed to the cell where Cullen was lying to look at his wound first. Unfortunately, while checking Cullen's wound, Cullen died. "Ed, you might as well get Alfred. He has a customer."

The doctor was able to patch the legs of the other two. He said, "Those two will be fine if they don't get an infection. But if something happens, come and get me."

After the doctor left, Milo pulled out the posters for the three men and showed them to the sheriff. "These are the three men you now have in your jail. Cullen, who is dead, was worth eight hundred dollars, Ben was worth eight hundred, and Carter is worth nine hundred," said Milo. "That comes to twenty-five hundred dollars."

"I will have to send away for the money," said Ed. "What about the remaining men at the ranch? Ike Evens, Frank Logan, Nate Garrett, Ernest Antrim, Wade Alsup, and Juan Aquilar?"

"We will be bringing them in soon," said Milo.

Leaving the sheriff's office, they rode back to camp. Once they were back in camp, Milo called the men together. "The ranch is down to maybe nine men, including Ernest Antrim, Wade Alsup, Nate Garrett, Juan Aguilar, Ike Evens, and Frank Logan. Do you think any of the regular hands will stand with Ike?" asked Milo.

Amos said, "I think I can get on the ranch and meet with Richard. If I can convince him that we are now working for you, he should get the word to the other men. I don't believe any regular hands will stand with Ike. The three still there of Ike's original men are mean and will fight."

"How are you going to get to Richard?" asked Garth.

"I believe that I can get to the back of his house, and if Izar is at the house, she can get Richard for me," said Amos.

"Maybe you should wait until dark," said Milo. "Richard might even be in the house at that time."

"I can go with you," said Garth. "Maybe I will be able to find some of the other men and talk to them. I think waiting until it is dark is good."

"We can eat early and then go where we can watch before we try to get to Richard," said Amos.

"I want to stay at the ranch tomorrow night," said Milo.

Frank had seen enough about the camp where Marshal Milo Ryder was staying. He knew that Ike would want to go after him with the information. So, after making his way back to his horse, he rode back to the ranch.

Going to the house, he found Ike in the office. Ike asked, "Did you follow them to town?"

"No," said Frank. "I waited a little, and it was good, as three men followed them. One of them was Amos."

"Amos was with them?" asked Ike. "Where did they go?"

"About four miles from here, Amos left them and went to their camp," said Frank. "I wanted to find out if the other missing men were with Amos."

"You know where they camped?" asked Ike.

"Yes, and they have a woman with them," said Frank. "The rest of the missing men are at the camp."

"When Cullen, Ben, and Carter get back, we will pay them a visit in the morning," said Ike. "We will hit them before the sun comes up."

"They have a lot of men there," said Frank. "I counted seven men and the woman, besides the five men from the ranch."

"Do you think the men from the ranch will fight with them?" asked Ike.

"They were free to walk around the camp and had their guns with them," said Frank.

"After the men get back, I will put together a plan," said Ike. "Go find Archie and Juan and tell them to be ready to go in the morning."

It was late afternoon, and Ben, Cullen, and Cater had not returned. Ike began to wonder what was going on. Frank said, "You know the sheriff isn't that good. I bet they locked him up and went to the saloon to celebrate."

CHAPTER 12

Hannah heard that Amos and Garth were going to go to the ranch. They wanted to try to talk to some of the men at the ranch. Because they would leave early, she would plan on an early supper.

While eating supper, Burt sat with Amos and Garth, trying to get some information on the layout of the buildings at the ranch. "Are you sure you will be able to get in and out without being seen by Ike?" asked Burt.

"Si," said Amos. "I have a signal that Richard and I have used to let each other know who is coming. When he hears that, I know he will want to know what is happening."

Before it got dark, Amos and Garth rode back to the ranch. They stopped where they had been watching the ranch before and waited for dark. While they were watching, they saw Richard return to his house. Garth noticed that Brad Gosset, who lived next to Richard's house, was also in for the night.

After dark, they rode to the back of the ranch, left their horses, and made their way to the back of the two houses. Amos signaled Richard and waited.

Richard was sitting at the table with his wife when he sat up with a surprised look when he heard Amos. Looking at his wife, he said, "Amos is outside."

"What do you think he wants?" asked Izar.

"I need to see him and find out what is going on," replied Richard.

Getting up, Richard blew out the light before opening the door. He opened the door a little and looked out to see if anyone was watching who could see him leave the house. Outside he made his way around the house to where Amos was waiting. "Amos, where have you been?" asked Richard.

"I have been with the ranch's new owner," said Amos. "He wants to take it over tomorrow. We have three of Ike's men in jail now. I need to know if any of the regular hands will help Ike?"

While they were talking, Brad and Garth joined them. Brad asked, "What is going on? Garth told me that five of our men are with a US marshal who owns this ranch."

"That is right," said Amos. "The man's name is Milo Rider. He bought the ranch, but Burt Ware will be running it."

"What do you want us to do?" asked Richard.

"We need you to get word to the rest of the men that we will be coming in to take over the ranch in the morning," said Amos. "They should not help Ike if they want to have a job when the new owner takes over."

Brad said, "Five of Ike's men are still here. Ernest Antrim, Wade Alsup, Archie Garrett, Juan Aguilar, and Frank Logan. We will have to be careful telling the others what will happen in the morning."

"Brad is right," said Richard.

"You will have to ensure that Ike does not find out," said Amos.

"We will tell them," said Richard. "If we can help, we will. I will have the men make sure they have their guns."

"Milo has six men with him, and his wife," said Amos. "I think if you can keep everyone out of the way if there is a gunfight, it will be best. Besides Milo and his men, Carter, Jasper, Eugene, Reeve, and I are with him."

"We will make sure that the women and children are safe," said Brad. "I overheard Frank saying to Ike that he found your camp. They are waiting for Ben and the others to return to go after you."

"Those three are in jail," said Amos. "We will not have to worry about them."

Thanking Brad and Richard, Garth and Amos left to return to camp.

Milo was waiting for them when they arrived. "How did it go? Were you able to talk to Richard?" asked Milo.

"We talked to Richard and Brad," said Amos. "They will make sure that the women and children are safe."

"Brad said that Frank knows where our camp is," said Garth. "I think that we will need to keep a guard. They might decide to raid us."

"We can do that," said Milo. "I wonder how he found the camp?"

"If Ike is waiting for Ben, Cullen, and Carter before he would come here, we may not have to worry," said Amos.

"Do you know how many men Ike still has at the ranch?" asked Burt.

"Brad said there are five men with Ike," said Garth.

"Just to be safe, tomorrow we all will go to the ranch, including Hannah," said Milo.

After Milo finished talking to Garth and Amos, he went to find Hannah. When he found her, he said, "Tomorrow after we eat breakfast, I want you to pack up, with the help of some of the men from the ranch, and follow us to the ranch," said Milo.

"What happened?" asked Hannah.

"Garth said that they know the location of our camp," said Milo. "We will take over the ranch in the morning, and I want to stay at the ranch tomorrow night."

The following morning activity at the camp was bustling. With the help of Jasper and Reeve, Hannah had breakfast ready before sunrise. Once everyone had finished eating, Milo and Amos and the rest of Milo's men rode out.

Ike kept pacing the house, wondering what had happened to Ben and the others. *They should have been back here by now, even if they stopped at the saloon. Did something go wrong, and why didn't Frank follow them to town? I would know what happened to them if he had, but he would not have found the marshal's camp. I will send Frank to town to find out where the men are in the morning.*

That night sleep did not come to Ike. Things had changed since that marshal showed up to look at the ranch. If something happened in town and his men were arrested, maybe he needed to leave the area before something happened to him.

The following morning Ike got up and went to the kitchen for breakfast. Loretta, the cook, was acting differently when she served him breakfast. "What's wrong?" asked Ike.

"I did not sleep well last night," lied Loretta.

Early that morning, she had gone outside, where Richard found her. He told her that she needed to get away from the house as soon as possible. When she asked why, Richard told her there would be trouble and that it could be a gunfight.

Not wanting to say any more, she quickly served his breakfast and returned to the stove, waiting for Ike to finish.

While Ike was eating, Frank came in.

"Did Ben return last night?" asked Ike.

"No," said Frank. "None of them came back last night."

"I want you to go into town and find out what happened," said Ike. "Sit down. You eat something first."

Frank sat down at the table.

Loretta heard Ike tell Frank to eat, so she got a plate and gave it to Frank, filled with eggs, potatoes, biscuits, and gravy. Once she fed Frank, she left the kitchen to go to her room. While they were eating, Ike heard a commotion going on outside. "What the hell is going on?" said Ike.

Ike and Frank got up and went to the front door to find out what was happening. When they went to the front door, Loretta went out the back door, going to Richard's and Izar's house, where she would be safe.

When Ike opened the door, he saw the people moving away from the house like they were trying to get away. He then saw riders coming up the road toward the ranch. Seeing the number of riders, Ike knew that it wasn't Ben. Reaching behind the door, he grabbed a rifle before going out and holding it as the riders came into the yard.

"You are trespassing," said Ike, as Milo and his men stopped in front of him.

"You are the one trespassing, and you are under arrest," said Milo. "I own this ranch."

Cody was next to Milo when Ike started to raise his rifle. Cody didn't wait but drew his Colt and fired, hitting Ike in the shoulder, causing him to drop his rifle. Frank had started to draw his pistol but changed his mind.

Off to the side near the barn, Ernest and Archie started to raise their rifles when Richard and Dusty held their Colts on them. Richard said, "Drop your rifles."

Ned turned and saw that they were covered and dropped his rifle, and Ernest did the same.

Cody heard the commotion at the barn and looked over as two men came out of the bunkhouse, shooting at them. Cody returned fire, killing one of the men but not before he had wounded Nate. As he was firing, Billy wounded the second man, causing his shot to go wild. Brad and Jesse grabbed the two men, taking their guns away from them before they could recover.

Cody and Billy rode over to give Brad and Jesse a hand.

Milo looked at Frank and said, "You are also under arrest. Amos, I will give you the privilege of tying these two up."

"Thank you," said Amos. "I have wanted to do that for a long time."

With Ike and Frank taken care of, Milo turned his attention to what Cody and Billy were doing. The rest of Milo's men got off their horses and went to help round up the four men. Then, with no more shooting, the people started coming out in the open. Amos said, "This is US Marshal Milo Ryder." The people gathered around to hear Amos. "He is the new owner of the T Bar Ranch, and these are his men. You will have a chance to meet them and his wife."

Nate walked over to Milo, and Milo saw that Nate was wounded. He had been hit in the shoulder.

Loretta came out of the house with Izar and walked over to where Ike was bleeding. She looked up at Milo and asked, "Do you want me to stop his bleeding?"

"If you can, take a look at Nate before Ike. Then maybe we can take him to jail," said Milo. "Could we get a wagon to take them?"

Izar came out of the house, and Loretta said, "Izar, help me with these two men." Then, pointing to Nate, she said, "We want to look at his wound first."

The two women helped the wounded into the kitchen.

"I am Richard Fleming," said Richard, coming over to Milo. "I have been the foreman here for several years, and Izar is my wife. The woman who offered to stop the bleeding was Loretta. She is the cook."

"Thank you," said Milo, shaking Richard's hand. "I hope you will want to remain as the foreman at this ranch. Can you have someone get us a wagon?"

Richard turned to one of the men and said, "Dusty, get Mr. Ryder a wagon."

Burt, who had been helping with the prisoners, walked over to Milo. Milo said, "Richard, I want you to meet the man overseeing the operations here. Burt, this is Richard Fleming. Richard, this is Burt Ware. Burt, Richard has been the foreman for several years, and I believe you will want to keep him as the foreman."

Burt shook Richard's hand and said, "I hope we can get this ranch back in order now that we have gotten rid of Ike and his men."

While they were talking, Hannah rode in with the rest of the men and their equipment. Milo said, "Richard, I want you to meet my wife, Hannah."

Hannah got off her horse and said, "It looks like you have taken over the ranch."

"We have control, and as soon as Loretta finishes with Nate and Ike, we are taking the last of Ike and his men to jail."

"Who is Loretta?" asked Hannah.

"She is the cook," said Richard. "If you come with me, I will introduce you to her and my wife."

Hannah went with Richard into the house. The front room was the first room that she saw. There was a fireplace on the wall to the right, and two couches and three chairs were in the room. A coffee table sat in front of both couches. A gun case was on the wall to the left, filled with rifles. A hallway was next to the gun case, hidden by stairs leading to the second floor. A doorway led from the kitchen to the back of the room. After following Richard to the kitchen, Hannah found Cody with Nate, Ike, and two women.

"Hi, Hannah," said Cody. "Did you have any problems?"

"No, Jasper and the others helped pack everything up," said Hannah. "It looks like you had a little trouble here."

"Mrs. Ryder, I want you to meet my wife, Izar, and the cook, Loretta. Ladies, this is Mrs. Ryder, the new owner's wife," said Richard.

"Ladies, please call me Hannah. We are very informal on the ranch," said Hannah. "How bad is Nate hurt?"

Izar was finishing cleaning his wound and putting a wrapping on it. She looked at Hannah and said, "The bullet just left a ridge on his shoulder. He will be fine."

Nate said, "I what to thank you for taking care of it."

Loretta had finished wrapping Ike's wound, and Cody was getting ready to take him back out. "If you will excuse me," said Cody, "I think I will get rid of this and take him to jail."

Loretta looked at Hannah and asked, "You will be staying here, no?"

"No, I will not be staying here," said Hannah.

"If you are not staying here, who will be staying here?" asked Loretta.

"One of our men, Burt Ware, will be staying here to run the ranch," said Hannah. "My husband and I have two more ranches east of here."

"Is he married?" asked Loretta.

"No, but I think he will be before long," said Hannah. "However, we will be staying here for a few days to understand the operations and ensure that those who want to remain working here do."

"Most of us have no place to go," said Loretta. "When Ike and his men came here, they caused us nothing but trouble. His men would have their way with any woman here, and Ike would do nothing to stop it. So it will be a relief to all of us with Ike and his men gone."

"I am sure you will like the change," Hannah said.

"So, how many people will be staying for a while?" asked Loretta.

"With me, there are eight of us," said Hannah. "How many bedrooms are in the house?"

"We have five bedrooms on the second floor," said Loretta. "I have a room on this floor."

"We will need four of the bedrooms," said Hannah. Burt will need a room that he will continue to stay in. The other three are for Cody, Milo and me, and Luke."

"I will help you get them ready," said Izar to Loretta.

"I am sure the ranch women will want to celebrate and welcome you here," said Loretta. "They know how to make the food and set it up."

When Cody had Ike back outside, Dusty had the wagon at the house.

Cody loaded Ike in the back, where Frank, Ernest, Ned, Juan, and Wade were already tied.

Milo asked, "Cody, can you take them to the sheriff? While you are there, check his posters for these other four."

"I will do that," said Cody. "I will ensure that the sheriff knows we are on the ranch."

Richard stood there and said, "Dusty, you drive the wagon for Cody."

Milo said, "Take two men with you on horseback in case there is any trouble."

"Señor, can Jesse and Brad be the two men to ride with you?" asked Amos. "They have suffered the most from them, and I know they would like to see them in jail."

Milo handed Cody the wanted posters to show the sheriff. Putting the posters in his pocket, Cody and the three ranch hands started for town with the prisoners.

CHAPTER 13

With Ike and his men taken to jail, Milo wanted to look the buildings and ranch over. Amos walked around the ranch with Milo, answering questions as they went. Burt got with Richard to discuss the operations and talk to the hands.

Hannah was in the house talking to Loretta and Izar. The rest of the men put up their horses and talked to some of the hands.

Milo and Amos went to the bunkhouse first to see what the condition of the building was. Then, going inside, Milo found that it had been well cared for and didn't need significant repairs. Amos pointed out that because Richard had a house to live in with his wife, the top hand lived in the foreman's room. From the bunkhouse, they went to the barn. Again Milo didn't find any problems. They looked at the horses in the corral next. Milo decided that he would have Billy take a look at them. From what he saw, they were in good shape.

Amos said, while walking around, "Most of the men want to stay on."

"How have the men taken to Richard running the ranch as the foreman?" asked Milo.

"He has been strict about making sure everything is correct. He is a fair man," said Amos. "I am sure that he will get along with Mr. Ware."

"I am sure that Burt will want you to call him Burt," said Milo. "We have always been like a family at the other ranches."

"He is single, no?" asked Amos.

"Yes, he is single, but I believe he will be married to a woman from El More soon," said Milo. "She will be coming here after they marry."

"Will she replace Loretta?" asked Amos.

"No," said Milo. "Loretta will remain as the cook."

When Milo finished looking the ranch over, he found Hannah back at the house in the kitchen with Loretta and Izar, talking at the table. When he walked in, Loretta asked, "Would you like a coffee?"

"Thank you," said Milo. "I know that we have upset your day by being here. However, I believe things will settle down and return to normal."

After getting Milo coffee, Loretta said, "Dinner will be ready soon. Izar is helping me with all the excitement. We will have your rooms ready this afternoon where you can put your gear."

"It is nice to know that life will be back to how it was before Mr. and Mrs. Tilghman were killed," said Loretta. "You can see that the men are glad that Ike is gone, and the women already want to put on a celebration in your honor."

It wasn't long before Burt walked in with Richard. Once they sat down, Milo asked, "What do you think of the operation?"

"I had a chance to talk to some of the men. Amos had the word spread to them that if they did not interfere with us taking over the ranch, they would keep their jobs," said Burt. "The ones I talked to were happy that they would remain working here."

"We will spend a couple of days here," said Milo. "That should give Sheriff Ed Drew time to get the reward money together, and we can set up a bank account so you will have money to operate with."

"Once I get settled, I would like to contact Shellie and get married," said Burt.

Loretta heard Burt talk about a wedding and asked, "Will you have the wedding here?"

"No, I am sure her parents would like to have it in El More, where they live," said Burt.

"May I ask what will happen to me when you get married?" asked Loretta.

"You will remain here," said Burt. "I do not plan on changing anything unless I see something wrong that needs changing. We want to raise a family, so I am sure that with all the men and starting a family, we will need your help."

"Thank you," said Loretta. "When you marry, we will have a big celebration when you bring your new wife home."

Izar said, "Richard, go ring the dinner bell. Dinner is ready."

Richard got up and rang the bell, and it wasn't long till all the men were in and sitting at the table.

Izar, Loretta, and Hannah put the food on the table and sat down.

Jesse Salazar asked, "Mr. Ware, are you going to keep us who are here now?"

"First of all, you can all call me Burt. I don't know all of your names, but I will call you by your first name as I get to know you," said Burt. "Like I told Amos, if you are not attached to Ike, then you will retain your job with the ranch."

"Will you make changes to the operation?" asked Jesse Salazar.

"Like I told Loretta," said Burt, "I don't plan on making changes unless I see something wrong that needs changes. If you have suggestions for improving the operations here, feel free to give them to me."

"What about you, Mr. Ryder?" asked Jesse.

"Burt will be running the operations here," said Milo. "I still have a ranch outside of Stonewall that I will be running."

"You will not be staying here?" asked Jesse.

"Hannah and I will be here for a couple of days, and then we will go back home," said Milo.

After eating, the men got busy with the chores that needed completing. The women got busy planning to celebrate the new owner. They wanted to put on a feast with music and plenty of food.

Cody rode in front of the wagon holding Ike, Frank, Ernest, Ned, and Juan. Jesse and Brad followed the wagon, driven by Dusty. When they arrived in town, some townspeople stopped and watched as they drove up to the sheriff's office. Nora from the café was out front when they drove by.

When she saw Ike in the wagon tied up, she smiled, knowing that the T Bar Ranch was out of Ike's control.

Sheriff Drew came out when they stopped in front of the sheriff's office. Looking at Cody, he said, "What is going on?"

"Sheriff, these men are under arrest," said Cody. "You need to lock them up with the others we turned over to you and hold for trial. I have wanted posters on some of them. I want to look at any posters you might have on the others. Once we determine who has posters, you need to get the reward money to US Marshal Milo Ryder."

"Bring them in, and I will lock them up," said Sheriff Drew. Walking away from Cody, he was cursing that he now had more prisoners to watch.

Once he locked them up, he asked Cody, "Are all these men charged with rustling?"

"They are under arrest for rustling cattle of the T Bar Ranch," said Cody. "They are wanted on the charges on posters we found on them. You will have to let us know when the judge will be here for the trial, but first, let's look at your posters."

While Cody was going through the posters, Sheriff Drew asked, "Who will testify against them for rustling cattle?"

Dusty said, "I, along with some other men at the T Bar, witnessed these men taking cattle and selling them."

"From what I know, Mr. Ryder only purchased the ranch in the past few days. So how can they say these men rustled the cattle?" asked Sheriff Drew.

"They sold cattle that did not belong to them, as the bank was the owner until Milo Ryder purchased the ranch," said Cody.

When Cody finished going through the posters, he found posters on all the men. "You need to get the reward money together for all the men in your jail and get it to Milo. We are the ones who arrested these outlaws. Will that be a problem?"

"No, I will get it together," said Sheriff Drew. "I will get in touch with the judge and let them know at the ranch when he will be available."

"How long will it take you to get the money?" asked Cody.

"It will be here the day after tomorrow," said Sheriff Drew.

Cody, along with Dusty, Jesse, and Brad, walked outside. Cody said, "I think this calls for a drink on Milo. Dusty, do you know of a saloon?"

"Si, the El Tarro," said Dusty. "It is just down the street."

Taking their horses and wagon, they rode to the saloon and went in. Finding a table, the four men sat down. It wasn't long until the barkeep came over. "Dusty, you have not been in here for some time. What happened?" asked the barkeep.

"We have a new boss," said Dusty. "Senior Ryder bought the T Bar, and this is one of his men, US Marshal Cody."

"What can I get for you men?" asked the barkeep.

"Bring us a round of beer," said Cody.

While waiting for their beer, Brad said, "Do you think Sheriff Drew will get you the reward money? He did not look too happy about having Ike in jail."

"He does not have a choice," said Cody. "If he does not get it, he will end up in jail, if I know Milo."

"It is good to see those men in jail," said Jesse. "They have done terrible things to the women of the ranch. I know that they will all be happy now."

When the barkeep returned with their beer, he said, "I saw you come into town with several other men. What happened to them?"

"That was Ike Evens and his men," said Cody. "They were arrested for rustling cattle at the T Bar Ranch."

"Word was that Ike was running the ranch," said the barkeep. "What happened?"

"The bank owned the ranch, and Sheriff Drew was afraid to run Ike and his men off the ranch," said Cody. "Milo Ryder bought the ranch, and with the help of these men, we arrested Ike. He will go to trial and could hang."

"It was a sad story when we heard that Mr. and Mrs. Tilghman was killed," said the barkeep. "I know I have seen you three men here before, but I do not recall when I saw you."

Cody replied, "I run one of Mr. Ryder's other ranches. You will probably get to know the man running the T Bar ranch. His name is Burt Ware."

"We are looking forward to working for Mr. Ware," said Dusty. "Mr. Cody and Mr. Ryder are both US marshals. We will again have a good ranch at the T Bar."

"It is good to meet you, Marshal. I look forward to meeting this Burt Ware," said the barkeep, going back to the bar.

Once they finished their beers, Cody said. "Let's head back to the ranch. We should be there in time for supper."

Getting up, they left and rode back to the ranch.

CHAPTER 14

When Cody and the others rode into the ranch, several men gathered at the table the hands ate at. Dusty, Jesse, and Burt joined them while Cody went to the house. When Cody sat down with the men in the house, Milo asked, "Did you have any trouble?"

"No," said Cody. "I don't think Sheriff Drew is happy holding the prisoners."

"Did you find anything on the ones we didn't have the papers on?" asked Milo.

"Sheriff Drew had posters on all the men," said Cody. "When we figured it out, eleven thousand dollars in reward money should be coming."

"What did Sheriff Drew say about the reward money?" asked Burt.

"When I asked him when the reward money would be available, he said that he would have it the day after tomorrow," said Cody.

"What about the rustling charge?" asked Burt.

"The sheriff didn't want to contact the judge for a trial until Dusty told him that he and some men at the ranch saw Ike take and sell some cattle," said Cody.

"We don't have to remain here for that trial," said Milo. "We will wait for the reward money to come in."

"Mr. Ryder, the women would like to set up a celebration in your honor for freeing them of Ike," said Loretta.

"Please call me Milo," said Milo. "That is nice of them. When would they like to do that?"

"They would like two days to prepare the food and set everything up," said Loretta. "They would like to cook a young steer with your permission, Mr. Ware," said Izar.

"Please call me Burt," said Burt. "Have Amos or one of the men get a steer for them."

"What will we need to do to help them?" asked Hannah.

"They will take care of all of it," said Izar. "I was talking to some of the women earlier, and they are excited that they will not have to put up with Ike or his men. They will now feel free to walk around the ranch and not worry about being mistreated."

Burt asked, "Do we need to get supplies for the ranch?"

Richard said, "We got some supplies for the ranch four days ago. So I think we are good for now."

"How about the house?" asked Hannah.

"I will have to take a look," said Loretta. "I believe we are good, but I will check to make sure."

"Tomorrow, I want to ride out and move those cows back to the ones we took them away from," said Burt. "I want to locate the rest of the herd while we are there."

"I will have some men move them back while you and I go look at the rest of the cattle," said Richard.

Milo asked, "Did any other men come and talk to Ike while he was here?"

"Three other men came with Ike when he first arrived," said Amos.

"Do you know their names?" asked Burt.

"Tobias Averill, Chris Spence, and Harris Poole," said Richard.

"What happened to them?" asked Milo.

"They did not like being on the ranch," said Amos. "One day, they just took their gear and left. I think Ike and them had words."

"I thought I saw them one other time," said Richard.

"Where was that?" asked Milo.

"When we were rounding up the cattle to move them, I thought I saw Ike talking to them," said Richard. "He didn't notice that I had seen them. They may have taken some of the cattle that are missing."

"Burt, you may have to watch for them if they decide to come back," said Milo.

"That was several months ago," said Richard. "Since then, I believe that it was only Ike who was taking and selling the cattle."

"I don't understand why Ike would be content to remain on the ranch. His background is in robbing banks," said Milo.

"He would sometimes leave for a few days," said Amos. "When he came back, he always had money, and his horses looked like they had been ridden hard."

"Did Sheriff Drew ever come out here?" asked Burt.

"No," said Richard. "Sheriff Drew would avoid Ike even when he was in town."

"Do you think he knew what Ike was doing?" asked Cody.

"If he did, he was afraid to confront Ike," said Richard.

"That must be why the bank was willing to sell the ranch for what it owed the bank," said Milo. "Whoever bought it would have to deal with Ike."

"Billy, I would like you to look at the horses tomorrow and let me know what kind of shape they are in," said Burt.

"I will have Garth go with you," said Richard. "He has been the one training and caring for the horses. I will introduce you to him in the morning."

"Thanks," said Billy. "I look forward to meeting him."

"I heard Amos say that you have a way with animals and have been training the horses at the main ranch," said Richard. "I am sure that Garth will want to ask you about what you do to train horses."

"We have another man, Jose, at the Lazy S Ranch with a palomino he trained that works cattle like no other horse I have seen," said Billy. "He got on him one morning and went through his exercises without using a saddle or reins."

"Garth has done something with the horses here that I am sure you will want to see," said Richard.

Richard got up and said, "Thank you for supper. I need to go and check on the men. Izar, I will see you at home when I have finished."

The rest of the people got up, and the men entered the living room. Hannah, Loretta, and Izar started to clean up.

In the living room, Burt found glasses and whiskey and handed them to Milo and the rest of the men. "This is to celebrate moving into the new ranch," said Burt.

After the men sat down, Milo asked, "Burt, do you have any questions about the ranch?"

"I don't think I will have any trouble, if that is what you mean," said Burt.

"I want to get things set up with the bank and the mercantile," said Milo.

"There may be a bill at the mercantile," said Burt. "Richard said they had gotten supplies a couple of days ago."

"We will have to see," said Milo. "I want to see you get a fresh start in San Luis de la Culebra. I am not sure about Sheriff Drew. He does not seem like a sheriff who takes the law to heart. The bank could have asked more for the ranch if he had done something about Ike."

"Burt, when will you and Shellie be married?" asked Billy.

"I will have to get settled here before marrying Shellie," said Burt. "Maybe I could invite her and her folks to come and see the place before we get married."

"I think that is a good idea," said Hannah, walking into the living room and hearing what Burt said.

"When we go to town, you can send her a telegram," said Milo.

"I am sure she will like it here," said Hannah. "Loretta will make her as welcome as she has me."

"When everyone is ready, I will show you where you can sleep," Loretta said, when she entered the living room.

When Billy and Nate got up, Billy said, "Richard arranged for Nate and me to sleep in the bunkhouse. We will see you in the morning."

It wasn't long after Billy and Nate left that the rest decided to go to bed. Loretta had already helped Burt get set up in the primary bedroom, so he knew where he would sleep. Loretta showed Cody, Milo, and Hannah their rooms.

Once Milo and Hannah were alone, Hannah said, "This is a nice ranch. I am sure that Shellie will like living here."

"What do you think about Burt having a bigger house than we have at the Rocking R?" asked Milo.

"I am happy where we are living," said Hannah. "We do not need all the rooms here, and if Burt and Shellie are going to raise a family, they may need all the rooms when her parents and we come to visit."

Milo sat quietly for a while.

Hannah asked, "Is something wrong?"

"Burt wants to buy half of the ranch," said Milo.

The statement took Hannah by surprise. "Are you going to let him?" asked Hannah.

"I am going to," said Milo. "With him owning half the ranch, it will cause him to be more astute to its operation. That will lighten my worries about it failing or if we have enough money to keep it operational."

"When are you going to tell him?" asked Hannah.

"I will tell him in the morning," said Milo.

The next morning after breakfast, Milo called Burt aside. Burt went into the office and asked, "What do you need?"

"Remember when you asked me if you could go in as a partner with this ranch?"

"Yes," said Burt. "Because you had not said anything, I figured you did not want to do it."

"I have to admit that I had doubts about what I should do," said Milo. "I have decided to let you buy into the ranch. The cost was ten thousand dollars, so we will be partners if you want to invest five thousand. Because you will be running the ranch, I want thirty percent of the profits after expenses. So that will give you seventy percent."

"Thank you," said Burt. "I believe that it is more than fair of you. We can have the paper drawn up with the terms of the partnership and make it legal. I will have the bank release the five thousand dollars to you in Stonewall and have it available when you go home."

"Why don't you put up two thousand against the loan at the bank as I did?" asked Milo. "Then we will use the money that the ranch raises to pay off the loan. If we put an additional two thousand in the ranch fund in the bank for operating expenses, that should get the ranch going. I plan on splitting the reward money with our men. We could take our shares and put it in the ranch fund."

After shaking hands, Burt went looking for Richard.

Hannah saw Milo coming out of the office and asked, "Did you tell Burt?"

"Yes," said Milo. "Tomorrow, when we go into town, we will have a paper drawn up stating the conditions, and it will be legal."

"When are you going to tell the rest of the men?" asked Hannah.

"After we have the document signed," said Milo.

"Are you going to let some of the men do the same?" asked Hannah.

"I will have to wait and see," said Milo. "Cody might want to do something like that with the Simms ranch. If he does, we could add another ranch."

Milo went outside while Hannah went to see Loretta.

When Milo walked up to the corral, Billy was checking out the horses with Garth. "What do you think?" Milo asked Billy.

"There are some fine horses in this bunch," said Billy. "Garth has been telling me what he has been doing with them. I would have to say that he has done a good job. Garth, I want you to meet Milo Ryder. He is the new owner of the ranch."

"Mr. Ryder, I am glad to meet you," said Garth, holding out his hand.

Milo shook his hand and said, "I am glad to meet you. Billy has been working with my horses at the Rocking R Ranch."

"He has been telling me about your paint," said Garth. "He sounds like some kind of horse."

"Jose, who works at the Lazy S Ranch, has a palomino that is a wonder to watch work cattle," said Milo. "Have you seen Burt?"

"He rode out with Richard," said Billy.

"If you want to join them, I can get you a horse," said Garth. "Billy and I were going to look at the horses we have in the pasture. I believe that is where Richard was taking Mr. Ware."

"Thanks," said Milo. "I will ride with you."

After saddling their horses, they rode out. They found Burt and Richard looking at the land where they could cut grass for winter feed, but they would have to keep the livestock off it. As Milo rode up to them, Burt was telling Richard that they needed to fence it.

"Hi, Milo," said Burt. "I was telling Richard that we could use this field for hay. But we would have to fence it to keep the cattle off it."

"Have you had a chance to look over all the cattle?" asked Milo.

"This is the first area we started looking in," said Richard. "I sent some men to where you had moved the cattle to bring them back. There are three different areas where we have pastured cattle during the summer. We try not to run the grass down."

Burt spent the day with Richard getting to know the ranch's boundaries. Then, back at the ranch, he talked to the men about how they had operated in the past. He learned some of the men by their first names and encouraged them to call him Burt.

CHAPTER 15

THE MORNING SHERIFF DREW HAD the reward money available, Burt and Milo rode to town. It was the middle of the morning when they stopped in front of the sheriff's office. Entering the office, they found Sheriff Drew sitting at his desk. He looked up and said, "I suppose you are here to get your money."

"That would be right," said Milo.

"Have you heard when the judge will be here?" asked Burt.

"He won't be here until next Tuesday," said Drew. "I will need the men from the ranch to testify at their trial."

"The men already said that they would," said Burt.

Sheriff Drew got up and went to his safe. After taking out the reward money, he handed it to Milo. "That is a lot of money to be carrying around," said Sheriff Drew.

"I think we can handle it," said Milo.

Leaving the sheriff's office, they went to the bank. Seth Brewer, the owner, saw them come in. Getting up, he went to greet them. "Mr. Ryder, what can I do for you?" he asked.

"We need to make some changes to the title of the ranch," said Milo. "Burt will purchase half the ranch as a partner of mine. Will that be a problem?"

"No, not at all. Come into my office," said Seth. "How would you like it written?"

"We will need both names on the title," said Milo. "Burt will be putting additional money toward the purchase."

"What will you add to the initial payment?" asked Seth.

"I will have two thousand dollars transferred from the bank in Stonewall to you and applied to the loan," said Burt. "The loan will have to be changed to both Milo's and my name. After we finish and leave here, I will telegraph the bank and have them transfer the two thousand dollars. We also want to set up an account for the ranch with your bank, where we will deposit three thousand dollars."

"Will you have that transferred to the bank?" asked Seth.

"No," said Milo. "That money we will deposit today."

"How will this partnership work?" asked Seth.

"Because Burt will be running the ranch, we have agreed that I will get thirty percent of the profit, and Burt will get seventy percent," said Milo. "Funds will be kept in your bank, and once a year, my share of the profit will be transferred to my bank in Stonewall."

"Burt, you will be doing the banking here?" asked Seth.

"Yes," said Burt. "Milo will be able to access the account if something happens to me."

"Will there be any other changes?" asked Seth.

"No, I think that will take care of the partnership," said Milo. "How long will it take you to change the title and loan?"

"Give me an hour, and I will have the papers ready to sign," said Seth.

"We have some other business to take care of in town. So when we finish, we will be back," said Burt.

Leaving the bank, they walked to the telegraph office, where Burt sent two telegraphs. The first one he sent to the bank in Stonewall requesting that two thousand dollars get sent to the bank in San Luis de la Culebra.

The second telegraph he sent to Shellie and her parents. He requested that they come to visit the ranch and make plans for the wedding.

SHELLIE MARKER: I HAVE PURCHASED A RANCH IN SAN LUIS DE LA CULEBRA WITH MILO RYDER. STOP: I NEED A MONTH TO GET THE RANCH GOING THE WAY I WANT IT TO GO. STOP:

I WOULD LIKE YOU AND YOUR PARENTS TO COME AND VISIT TO MAKE SURE YOU WOULD LIKE TO LIVE HERE. STOP: WE CAN SET A DATE WHEN YOU WANT TO HAVE THE WEDDING WHEN YOU ARE HERE. STOP: BURT

Finished with the telegraph, they went to the mercantile. Ernest Crawford, the owner, met them. "Gentlemen, what can I do for you?" he asked.

"We are the new owners of the T Bar Ranch," said Burt. "My name is Burt Ware, and I will be here. My partner, Milo Ryder, will be here sometimes but mostly at his ranch in Purgatoire Valley."

"Glad to meet you. My name is Ernest Crawford."

"I understand that supplies were gotten a few days ago, and I need to know if there is an account and if money is due," said Burt.

"Let me check," said Ernest, going behind the counter and pulling out a box of cards with accounts. Finding the T Bar Ranch card, he said, "There is a balance of ten dollars due."

Burt took out the money and paid the bill. While he was paying, a woman walked in from the back.

Seeing his wife, Ernest said, "Gentlemen, this is my wife, Gwendolyn. Gwendolyn, I want you to meet Mr. Ware and Mr. Ryder. They are the new owners of the T Bar Ranch."

"I believe I met your wife, Mr. Ryder," said Gwendolyn. "I believe her name is Hannah."

"That is my wife," said Milo. "She was in to get supplies for us one day."

"She seemed very nice," said Gwendolyn. "I look forward to seeing her again."

"We live by Stonewall," said Milo. "Burt will be running the ranch here."

"I look forward to meeting your wife," said Gwendolyn.

"I am not married," said Burt. "However, I do hope to change that soon."

"Well, when you do, I will look forward to meeting her," said Gwendolyn.

"Will you be the only one getting supplies?" asked Ernest.

"No," said Burt. "Amos Chavez, Richard Fleming, and Loretta Gonzolez will come after supplies besides myself."

"Do you want to set up a new account?" asked Ernest.

"The ranch has an account now, and it is clear," said Burt. "We can just keep it the way it is."

"We are glad to see that Ike is gone and you have taken over the T Bar Ranch," said Ernest.

When they finished at the mercantile, it was time to return to the bank.

They found that Seth had finished drawing up new papers for Milo and Burt to sign. Thanking Seth, Milo and Burt got up to leave after signing the papers.

"Seth, if you are available tonight, bring your wife to the ranch. The women at the ranch are planning a celebration," said Milo.

"What is the occasion?" asked Seth.

"They are happy that Ike and his men are in jail," said Burt.

"Thank you," said Seth. "I will see if we can make it."

Leaving town, they rode back to the ranch.

Riding into the ranch, they saw all the women and men working in the yard setting up tables and cooking in preparation for the celebration. Everyone looked like they were having a good time. Some stopped and waved to Milo and Burt as they rode in.

"It looks like it will be a big celebration," said Milo.

"I told Seth that if there were others who would like to come out, they were welcome," said Burt. "If more people from town come, it will be a good chance to know them."

After putting up their horses, they went to the house.

Milo called Cody, Nate, James, and Billy into the office. Once they were in, Milo gave each one $1571. "Men, this is your share of the reward money," said Milo.

Nate said, "That is the most money I have ever had at one time. I want to thank you, Mr. Ryder."

"You earned it," said Milo.

Cody said, "Milo has always shared the reward money with the ones he takes along where rewards are involved. Some of us have saved enough that we might want to get our own ranch."

"I also want to let you know that Burt is becoming a partner on this ranch and is putting up half the money," said Milo.

"I didn't know that Burt would want to buy a ranch," said Cody.

"Burt had mentioned it to me," said Milo. "I have been thinking that if

I keep buying ranches, there may be a chance for some of you to become a partner with me. Of course, that is, if you would like to."

The men looked at each other but said nothing at the time. Then, thanking Milo, they left, going outside. Outside they talked among themselves, thinking it could be an excellent way to get their own ranches. Once they finished talking among themselves, they went to help prepare for the celebration.

Outside, the ranch women were busy getting ready for the celebration. There were a lot of activities in preparation. Some men were putting up tables. They had dug a pit, and a young steer was cooking over it. You could smell the beans cooking, tortillas baking, peppers roasting, and rice, making their mouths water.

Everyone was in a good mood and waiting for evening, when the party would begin.

Loretta and Izar were helping the women with some of the cooking in the main house. Hannah tried to help, but Loretta said, "Hannah, please sit down. We are doing this because of what you and your husband have done for us."

"There must be something I can do to help," said Hannah. "I feel bad that all of you are working and I am doing nothing."

"If you must do something, why don't you go out and see if the women there need me to get them something," said Izar.

Hannah got up and started for the front door as Milo came out of the office. "Why the long face?" asked Milo.

"Everybody is busy getting ready to celebrate, and I have nothing to do," said Hannah.

Milo laughed and said, "Come, let's go for a walk, and I will show you the ranch."

Outside Hannah saw that even the children were busy helping their mothers prepare for the celebration. The women would stop and smile and say hello as they walked around.

"I think Burt and Shellie will like it here," said Hannah. "These folks are so nice."

"While we were in town, Burt sent a telegram to Shellie and her folks asking them to come and see the ranch," said Milo.

"I hope that they come," said Hannah. "I wonder when they will have their wedding. With starting a new ranch, when will Burt be able to go to El More?"

"I think he could leave Richard in charge while he gets married," said Milo. "He has a lot of good men working here. It isn't like when we bought the Lazy S and lost two men. The men we lost here were extra, and Burt still has the men needed to run the ranch."

"Did you talk to the other men about Burt becoming a partner?" asked Hannah.

"Yes, I did," said Milo. "I think some of the men are starting to think about it. Maybe Cody will want to buy into the Lazy S Ranch. If he does, we could expand both the Lazy S and Rocking R."

As Hannah and Milo walked around, Hannah spoke to some of the women, asking if there was anything they needed. All the ladies said that they did not need anything.

Burt was working with Richard, talking about some of Richard's concerns with the ranch. Seeing Milo and Hannah, he motioned for them to come over. "Richard has been telling me about some land they have been using during the summer for the cattle that no one owns—located back in the mountains where the access is only through the T Bar range. Maybe we should look into seeing if we can buy it."

"If no one owns it, maybe we can incorporate it into the ranch," said Milo.

"We could use it for hay," suggested Richard.

"Let's ride out there tomorrow and look at it," said Milo. "If it is hidden, we might be able to use it for hay for winter feed."

Early that afternoon, people from town started to arrive. Burt was busy getting to know them. Nora McNab from the café was one of the first to arrive. Burt greeted her. She asked if there was anything she could do to help. "You can go in the house and talk to Loretta," said Burt. "She is in charge of what is going on."

Later, Ernest and Gwendolyn Crawford arrived with Seth Brewer and his wife, Mabel, followed by several townsfolk. It wasn't long, and the celebration was going in full swing. Some of the ranch hands brought out their instruments and started playing when everyone finished eating.

When Ernest arrived, he had a telegram for Burt from Shellie.

BURT WARE: I GOT EXCITED HEARING FROM YOU. WE WILL BE THERE IN THREE DAYS BY THE STAGE. CANNOT WAIT.
SHELLIE

After reading the telegram, Burt let Milo and Hannah know that the Markers would be there in three days.

The celebration lasted until after dark before folks started for home.

CHAPTER 16

WHILE THE CELEBRATION WAS GOING on, three men rode up to the ranch but stayed far enough away not to be recognized. They waited where they could watch the ranch. Because of the people from the town who were there, they did not see any of Ike's men. Chris Spence said, "I wonder what happened to Ike. I don't see Ben or any of the other men there either. That one man I see there, I believe, is a US marshal. I wonder if he had anything to do with Ike. Let's ride to town and see if we can find out what is going on."

Before Milo and his men had taken over the ranch, Ike had gotten word to Chris that he wanted to see him.

When the three men rode into San Luis de la Culebra, they stopped at the Delta Saloon. Inside they found a table and sat down. It wasn't long, and the barkeep came over and asked what they would have. Harris Poole said, "Bring us a bottle and three glasses."

When the barkeep returned with the bottle and glasses, Tobias Averill asked, "Have you seen Ike Evens around from the T Bar Ranch?"

"Ike and some of the men from the T Bar are in jail," said the barkeep.

"What happened?" asked Chris.

"The ranch was sold to a US marshal," said the barkeep. "He and his men arrested Ike and some other men and put them in jail."

"When did this happen?" asked Wade.

"Over the last few days," said the barkeep.

"Was there a gunfight?" asked Chris.

"I did not hear of a gunfight," said the barkeep. "A few days before, there was a gunfight at the sheriff's office, and one man was killed."

"Do you know who was killed?" asked Harris.

"I believe the man's name was Cullen," said the barkeep.

When the barkeep returned to the bar, Chris said, "We need to talk to the sheriff. I didn't think he would hold Ike."

"If the US marshal arrested him, he might not have a choice," said Tobias.

"What do you think we should do?" asked Harris.

"I think we need to get Ike out of jail," said Chris. "With many of the people from town at the ranch, now would be a good time to do it. We need to find out how many men are in jail."

"If Cullen was the only one killed," said Tobias, "Ike, Frank, Ernest, Ned, Juan, and Wade would be left."

"We need to find some horses," said Chris. "Let's go to the livery and see if their horses are there."

Getting up, the three men left the saloon and rode to the livery. Finding no one, they took six horses and headed to the sheriff's office. While Tobias and Harris waited with the horses, Chris quickly opened the door and entered the office with his gun drawn. When Sheriff Drew saw the gun, he said, "What do you want?"

"I want you to let Ike and his men out of jail."

Sheriff Drew got up and got the key. Then, going to the back of the jail, he opened the cells to the prisoners. Once they were out, Chris forced Sheriff Drew into a cell and hit him over the head, knocking him out.

Ike said, "It's good to see you. How did you find out we were in jail?"

"We went to the ranch and saw that you were not there, but many other people were celebrating, so we came to town, and I heard about it at the saloon."

"Who is with you?"

Chris said, "Tobias and Harris are outside with horses."

All the men gathered guns and went outside. Then, mounting horses, they rode out of town. Chris asked, "Do you want to go to the ranch?"

"No," said Ike. "The marshal has too many men there, and with the help of the ranch hands, we would not have a chance. I need to think of a way to get back at him. I heard that he has a ranch near the Purgatoire Valley. We need to find a place to hide for now. We will need some money, and I had put together a plan to get money from a bank in Durango before we were arrested. Then we can work on getting that US marshal."

"What about the ranch here?" asked Tobias.

"We can come back to that later," said Ike. "We will go to Conejos and get supplies. Then, once the town discovers we are gone, they will contact that US marshal and start looking for us."

They continued to ride west until dark.

Sheriff Ed Drew woke up, finding himself on the floor of one of his cells. At first, he couldn't see clearly and almost fell again as he tried to stand. Ed felt the knot on the back of his head as he remained standing and his vision started to clear.

Going to his office, he collected his gun and hat before getting his horse. Outside his office, he ran into Albert Jones, the doctor. Albert asked, "What happened? I saw Ike and his men ride out of town. I thought you had them locked up waiting for the judge."

"Chris Spence broke them out," said Sheriff Drew. "Did you see which way they rode out?"

"They headed south," replied Albert.

Not knowing where Ike and his men would head, Ed decided that he needed to let US Marshal Milo Ryder know that they were loose. Riding to the T Bar Ranch, he was surprised when he found a lot of people from town there celebrating.

Richard saw Sheriff Drew ride into the yard and recognized him. "Sheriff, what can I do for you?" asked Richard.

"Is Marshal Ryder here?" he asked.

"I believe that he is in the house," said Richard. "If you get down, I will take you to him."

When the sheriff got down, Richard had one of the men take the sheriff's horse while he took the sheriff to the house. Milo was coming out as Richard and Sheriff Drew approached the house.

"Sheriff, what brings you out here?" asked Milo. "Did you come to join in the celebration that the wives of the hands are putting on?"

"No. There has been a jailbreak, and I came to warn you," said Sheriff Drew. "Ike and his men are gone."

"What happened?" asked Milo.

"One of the men known to ride with Ike, Chris Spence, barged into my office with his gun drawn, and before I could react, he forced me to let Ike and his men go," said Sheriff Drew. "Before he left, he hit me over the head, and when I came to, they were gone."

"I remember Richard saying that Chris Spence had been here with Ike," said Milo. "He also said that two other men had come. Were they with Chris when he broke Ike out of jail?"

"They could have been outside," said Sheriff Drew.

"He must have come here after you arrested Ike," said Richard. "If Chris were here, I would bet the other two were with him. They have come back here before, and I heard that Ike had sent word to them. Maybe he was planning something and needed their help."

"Do you know which way they were heading?" asked Milo.

"The doctor said that he saw them ride out of town heading south," said Sheriff Drew. "They could be hiding out, waiting to come after you, so I came out to warn you."

"Are you going to go after them?" asked Richard.

"If he didn't come this way, by now he is out of my jurisdiction," said Sheriff Drew.

"Now you can add jailbreak to Ike's list of charges," said Richard.

"Have you notified the sheriffs in the towns around here to be on the lookout for Ike and his men?" asked Milo.

"No," said Sheriff Drew. "I wanted to let you know if they were heading your way."

"Thank you for letting me know," said Milo. "We will keep guard, and if he does try something, we will be prepared."

"What will you do if he does show up?" asked Sheriff Drew.

"If he doesn't surrender, he may end up dead," said Milo.

"I thought you would return to Purgatoire?" asked Sheriff Drew.

"We are," said Milo. "I am leaving Deputy Marshal Burt Ware here. If Ike and his men return, Burt is authorized to deputize as many men as he needs to take care of Ike. I believe that you have met Burt. He will be running the ranch. He is my partner in the ranch."

"Yes, I have," said Sheriff Drew.

"If you would like, you can join the celebration. There is plenty of food," said Milo.

"Thank you," said Sheriff Drew. "I think I need to go back to town and send some telegraphs."

The sheriff got his horse and rode back to town. Burt saw the sheriff as he was leaving and went to find out what he wanted.

"Was that Sheriff Drew?" asked Burt.

"Yes, it was," said Milo.

"What did he want?" asked Burt.

"He came to tell us that Ike and his men escaped from jail," said Milo.

"He said that Chris Spence and two others got them out of jail," said Richard.

"Did he want us to go after them?" asked Burt.

"No, he felt that he needed to warn us in case they tried to get revenge," said Milo.

Milo, Richard, and Burt went out to where everyone was dancing. Milo found Hannah talking to Gwendolyn Crawford and Mabel Brewer from town. Burt and Milo ended up talking to their husbands, Ernest and Seth.

Seth asked Milo, "When are you going to start for home?"

"Burt just got word that his fiancée and her parents are coming in the next day or two. Hannah and I will wait until they get here," said Milo. "I will send some men back to attend to the two ranches there," said Milo.

It wasn't long before the people from town started to leave. Before leaving, they stopped and thanked Burt, Milo, and Hannah for inviting them. They looked forward to seeing them again.

The next day Milo decided to send some of the men back to Purgatoire. Only Billy stayed with Milo and Hannah.

CHAPTER 17

NED WAS COMING OUT OF the bunkhouse when a rider rode into the yard. At first, he didn't recognize Tommy Nile from the telegraph office. When Tommy stopped, Ned said, "Hi, Tommy. What brings you out here?"

"Hi, Mr. Davis. Is Miss Shellie home? I have a telegram for her," said Tommy.

"I believe that she is in the house. Come on, and we can see if she is there," said Ned.

Inside the house, they found Shellie in the kitchen. Turning around, she saw Tommy with Ned. "Hi, Tommy," said Shellie.

"Hi, Miss Shellie. I have a telegram for you," said Tommy, handing the telegram to her.

"Is it bad news?" asked Ned.

"I don't think so," said Shellie.

"Good. I need to get to the barn. Your pa will need help," said Ned, leaving.

"Thank you," said Shellie. Then, taking the telegraph and reading it, she called for her mother.

Wanda was out back when she heard Shellie calling for her. Hurrying in, she asked, "What's wrong?"

"Mom, it's a telegram from Burt," said Shellie. "He has a ranch in San

Luis de la Culebra, and he wants us to come to visit him there. He said that we could make wedding plans."

"Did he buy the ranch?" asked Wanda.

"He said that he bought it with Milo Ryder," said Shellie. "I would like to go see it, and we can make plans for the wedding."

"Let's tell Pa," said Wanda. "Tommy, can you wait here till we talk to him?"

"Yes, ma'am," said Tommy.

"Come on, Shellie. Pa is in the barn," said Wanda.

Wanda and Shellie walked out to the barn and found Ned and Albert working on fixing a stall that one of the horses had broken. When they entered the barn, Shellie called out to her father, "Pa, I got a telegram from Burt. He wants us to visit him at his ranch."

"What do you mean his ranch?" asked Albert.

"Burt said that he bought a ranch with Milo Ryder," said Shellie. "He also wants us to make wedding plans."

"Where is this ranch located?" asked Ned.

"It is at San Luis de la Culebra," said Shellie. "Can we go?"

"I thought he would come here when he got done helping Milo," said Albert.

"He wants Shellie to see it so she can see if she will like moving there," said Wanda. "He invited us to come to the ranch with Shellie. He said it would take him a month to get the ranch in order."

"How do you want to go?" asked Albert.

"We can take the stage," said Wanda.

"Thanks, Dad. I will give Tommy a telegram to send to Burt and let him know," said Shellie.

Running back to the house, she quickly wrote a telegram and gave it to Tommy.

Albert watched as Shellie ran back to the house. "I ain't seen that girl that excited in a long time," Albert said, smiling. "I don't think we will have a daughter at home much longer."

"I think you are right, Pa," said Wanda.

"I will go and pack, and we can leave tomorrow," said Wanda.

The following day Ned took Wanda, Shellie, and Albert into El More, where they got on the stage.

Burt rode into town the day after the celebration to find out when Shellie and her parents' stage would arrive. At the stage office, he was told that the stage would arrive at about three in the afternoon. Back at the ranch, he informed Hannah and Loretta when the stage would be arriving so they could make sure to have rooms and supper available for their arrival.

"Do you want us to go to town with you tomorrow?" asked Hannah.

"I don't know," said Burt. "I am excited about Shellie being here, and I hope she likes it."

"I am sure that she will like it," said Hannah.

"How many will be here?" asked Loretta.

"It will be Shellie and her parents," said Burt. "They will need two rooms."

"That won't be any trouble, as Milo sent most of the men home," said Loretta. "I will get Izar to help me prepare the rooms. We will have a big meal for them when they get here. Several of the women will want to meet Shellie and welcome her."

"I am sure they will make Shellie and her parents welcome," said Hannah.

The following morning Burt was nervous and could not concentrate on the work that needed to be done in preparation for their arrival. Finally, Loretta said, "Burt, you need to go outside and let us women do our work."

Going outside, Burt went looking for Richard. When Richard saw Burt, he called him over. "I have two men watching the road, making sure Ike and his men haven't come back," said Richard.

"I am hoping they will leave the area," said Burt.

"You look a little nervous," said Richard. "Are you worried about Ike?"

"No," said Burt. "I am worried that Shellie won't like it here."

"I am sure she will be made to feel welcome," said Richard. "Most of the women here are looking forward to meeting her."

"It is still new to me having a fiancée," said Burt. "Her parents will be with her, and we are supposed to make our wedding plans."

"I can see where that would make you worried. It is a bigger step than taking on Ike and his men," said Richard, laughing. "How many people are going to town to get your fiancée?"

"Milo and Hannah will be going with me," said Burt. "We will need two buggies."

"I think I will send Amos and Dusty to ride with you," said Richard. "Until we know Ike is not around, we don't want to take any chances."

"That is good," said Burt. "Tell them that we will be leaving right after dinner."

"I will have the buggies ready, along with Amos and Dusty," said Richard.

Burt walked over to the corral where Billy and Garth were working with one of the young horses. When Billy saw Burt, he walked over to him and asked, "When will Shellie be here?"

"She will be on the stage at three o'clock this afternoon," said Burt.

"Do you want me to ride with you?" asked Billy.

"Richard has Amos and Dusty riding along with Milo and Hannah," said Burt. "If you want, you can ride along. Seeing more familiar faces might help her become comfortable."

When Garth walked over, Burt asked, "How is it going?"

"Billy is showing me some of the things he does to train horses," said Garth. "I can see where it is very effective."

"Billy does have a way with animals," said Burt.

"When are you leaving for town?" asked Billy.

"We will be leaving right after dinner," said Burt. "The stage will arrive at three."

"I will be ready," said Billy.

Burt went back to the house and decided that he needed to look at the books. Going into the office, he found Milo. "I thought I would come and look at the information in the books," said Burt.

"I have been looking at what is here," said Milo. "It looks like no entries have been put in the books since Ike took over. You will need to get a count on the cattle, and you know what money we put in the bank to run the operation."

"I figured that might be the case," said Burt. "At least I will start fresh."

Milo got up and let Burt get behind the desk. Burt looked at where entries to the books had stopped when Tilghman was killed.

Burt said, "I can adjust them to show the correct number of cattle and what's in the bank. That way, we will know how the ranch is doing from this day on."

While looking at the books, Loretta said dinner was ready. Going to the kitchen, Burt and Milo joined the rest. When they finished eating, those going to town got ready to leave. Burt drove the front buggy while Milo and Hannah followed with the second buggy. Billy rode with Amos and Dusty.

The trip to town went without any incidents. They arrived before the stage arrived. Sheriff Drew saw them come in and went to talk to Milo and Burt. "What brings you to town?" asked Sheriff Drew.

"We are here to meet the stage," said Burt. "My fiancée and her parents are due to arrive on it."

"Congratulations," said Sheriff Drew. "I may have some good news for you. I received a telegram from the marshal in Durango. It seems that Ike and his men tried to rob the bank there. There was a shootout, and five of Ike's men were killed, but Ike got away."

"Do you know how many got away?" asked Milo.

"The telegraph did not say," said Sheriff Drew. "From those who got Ike out, I have to say that Ike only has four men with him."

"At least we know where Ike headed when he left here," said Burt.

"Did he get away with any money?" asked Milo.

"They were caught coming out of the bank, and the money was recovered," said Sheriff Drew. "If they are short on money, they may try to rob another bank."

"If they are that short of men, Ike may have to try and get more men first," said Milo.

"Thank you for the information," said Burt. "We will keep looking for him in case he comes back here."

"Here comes the stage now," said Hannah. "I think your wait is over, Burt."

Burt stood with Milo, Hannah, Billy, Amos, and Dusty on the boardwalk, waiting for the stage to stop. The first one off the stage was Shellie. When she saw Burt, she went running to him and hugged him. "I didn't think we would ever get here," said Shellie, as she continued to hug Burt.

While Shellie was busy with Burt, Milo helped Wanda and Albert off the stage. Once they were off the stage, the driver started handing down their luggage. Amos, Dusty, and Billy took their bags and loaded them in the buggies.

Once everyone was introduced, Milo said, "If you are ready to ride some more, we can go to the ranch." So Wanda and Hannah got in the back of the buggy while Albert and Milo got in the front. Shellie got in the buggy with Burt.

During the ride to the ranch, Burt and Shellie talked about what had happened since the last time together.

Richard spotted them on the road and rang the dinner bell, calling all the hands to the house. When Burt and Shellie drove into the yard, everyone was there to greet them. They were standing in front of the house.

Shellie saw all the people and asked, "Who are all these people?"

"They work on the ranch," said Burt.

"Do all these women work on the ranch?" asked Shellie.

Burt said, "The women are married to the hands and live here on the ranch."

After Burt stopped in front of the house, Loretta came over to the buggy and said, "You must be Shellie. I am Loretta, the housekeeper. I am happy to meet you."

"Yes, I am Shellie."

"Welcome to the T Bar Ranch. Let me help you with your things," said Loretta.

"Thank you," said Shellie.

Burt helped Shellie down from the buggy while some of the hands took care of their luggage. Milo introduced Wanda and Albert Marker to Richard and Izra.

Wanda looked at the house and all the people, wondering how Burt could afford all of this. "Albert, I never expected to see something like this," said Wanda.

"It looks like Burt is doing well," said Albert.

"Please follow me into the house, where you can freshen up, and supper will be ready soon," said Loretta.

As they walked to the house, several people who came to greet them started to go back to work. Shellie overheard one of the women say, "Did you see how beautiful she is?" Smiling, Shellie hugged Burt's arm as they went to the house. Inside, Shellie met more surprises. The house was more extensive than she had imagined. Loretta said, "Shellie, let me show you to your room, where you can freshen up. Then, Mr. and Mrs. Marker, if you will follow me as well, I will show you your room. After you have had a chance to freshen up, come to the kitchen."

"Albert, when you get a chance to relax, I will show you around the ranch," said Burt. "I know that all of you must be tired after your trip."

Shellie looked at Burt and said, "I am just too excited to be with you that I don't think I can relax. So let me get freshened up, and I will be right back."

Loretta took them to their rooms and asked Shellie if she would want a bath. "Right now, I want to be with Burt," said Shellie. "I will want one before I go to bed tonight."

"I will ensure that the tub with hot water is in your room," said Loretta. "We are happy to meet you and look forward to you living here."

"I am sure that when Burt and I are married, I will enjoy living here," said Shellie. "Everyone seems so nice."

Loretta left her and returned to the kitchen while Shellie washed up and changed clothes.

Burt was waiting for Shellie in the living room with Hannah and Milo. Wanda and Albert were the first to return. After they sat down, Loretta came in with fresh lemonade.

"Milo," said Albert. "I understand that you and Burt are partners in this ranch."

"That is correct," said Milo. "Burt bought into the ranch by paying for half."

"How does that work?" asked Wanda.

"Because Burt will be here running the ranch, he will receive seventy percent of the profits, and I will get thirty percent," said Milo.

"We are hoping that once the ranch gets back to a normal operation, It will pay all expenses and leave us a profit," said Burt.

"It looks like you have a large crew of ranch hands," said Albert. "Who has been running the ranch?"

"Richard is the foreman," said Burt. "Izar is Richards's wife, and they live in the house next to the main house. He has been the foreman for several years. Most of the men working here have been with the ranch since the Tilghmans owned it."

"Can they be trusted, seeing that they were here with that Ike Evens?" asked Albert.

"These are some of the men that helped us capture Ike Evens and his men," said Burt.

Shellie came walking into the living room while Burt was talking. She came over and sat down next to Burt.

"Would you like some lemonade?" asked Hannah.

"Thank you," said Shellie. "Who is Ike Evens?"

"Ike Evens is an outlaw who took over the ranch after the Tilghmans were killed," said Milo.

"Are they in jail?" asked Albert.

"They were," said Milo. "Some of his men who were not here got them out a few days ago."

"Aren't you worried they will return?" asked Wanda.

"Today, we heard from the sheriff in town that they robbed a bank in Durango, and five of his men were killed," said Burt.

"What if they do come back?" asked Wanda.

"Richard has men watching," said Burt. "If he lost five of his men, he won't be coming here."

Loretta came in and said, "Supper is ready. Do you want to call the men, Burt?"

Burt rang the dinner bell, and those who were not married came to the house to eat, along with Richard and Izar.

The men got to know Shellie and her parents while they were eating, and Shellie got to know them. After supper, Hannah and Wanda got up and helped Loretta and Izar clean up while Burt and Shellie went for a walk.

While Shellie and Burt were walking, Burt asked Shellie, "When would you like to have the wedding?"

"I want to get married as soon as we can," said Shellie.

"What do you think about making this your home?" asked Burt.

"I will be happy anyplace we live as long as I am with you," said Shellie.

"I wish we could be married tomorrow, but I know Mom wants the wedding in El More, at our home there."

"Tomorrow, let's talk to your parents and make the arrangement," suggested Burt.

CHAPTER 18

THE FOLLOWING DAY BURT WAS the first one in the kitchen, waiting for breakfast. Loretta brought him a cup of coffee and said, "Shellie is a beautiful and friendly woman. I am going to enjoy her being here. When are you going to have the wedding?"

"We talked some last night, and Shellie would like it to be as soon as possible," said Burt.

"Will it be here?" asked Loretta.

"She wants it to be in El More, where her parents live, and near her brother," said Burt.

While they were talking, Shellie, Albert, and Wanda came into the kitchen. "Have a chair, and I will get you some coffee," said Loretta. "Breakfast will be ready soon."

"Do you want some help with breakfast?" asked Shellie. "I know that if I am going to live here, I want to help in the kitchen."

"Thank you," said Loretta. "If you don't mind, you can set the table. I have the meal cooking. Bread will come out of the oven shortly, and Izar will come in to help."

Hannah and Milo walked in and sat down at the table. Hannah was surprised to see Shellie helping Loretta and offered to help them.

"You can relax," said Loretta. "I don't know what to do with all this help."

Shellie got Hannah and Milo coffee and went back to help Loretta.

It wasn't long before the rest of the men arrived for breakfast. Shellie,

Loretta, and Izar put the food on the table and then sat down. While eating, Burt said, "Richard, I would like to get a count of the cattle we have. How long do you think it would take?"

"We have cattle in two different pastures," said Richard. "I will send men to each pasture, and we should have a count by tonight."

"Once we have a count, we will know how much hay we need this winter," said Burt. "I want to know if that valley where we hid the cattle before is available. That looks like it could feed them this winter if we keep the cattle off it."

When everyone finished eating, Richard sent the men out to count the cattle while Burt, Shellie, Albert, Wanda, Hannah, and Milo sat at the table to talk about the upcoming wedding.

"Last night, Burt and I talked about wanting the wedding as soon as we can," said Shellie. "I know you want it in El More, and we will need some time to get everything ready."

"What do you want?" asked Wanda.

"I want to spend a few days here getting to know everyone before I return to El More," said Shellie. "I need someone to make me a wedding dress, and bridesmaids. Oh, so much must be done before the wedding."

When Shellie was talking about having a wedding dress made, Loretta walked in and said, "Shellie, the women here can make you a dress. I know that they would love to have a hand in your wedding. If you know what material you want to use, we can have a dress made before you go home."

"Oh, Mother, maybe we can go to town and find the material," said Shellie. "That would be so nice of the ladies here. That way, they could feel like they are part of the wedding."

"Hannah would like to go to town with us?" asked Wanda.

"When you are at the mercantile getting your material, charge it to the ranch," said Milo.

"I will have Richard assign some men to go to town with you," said Burt.

"I am sure that we will be all right," said Wanda.

"I will feel better if some men accompany you, not knowing where Ike is," said Burt.

"Let's get ready," said Hannah. "We can have dinner in town."

While the women got up to get ready to go to town, Loretta informed some of the women that they would be making the wedding dress for

Shellie. Burt went to find Richard and have him get a buggy and men ready to take the women to town.

When the women were ready, Richard had a buggy and three men ready to accompany them to town. After they left, Albert sat with Milo while Burt and Richard rode out to see how cattle counting was going.

By the middle of the afternoon, everyone had returned to the ranch. The women had gotten the material for the wedding dress, and Loretta had the ladies lined up to start working on it. Izar took Shellie and her mother to her house, where they would make the dress.

CHAPTER 19

IKE AND HIS MEN RODE out of San Luis de la Culebra after Tobias got them out of jail. Now that they were kicked off the T Bar Ranch, he needed to get some money. There was money hidden at the ranch, but there wasn't any way that he would be able to get to it without risking being killed. They rode west and found a spot where they could hole up to make sure that no one was following them.

Once they stopped, Tobias asked Ike, "What do you want to do about the ranch?"

"Right now, that US marshal has too many men to protect it," said Ike. "We need to get some money. I heard that the bank in Durango had a lot of money, so I asked Chris to come. I put together a plan to rob it."

"When do you want to hit the bank in Durango?" asked Frank.

"We can ride to Durango and be there late today," said Ike. "We can hit the bank in the morning."

"Where do you want to go after we hit the bank?" asked Tobias.

"We will head north for a while," said Ike. "Once things get quiet, we will go after that US marshal."

"Do you know where his other ranch is?" asked Harris.

"I heard it is in the Purgatoire Valley," said Ike. "He doesn't know Tobias, Chris, or Harris, so I can send one of them there to find the ranch. In the meantime, we will take the Durango bank."

After ensuring they were not being followed, they rode on toward Durango. It was late in the day when they stopped outside the city.

"Let's split up and go into town two at a time," said Ike. "We will meet at the Dimond Saloon."

Ike and Frank were the first two to enter Durango. Riding slowly, they stopped in front of the Dimond Saloon. Getting off their horses, they looked up and down the street. After checking the street and seeing nothing to alert them of trouble, Ike said, "Frank, go to the mercantile and get some supplies.

Frank went to the mercantile while Ike entered the saloon. Finding a table in the back of the room, Ike sat down and waited for the barkeep. "What can I get you?" asked the barkeep.

"Get me a bottle and two glasses," said Ike.

Shortly after he got a bottle and glasses, Tobias and Chris came and joined him.

"Where's Frank?" asked Tobias.

"I sent him to the mercantile to get some supplies," said Ike. "Chris, why don't you go help him carry what we need."

Chris got up and went to help Frank. When Chris got to the mercantile, he found Frank finishing paying for the supplies. Leaving the mercantile, they loaded them on the horses before they returned to the saloon, where they joined Ike and Tobias.

Ike was surprised at how empty the saloon was. "I wonder why there are not more men in here," he said to Tobias.

"Maybe something is going on in town keeping them away," replied Tobias.

"You could be right," said Ike.

A few minutes after Chris and Frank returned, the rest of the men started entering the saloon and taking tables near where Ike first sat.

The barkeep thought that it was strange that so many strangers had come in this late in the day. He kept watching them, wondering who they were. When he took a bottle to the second table, he overheard one of the men call Ike by his name. When he heard Ike's name, he remembered that Marshal Clayton Ogsbury had informed him to be on the lookout for a gang of men led by Ike Evens. As long as they were not causing any trouble, he went about serving other customers and not paying attention to them.

An hour after Ike and his men arrived at the saloon, Marshal Ogsbury came in. Walking up to the bar, he called Charlie, the barkeep, and ordered a beer. When Charlie brought the marshal his beer, Charlie said, "Marshal, those men sitting near the back of the room are with Ike Evens."

"How do you know that?" asked Ogsbury.

"I overheard one of the men call Ike by name," said Charlie.

"Which one is Ike?" asked Ogsbury.

"He is the one with his back to the wall; he's wearing a black hat and keeps talking to the man on his right," said Charlie.

"Do you know how many are with him?" asked Ogsbury.

"Ten men came in shortly after he did," said Charlie. "They are all sitting near the back of the room together."

"Have they caused any trouble?" asked Ogsbury.

"No, but I find it strange that when one of the girls asked them to buy her a drink, they sent her away and told her not to bother them."

Frank called out to Charlie about that time and said, "Bring us another bottle."

Charlie left the marshal and took another bottle to their table.

While the marshal finished his beer, more men from the town and local area came into the saloon. He got up and left. *If that is Ike Evens,* he thought, *I need to get some help in case there is trouble.* Because all the shops were closed, he would have to warn them in the morning. In the meantime, he located some men he had counted on before to help him. He told them to be ready, that Ike Evens and his gang were in the area and might cause trouble.

After talking to some men, Marshal Ogsbury returned to his office, where he could watch the saloon and see if Ike and his men would leave.

An hour later, Ike got up to leave. They still needed to find a place to camp for the night. When Ike got up, the rest of the men got up and left with him. Charlie was sure that all the men were with Ike Evens.

Marshal Ogsbury saw Ike and his men coming out of the saloon. He stood by the window and watched as they mounted their horses and rode north out of town. Feeling relieved that they had left, he still felt that it was not the last time he would see them.

Ike and his men rode north for two miles, where they found grass and water along the Animas River and set up camp. With the supplies that Frank had picked up, they could make coffee. The following morning Ike laid out his plan to rob the bank. When he got the men together, Ike said, "Tobias, Chris, Ben, and I will go into the bank. I want the rest of you to wait with the horses outside the bank. Be prepared to start shooting if anyone comes to see what is happening. I want two at a time to ride into town and spread out and wait. The four of us will ride in after the rest of you are in town. We will wait one hour to give you time to get to town. Wade, I want you to stop by the bank and watch for us to arrive. You will stay out and hold our horses when we go into the bank. We will head north after getting the money, so be prepared to ride hard."

The men who were to stagger going into town saddled their horses and rode out. Ike waited an hour before he and the rest of the men rode to town. Wade was at the bank waiting for Ike and the rest to arrive.

Dan Bogan was in front of his blacksmith shop when Ike's men started to come into town. Watching them, not knowing them, he thought it strange that so many strangers were in town. Dan continued to watch as each pair of men seemed to find a different place to stop and wait. Dan, went to find Marshal Ogsbury. Finding the marshal in his office, he went in.

"Hi, Dan, what can I do for you?" asked Clayton.

"Marshal, I just saw several groups of two men ride into town and stop at several of the businesses and watch like they are waiting for something," said Dan.

Clayton got up and went to the window. Looking across the street, he saw two men standing by their horses. He recognized them from the saloon last night as men who rode with Ike.

"Go back to your shop, get your rifle, and watch the street," said Clayton. "I have a feeling that Ike Evens and his gang are going to try something. Those men you saw come into town ride with Ike."

Dan returned to his shop while Marshal Ogsbury left his office, walking up the street where he found Slim by the Mercantile and told him to notify the men he had talked with to be ready.

Word of possible trouble spread fast through the town. When those Clayton had talked to got the word, they made their way to the main street where they could watch and not be seen.

Clayton walked over to the Dimond Saloon with his rifle and waited inside the door.

Charlie walked to the marshal and asked, "What's happening?"

"Dan told me there are some men who rode into town and are standing like they are waiting for someone or something," said Clayton. "These are some men who were here with Ike last night. So I want to be prepared if Ike Evens and his men start trouble."

While the marshal was talking, four riders stopped in front of the bank. The one man standing by the bank walked out to them and held their horses when they went into the bank. Right after they entered the bank, the men standing by their horses mounted and stopped in front of the bank.

"I don't like what I am seeing," said Charlie. "I think I will get behind the bar."

The marshal continued to watch the men in front of the bank. When the four who went into the bank came out with guns drawn, Marshal Ogsbury opened fire at the first one out of the bank. Marshal Ogsbuy hit Tobias in the shoulder, causing him to drop his saddlebags. Some townsmen started firing as the rest of Ike's men opened fire.

Chris saw that Tobias was hit and dropped the saddlebags. He reached for them. While reaching for the saddlebags, Chris was shot and killed. Ike was wounded as he started to mount, dropping his saddlebags. Ben grabbed Ike's saddlebags and mounted his horse. While he was riding away from the bank, he and his horse were shot. Both were killed. As Ike and the rest of his men tried to ride out of town, three more of Ike's men were killed.

When Ike and the remaining men escaped, they rode north. When they stopped, Ike had lost five men and had two others wounded, plus himself. Frank hung behind the others to watch for any pursuit coming from town. Not seeing any, he caught up with Ike and the rest. Frank said, " I haven't seen any pursuit from town."

Ike decided to stop and take care of their wounds before going on.

When the gunfight was over, Marshal Ogsbury was wounded, along with three men from town. The money was recovered. They found a saddlebag Ike dropped and one from two dead men who rode with Ike, and returned to the bank.

Charlie came out helped Marshal Ogsbury to the doctor's office. When he got the marshal to the doctor's office, Charlie asked, "Do you want to get a posse together and go after them?"

"Did they get away with the money?" asked Clayton.

"I heard that all the money is back in the bank," said Charlie.

With the money recovered and no one from town killed, Marshal Ogsbury, being wounded, decided not to form a posse to go after them.

Ike's upper arm had a bullet through it, causing his arm to hang limp. Once it had been taken care of, he went to check on the others who were wounded.

Tobias was wounded in the shoulders. Archie was hit in his leg, and Juan was hit in the side. After the men had been treated, Ike wanted to put more distance from Durango in case a posse did form to come after them.

They rode, taking it easy because of the wounded men. Frank kept trailing, watching for any pursuit. Finally, late in the afternoon, Frank saw there still wasn't any pursuit.

Tobias's wound was starting to give him trouble, so Ike started looking for a place where they could hide and rest up. Going further into the mountains, they found an abandoned cabin. A corral, able to hold the horses, was located next to a lean-to behind the cabin. Frank was the only one not wounded, so he cared for the horses.

Due to their wounds, Juan and Tobias had to be helped into the cabin. Archie's leg had stopped bleeding but still caused him pain as he tried to make his way into the cabin. Ike had put his arm in a sling and was able to help get Tobias into the cabin.

When Frank finished with the horses, he entered the cabin and took a look at Tobias and Archie's wounds. Frank did what he could do for them before he started to put food together. The cabin had a stove, pans, and a coffee pot. There was a table with four chairs. On the north wall was a bed that Jaun was lying on.

While Frank was getting supper ready, Ike asked, "How is Juan doing?"

"He doesn't look good. He has a fever, and I don't know what I can do for him," said Frank. "If he makes it through the night, he may have a chance."

The rest of the men had to sleep on the floor, with only the one bed in the cabin. Unfortunately, Juan died during the night, so Frank took him out and buried him in the morning.

Ike was down to only four men after they failed to rob the bank in Durango. He would have to hole up until everyone's wounds healed before they could go on.

CHAPTER 20

Activity at the T Bar Ranch continued to return to normal. Richard got the report on the number of cattle in the pastures. When the report came in, the men counted eleven hundred head of cattle. Burt made a new entry into the ledger, indicating the current cattle count. He had already deposited the money in the bank to operate with. Burt could now tell how the ranch was doing with a fresh start on the books.

Shellie had gone to Izar's house, where the women were fussing over her, taking measurements for making her dress. She was excited about the dress, and the women were getting to know each other. Wanda and Hannah sat back and watched Shellie as the women fussed over her and smiled.

"Do you think Shellie will want to wait until you are back in El More to get married?" Hannah asked Wanda.

"I am afraid she will not want to leave Burt but will want to stay here," said Wanda. "I don't know what I will do if that is what she wants."

"If she decided to get married here," said Hannah, "we could have a party in El More and have them come there."

"I don't know," said Wanda. "After Burt asked her to marry her, she was nervous and wanted to go with him. "I don't think she wants to leave here without Burt, even if it's only to go home and prepare for the wedding."

"If she wants to get married here, what will you do?" asked Hannah.

"I don't know," said Wanda. "I will mention it to Albert and see what he says."

Seeing Burt looking at the books, Milo got up to leave, and Albert asked, "Are you going out?"

"I thought I would go look at that piece of land where we took the cattle," said Milo.

"I was thinking about going for a ride to look the country over," said Albert.

"If you want, you can ride along," said Milo. "I may be able to give Burt some ideas on what he can do with that land."

Milo and Albert went to the barn to get horses. Amos saw them and went over and asked, "Can I help you get a horse?"

"Thanks," said Milo.

"Where are you going?" asked Amos. "Maybe I should ride with you."

"We thought we would go look at that pasture that no one is using," said Milo. "I want to see how hard it would be to fence off."

"If I go along, I could show you some of the other land around here," said Amos. "There are other places that one could use."

While they were talking, Richard saw them and went to where they were getting their horses ready. "Milo, if you and Albert are going for a ride, I need someone to go with you," said Richard.

"I thought I would go look at some of the land, and Albert and Amos offered to ride with me," said Milo.

"Good," said Richard. "I don't think going out alone is a good idea with us not knowing where Ike and his men are. If you like, I can have another man ride with you."

"I think the three of us will be all right," said Milo.

After getting their horses, the three men rode out.

After Shellie told Burt that she would be at Izar's house, where the women would be working on her wedding dress, Burt went into the office to look at the books and try to figure out what he could do to improve the operation. He had operating money, but the herd had been cut by Ike and his men to where he would not have the cattle to sell this year. Maybe he should talk to Richard and see if he had any ideas. Burt got up to look for Richard.

When Burt found Richard, Richard was working with Billy in the corral. Richard approached the fence and asked, "Do you need something?"

"I would like to sit down with you and get your ideas on keeping the operation going until we can sell some cattle," said Burt. "The cattle I have seen are not the ones we want to sell. I think Ike and his men have thinned the herd, leaving mostly mother cows."

"We can ride out and look at what might be available for a roundup," said Richard. "There are mother cows who will be dropping calves. Those won't be ready to sell until next year. Maybe we could sell some of the older cows to the Indians."

"Billy, do you want to ride along with us?" Burt asked.

"Yes, I would like to give this young filly some exercise," said Billy. "I think she will be one of your better horses."

Richard and Burt got their horses, and the three rode out.

Shellie came out of Izar's house to talk to Burt as he rode out. Watching him ride out with Richard and Billy, she wondered where they were going. Shellie, not knowing how long they would be gone or where they were going, went back to Izar's house.

When Wanda saw her, she asked, "What's wrong?"

"I was going to talk to Burt, but he, Richard, and Billy rode out," said Shellie.

"He has a ranch to run," said Hannah. "If he knew that you would not be busy here, I am sure he would have wanted to be with you."

"Come," said Izar. "You can visit with the women as they work on your wedding dress."

"I am sure he will be back as soon as he can," said Wanda. "As Hannah said, he has a ranch to run."

Loretta came over close to noon to inform the women that dinner would be ready soon.

Izar said, "Shellie, you, your mother, and Hannah go. I will get the ladies here something to eat."

The three women went with Loretta to the main house. While Loretta continued to make dinner, Hannah asked Shellie, "What do you think about how the dress is coming?"

"The women working on the dress are going to have it ready to try on by tomorrow," said Shellie. "Once they finish it, I don't know if I can wait very long to get married."

"You have a lot of family and friends in El More who, I am sure, are waiting for your return and the wedding," said Hannah.

"Gretchen and Veronica said they would have a big party for Burt and me when we returned after the wedding," said Shellie. "They said it would be like a second wedding."

"Those two were the ones who planned the celebration we just had," said Loretta.

"As fast as they put that celebration together, I cannot imagine what they will do with the time they will have to plan for the second wedding celebrations," said Wanda.

The men returned from checking the pastures and cattle in the middle of the afternoon. After putting up their horses, they went to the house to discuss their findings. They found that the women had returned to Izar's house when they entered the house. They went into the kitchen, where they could all sit. Loretta had a fresh pot of coffee and started pouring it. She also had bread and some meat leftover from dinner for them to eat.

Burt said, "We looked at the cattle and found that there are a few head that could go to market but not enough to support the ranch for a year."

"What do you think you want to do?" asked Milo.

"We have operating capital in the bank, and maybe between that and the cattle we can sell, we will be all right," said Burt. "Richard suggested that we could sell some of the older cows to the Indians. That would help to clean up the herd and leave the younger stock for breeding. Maybe we could bring one of the offspring from the, Aberdeen Angus, to help improve the herd."

"What is an Aberdeen Angus?" asked Amos.

"It is a smaller animal than the longhorns, but they produce more meat that is much more tender," said Milo. "We have started breeding with two bulls at our ranches by Stonewall."

"When would one of the bulls be ready to bring here?" asked Richard.

"We only started using them," said Milo. "It will be next year when the claves are born that we will know what offspring we will have. Then, if we get a good bull, we will move it here."

"What did you find about that land you went to look at?" asked Richard.

"The grass is good, and it looks like it is getting plenty of moisture," said Milo. "It wouldn't take much to fence it off to keep cattle from going on it. Then you could cut it for hay for the winter. From what I saw, there should be enough hay to make it through."

"I will have to get some fencing material," said Burt. "Richard, do we have the men to put up a fence?"

"We have done fencing before," said Richard. "That should not be a problem."

"Tomorrow, I will go into town and order the fencing," said Burt.

Amos and Richard got up and left. After they were gone, Albert said, "We need to be going home. We will need some time to set up the wedding."

Milo said, "We need to be going as well. It looks like you have everything under control here."

"Albert, would you like to take a buggy back with you?" asked Burt. "That way, it will be in El More after the wedding, and I can bring it back with Shellie."

"If you do that, Hannah, Billy, and I will ride with you," said Milo.

"I would feel better if the six of you were traveling together," said Burt.

"I will talk to Wanda and see when she will be ready to leave," said Albert. "I know Shellie will not want to leave until her dress is finished."

That evening after supper, Albert said, "Wanda, we need to start for home. When will you be ready to leave?"

"It will take the women two more days to finish Shellie's dress," said Wanda. "Once the dress is finished, we can go home."

"Shellie, are you ready to go home and make your wedding plans?" asked Albert.

"I would like to stay here," said Shellie. "Burt, how long will you have to stay here before you can come to El More for the wedding?"

"How long will it take you to make the wedding plans once you get home?' asked Burt. "I think I can tell Richard what I want to be done while I am gone."

"It will take us a week once we get home to put the wedding together," said Wanda.

"I don't want to be away from the ranch too long," said Burt. "If I can get everything ordered to build the fence, Richard can handle it from there."

"When would you come?" asked Shellie.

"If I can get things worked out with Richard, I could ride back with you," said Burt.

Shellie got excited and said, "That would be wonderful. That way, we won't be separated again."

"We can all ride back together," said Milo. "Let's plan on leaving in three days."

With the plans to leave in three days, Burt would go with them.

Burt needed to talk to Richard. Getting up, he said, "I will go over and talk to Richard so we can make sure it will be all right."

Shellie got up with Burt and walked to Richard's house with him. Richard answered the door when Burt knocked. Seeing Shellie, Richard asked, "Is something wrong?"

"Can we talk?" asked Burt. "We are trying to make plans for the wedding, and I will have to leave the ranch for a few days. There are some things that I need you to do while I am gone."

"Come in," said Richard. "Izar, Shellie is here, and Burt and I need to talk."

"Come into the kitchen," said Izar. "There is fresh coffee."

While sitting at the table, Burt explained to Richard about the fence and getting the material for it. "We will take a wagon into town and get the material for the fence," said Burt. "If it is not available, I will order it."

"When are you leaving?" asked Richard.

"As soon as Shellie's dress is ready," said Burt. "I believe that it will be ready in two days. We will leave the day after that."

"Are you going to go by the stage?" asked Izar.

"No," said Burt. "I want to take a buggy so we can bring Shellie's things back with us."

"Do you think Ike will return while you are gone?" asked Richard.

"From what Sheriff Drew said about Ike losing men and some of those who got away being wounded, I don't think he will be able to return at this time," said Burt. "You need to keep men looking for him just in case."

The following day Burt and Richard went to town and purchased the material to fence the parcel Burt wanted for hay.

Before leaving for El More, Burt was working in the office when a folder he set on top dropped behind the cabinet. When he moved the filing cabinet, he found a loose panel in the wall. Removing the panel, Burt found a canvas bag. He took out the bag and opened it. Inside the bag, he found money. There was over two thousand dollars in the bag. Not knowing where the money came from or who it belonged to, he looked for Milo.

Burt found Milo talking to Albert in the kitchen. "Milo, can I see you for a minute in the office?" asked Burt.

"Excuse us," said Milo to Albert.

In the office, Burt showed Milo the bag he found and the money in it. When Milo saw it, he asked, "Where did you find this?"

"It was behind the cabinet in the wall," said Burt. "There is a little over two thousand dollars in here. I don't know who put it there."

"There are no markings on where it came from," said Milo, after looking at it. "What do you want to do with it?"

"Maybe we could use it to help pay expenses this year," said Burt. "I don't think that Bass Tilghman would hide money here. Maybe it was hidden by Ike."

"No matter who hid it, there is no way to return it to the rightful owner," said Milo. "I think your idea to use it for the ranch is the correct thing to do. That could be the difference between having to sell more cattle or not."

"For now, I will put it back and take it to the bank later," said Burt.

"You could just keep it here and use it as needed," said Milo. "We still have the money in the bank to fall back on."

Burt returned the money and would use it as needed on the ranch.

On the morning of the third day, Hannah, Milo, Wanda, Albert, Billy, Shellie, and Burt were ready to start for El More. Wanda and Albert drove a buggy that was to be used to haul Shellie's items back to the T Bar Ranch. Everyone else rode horses. Billy led two packhorses carrying supplies. The party left right after eating breakfast.

Hannah and Milo lead the group, followed by Albert and Wanda in the buggy. Shellie and Burt rode behind the buggy, and Billy followed them with the packhorses.

It was late in the day when they rode into the Rocking R Ranch. Maria came out to greet them. Seeing Billy, she ran over to him and hugged him. "I am so glad that you are home," said Maria. "I was not expecting you back today. Are you hungry?"

"We are all hungry and will help you," said Hannah. "We weren't sure if we would be here by tonight."

While the men took care of the horses, Wanda, Shellie, Hannah, and Maria went into the house and started supper for those who had just arrived.

Hearing them arrive, the men from the bunkhouse came out to greet them as well. Nate, seeing Burt, walked over to him and said, "I thought you would be staying at the new ranch. What happened?"

"I came back to get married," said Burt. "Shellie is in the house with her folks, and we will go to El More so we can be married."

"When is the wedding?" asked Nate.

"Just as soon as we can make all the arrangements," said Burt. "I want to return to the T Bar Ranch as soon as possible."

"Will you be here longer than tonight?" asked Porter.

"I think Albert and Wanda want to head home in the morning," said Burt. "I will be going with them."

After eating supper, Burt and Shellie went for a walk before going to bed. Shellie slept in the house while Burt slept in the bunkhouse. The following morning everyone met at the kitchen table for breakfast.

CHAPTER 21

Ike's arm was healing, along with Archie's leg. Juan developed an infection with a high fever. Frank did what he could for Juan, but on the third night, Juan died. Now Ike was down to three men plus himself. Tobias's shoulder was not hurting, so he could help Frank with some chores.

Ike was looking at the supplies, and seeing that they were running low, he had to figure out where he could get new supplies. Frank being the only one not wounded, it would have to be him going to get supplies.

When Frank came in from feeding the horses, Ike called him over. "I need you to go into Animas and get supplies. I have put together a list of what we will need."

"Have you got the money for the supplies?" asked Frank.

Ike reached into his pocket, pulled a ten-dollar gold piece out, and gave it to Frank. "This should cover the supplies we need."

Frank got his horse and a packhorse before he rode out. Late that day, he rode into Animas. Frank rode down the main street, where there weren't a lot of buildings. The town was made up of about twenty buildings. The old mining town had a couple of saloons, and in the middle of the main street sat a mercantile. Not wanting to stay where there might be word about the bank robbery in Durango, he stopped in front of the mercantile. Inside the store, he ran into Oscar, the owner. Oscar asked, "What can I get for you?"

Frank took out his list and handed it to Oscar. Oscar looked at it and said, "I should have everything you need."

When Oscar finished gathering the listed items, Frank asked, "How much do I owe you?"

"That will be five dollars," said Oscar.

Frank handed him the ten-dollar gold piece. When Oscar saw the coin, he said, "I haven't seen one of these for a while. Most of the miners pay in gold."

"I am not a miner," said Frank. "I am only passing through. I am not planning on stopping again, so I need the supplies to last for a while, as I am heading north from here."

Oscar gave Frank his change and said, "Good luck."

Frank went to the saloon after putting his supplies on the packhorse. He ordered a beer and bought a bottle to take back to camp. While drinking his beer, the barkeep asked, "Did you hear about the attempted bank robbery in Durango?'

"No, I can't say I have," said Frank. "What happened?"

"Word that came here was that the Ike Evens gang were the ones who tried to rob the bank," said the barkeep. "It didn't turn out too good for them. Several men were killed, and those who got away were wounded. That is according to the word that got here. So we have been told to look out for them, as they think they are heading this way."

"Have you seen any of them?" asked Frank.

"You're the first stranger I have seen since I got the word about the robbery," said the barkeep.

"I will have to keep watching to make sure I don't run into them," said Frank.

While talking, Frank finished his beer and said, "I will take a bottle with me."

Taking his bottle, he returned to his horse and rode out of Animus, heading back to the cabin, where Ike and the others were waiting. About three miles from Animus, Frank made camp after finding a spot hidden from the road. The next day he returned to the cabin.

When Ike saw him, he said, "We began to wonder if something happened to you."

"The word about the robbery has spread, and everyone who escaped the holdup was wounded," said Frank. "The barkeep said that word had gotten to Animus. So they are on the lookout for us to show up there."

After bringing in the supplies, Frank returned to his horse and got the bottle. Ike opened the bottle and poured drinks for all of them.

"With the supplies you got and the deer that Tobias shot, we have enough food to last us a month," said Ike.

"What are we going to do?" asked Tobias. "Are we going to stay here for a month?"

"Once Archie can move around, we will travel and learn more about that US marshal Milo Ryder," said Ike. "I want to get him before we go back to the T Bar Ranch."

"Are you sure the marshal isn't living at the T Bar?" asked Archie.

"While we were in jail, I heard that sheriff talking to the man from the bank, and he said that the marshal had two ranches in the Purgatoire Valley," said Ike. "We will go near Stonewall and find out where his ranches are. We will wait here until Archie's leg heals."

Only a few days later, Ike and his men rode east. Instead of going to Stonewall, they headed toward El More. Outside El More, Ike found a deserted cabin and set up camp.

After setting up camp, Ike sent Frank into El More to get information. Frank went to the saloon and ordered a beer after finding a table near a window where he could watch the street.

The morning after, Milo and Hannah had returned to the Rocking R Ranch. Everyone wanted to know if anything had happened with Ike. Milo filled them in on what he had learned from the sheriff. "I don't think Ike will be doing much for a while," said Milo. "However, we need to be aware that he could come this way. When you get a chance, Nate, I want you to ride over and tell Cody about Ike and what happened to him. He will need to be watching for him as well."

The rest of the conversation was about the upcoming wedding. Billy asked Shellie, "When are you going to have the wedding?"

Shellie turned red and said, "I wanted to have it at the T Bar, but everyone wants it to be at El More. I am hoping that we can have it within the coming week. Burt has to return to the T Bar, and I look forward to making it our home."

After breakfast, Albert and Wanda loaded the buggy, and Shellie and Burt mounted their horses. Finally, everyone said their goodbyes, and the four were on their way to El More.

After Burt and the Markers were gone, Milo said, "I want to go into Stonewall and talk to Marshal Sieke."

"What do you want to talk to him about?" asked Hannah.

"I want to find out if he has heard more about Ike," said Milo. "If he hasn't, I want him to let me know if he does hear anything."

"If you are going into town, I will go with you," said Hannah. "Maria mentioned that we need a few things now that we are all back."

"I will have Nate get us a wagon," said Milo.

When Nate brought the wagon to the house, Maria had put together a list of supplies they needed. Nate asked Milo, "Do you want anyone to ride in with you?"

"I think we will be all right," replied Milo.

Milo helped Hannah on the wagon, and they headed to town. The first stop was at the marshal's office. Marshal Sieke saw them stopping in front of his office and got up to open the door. He said, "Hello, Hannah, Milo, please have a seat. What brings you to my office?"

"Hello, Tom," said Milo. "We returned from San Luis de la Culebra, where I purchased the T Bar Ranch, and we arrested Ike Evens and his gang. Unfortunately, while there, some of Ike's men broke him and those we arrested out of jail. The last word I heard was from Sheriff Ed Drew. He told us they had tried to rob a bank in Durango but failed. Some of Ike's men were killed, but Ike got away wounded. Do you have any more information about them?"

"I did hear about the failed robbery," said Tom. "I have not had any additional information come into my office. Are you expecting trouble from him?"

"I think he may try something," said Milo. "If not down there, he may come here."

"I will keep looking for more information about Ike," said Tom. "If I hear anything, I will get word to you at your ranch."

"Thanks, Tom," said Milo.

"I heard that you bought another ranch. Who do you have running it?" asked Tom.

"Burt Ware became a partner of mine, and we bought the ranch together, and he will be running it," said Milo.

"You left Burt there?" asked Tom.

"No, he is on his way to El More to get married," said Hannah.

"Get married?" said Tom. "Who is he marrying?"

"Do you remember the girl Shellie Marker we rescued in Silverton?" asked Milo.

"Yes, I do remember her," said Tom. "She was that pretty young woman you brought back who was kidnaped and testified at the trial."

"That is the one," said Hannah. "She fell in love with Burt and Burt with her. I believe they will return to the T Bar right after the wedding."

"I wish them the best of luck," said Tom.

"If you hear anything about Ike, if you would let me know, I would appreciate it," said Milo.

"If I hear anything, I will get word to you," said Tom.

"Thanks," said Milo, and they left to go to the mercantile.

When they entered the mercantile, Mabel was putting canned goods on the shelf. When she saw Hannah, she said, "Hi, Hannah, how are you?"

"Hi, Mabel," said Hannah. "We are doing fine. We just returned from San Luis da la Culebra."

"What were you doing there?" asked Mabel.

"Milo and Burt purchased another ranch, and we had some squatters we had to remove," said Hannah.

"Well, sometime you must fill me in on what happened. What can I do for you now?" asked Mabel.

"We need some supplies for the ranch," said Hannah, handing Mabel the list.

When they first walked in, Milo saw Ernest in the back room and went to talk to him. When Ernest saw Milo, he said, "I heard you were out of town. Maria was in one day to pick up some things and mentioned that you were gone."

"We went and looked at another ranch," said Milo.

"Did you buy it?" asked Ernest.

"Burt and I bought it," said Milo. "Now I am down another man, so if you hear of any good cowboys who are looking for work, send them to the ranch."

"I will do that," said Ernest. "Do you need anything special?"

"No, Hannah wants to get supplies for Maria," said Milo. "I wanted to talk to Tom at the marshal's office about an outlaw we ran across in San Luis de la Culebra."

"What is the name of the outlaw?" asked Ernest.

"Ike Evens," said Milo. "Have you heard of him?"

"I don't recall hearing that name," said Ernest. "But I will keep an ear open if I hear the name."

"Thanks," said Milo.

Mabel told Hannah that filling her order would take a while, and it was getting close to dinnertime. So Hannah called Milo and said, "Let's go to Millie's and get some dinner."

Betty saw them walking toward the café and was surprised to see them. When they entered, Betty said, "We haven't seen you in town for a while. Have you been gone?"

"Yes," said Hannah. "But we are back now."

"Take a seat, and I will be right with you," said Betty.

Shortly after they sat down, Cody walked in. Seeing Milo and Hannah, he went and joined them.

"Where is Rosie?" asked Hannah.

"She and Sadie stopped by the mercantile and said they would be right over," said Cody.

"Sadie feels safe to come to town?" asked Hannah.

"You didn't hear?" said Cody. "While we were gone, Sadie's ex-husband showed up at the ranch. When he tried to shoot Sam, Rosie shot and killed him. Sam told me all about it when I got back."

"I guess she doesn't have to worry about him coming back," said Milo.

"Do you know when the wedding will be?" asked Cody.

"They left this morning with Wanda and Albert for El More," said Hannah. "They are hoping to have the wedding within the week. Burt wants to get back to the ranch, and Shellie won't let Burt go without her."

"It sounds like Shellie has recovered from being kidnapped," said Cody. "Do we get to go to the wedding?"

"We can, but we will have to camp," said Milo. "The Markers do not have room for all of us to stay with them."

"We can take tents," said Cody. "I am sure that they will have enough room that we can be near the ranch where there is water."

"Now, all we have to do is wait to hear when the wedding will take place," said Hannah.

While Hannah was talking, Betty came over to the table and heard her say "wedding." "Are we going to have another wedding?" she asked.

"Yes," said Hannah. "But it will not be here. Burt is going to marry Shellie in El More."

"Oh, that's too bad," said Betty. "The last one was so nice."

The door opened, and Rosie and Sadie walked in. Betty, seeing them, pulled another table over to where the rest were sitting to make room for them. Then, going over to Sadie, Betty said, "I heard about your ex and am glad that you don't have to worry about him anymore."

"Thanks, Betty," said Sadie.

"What are you going to do?" asked Betty.

"I will keep working at the Lazy S," said Sadie.

After Rosie sat down, she said, "I understand that Shellie and Burt are going to get married. Do you know when?"

"They left for El More this morning," said Hannah. "They will let us know when the wedding will be."

Hannah and Milo returned to the mercantile when everyone finished eating and picked up their supplies. On the return trip home, Hannah said, "I wonder how the wedding plans are going?"

"I am sure that Shellie and Wanda have it under control," said Milo. "They will let us know when it will be so we can be there."

"I know," said Hannah. "I just miss not helping them. When will we go there?"

"I sent a telegram to Albert and told him we would be there the Thursday before the wedding," said Milo. "That should give you a day to help them get ready."

"What will we give them for a wedding present?" asked Hannah.

"We can wait and see what they need and send it to the T Bar Ranch," said Milo.

CHAPTER 22

THE DAY AFTER THE MARKERS and Burt returned to the Markers' ranch, Shellie and Wanda got busy making plans for the wedding. Shellie's sister-in-law, Rebecca, came to help. Shellie asked Rebecca to be her maid of honor. Burt sent word to Cody, asking him to be his best man.

Within three days, all the plans were complete, and the wedding was to be held the following Saturday. Telegrams were sent to the Ryders and other friends of the family, letting them know of the date.

Ned Albert's foreman got the men busy digging a pit to roast a steer and put up tables and benches for the wedding. With the excitement of the wedding, Burt was busy helping Ned, trying to stay out of the way of Shellie and Wanda.

Milo sent a telegram stating that there would be six people coming and would be arriving on Thursday before the wedding. Hannah, Milo, Rosie, Cody, Nate, and James would arrive with tents to stay in.

Albert talked to Burt about where Milo and Cody could put up the tents that would be out of the way and give them some privacy. After walking around the farm, they decided behind the house would be the best choice. There they would eat with the family.

With two days before Milo and the rest would arrive, plenty of work still needed to be done. Shellie needed to go into El More for some items she needed, so Burt hitched up a buggy and drove her to town.

While driving to town, Shellie wrapped her arm around Burt's and said, "I am so nervous. I hope the wedding goes well."

"You and your mother have done a great job preparing for it," said Burt. "It looks like everyone is excited about it. There is so much going on, I feel like I am in the way."

"You are not in the way," said Shellie. "I need you to keep me calm, or I will go nuts."

"Josh invited me to their ranch," said Burt. "With everything going on at your parents' place, I decided I wanted to be near you. So I told him he should bring Rebecca and the kids to our place after the wedding."

"What did Josh say?" asked Shellie.

"He said as soon as they could get away, they would," said Burt.

When they reached El More, Shellie went into the mercantile and told Burt to wait. Burt stood outside waiting for Shellie. When Shellie finished her shopping, they got in the buggy and stopped by the café. When they entered the café, Ruth, the waitress, greeted them. She said, "Hi, Shellie, who is your friend?"

"Hi, Ruth," said Shellie. "This is my fiancé, Burt Ware. Burt, this is a friend of mine, Ruth Meyer."

"Hi, Ruth," said Burt.

"I heard you were getting married," said Ruth. "When will the wedding be?"

"We are getting married this Saturday," said Shellie. "You are invited if you can make it."

"Thanks, I will be there," said Ruth. "Now, what would you like for dinner?"

"We will have the special," said Shellie.

"Two specials of steak, potatoes, and gravy coming up," said Ruth, as she went to the kitchen.

When Shellie and Burt finished eating, they went out to get in the buggy. Burt looked at the saloon and thought he recognized a man sitting by the window. Burt thought it looked like one of the men they had arrested on the T Bar Ranch, but he shook it off, figuring he had to be near the San Luis Mountains. Burt got in the buggy, and Shellie asked, "What were you looking at?"

"I thought I saw a man we arrested on the ranch," said Burt. "Last word I heard was that he and Ike were in the San Luis Mountains."

Leaving town, they drove back to the ranch.

Frank had been drinking in the bar for three hours when Burt and Shellie left the café. He caught a glimpse of Burt as he was getting into the buggy after they came out. He thought he knew who he was but wasn't sure. Wanting to find out who the man was, Frank got up and went to the café. Entering the café, he found a table and sat down.

Ruth came over and asked, "What can I get you?"

"I saw a couple come out of here, and I think I know the fellow," said Frank. "Can you tell me who they are?"

"Are you talking about the young blond lady and the dark-haired man?" asked Ruth.

"That is the couple," said Frank.

"That is a friend of mine, Shellie Marker, and her fiancé, Burt Ware," said Ruth. "They are getting married this coming Saturday."

"Oh," said Frank. "I guess I took him for someone else. I will have the special."

When Ruth walked away, Frank knew that Burt was one of the men who arrested him and the others at the T Bar Ranch. The waitress said that they were getting married this Saturday. Ike would want to know that.

After he finished eating, he rode back to the hideout. Tobias met him as he rode in. "How did it go?" asked Tobias.

"I saw one of the men from the T Bar Ranch who arrested us," said Frank. "He is in El More and will get married this Saturday."

"I am sure Ike would like to know this," said Tobias.

Frank found Ike sitting at the table, drinking coffee. "You are back early. What happened?" asked Ike.

"I saw one of the men who arrested us at the T Bar Ranch," said Frank.

"Where did you see him?" asked Ike. "I thought those men came from Stonewall. I didn't hear of any of them coming from El More."

"He was coming out of the café," said Frank. "I talked to the waitress after he left and found out he is getting married on Saturday. She said that his name was Burt Ware."

"Did you find out where the wedding will be?" asked Ike.

"No," said Frank.

"Maybe we can find out where this Burt Ware lives," said Ike. "We could start with him and find out where the others live. Tobias, I want you to go into town tomorrow and find out where he lives."

The next day Tobias rode into El More. Going into the saloon, he went to the bar and ordered a beer. When the barkeep brought him his beer, he asked, "Do you know where Burt Ware lives around here?"

"I don't recognize the name," said the barkeep. "Are you sure he is supposed to live in the area?"

"A friend of mine saw him in town yesterday with a woman," said Tobias.

"Sorry, I don't know him," said the barkeep.

After Tobias finished his beer, he went to the café. There, when Ruth asked him what he wanted, he ordered breakfast. When Ruth brought Tobias his food, he asked, "Do you know Burt Ware?"

"I only met him yesterday," said Ruth. "Why are you asking?"

"I met him a while back and thought if he lives around here, I want to look him up," said Tobias.

"He doesn't live around here, but he is getting married to a friend this Saturday," said Ruth.

"I didn't think he would marry," said Tobias. "Do you know where the wedding is going to take place?"

"I believe it will be at the Marker ranch," said Ruth.

"Do you know where the Marker ranch is located?" asked Tobias.

"It is three miles south of town," said Ruth.

"Thanks. I will have to see if Burt is there so I can say hi," said Tobias.

After breakfast, Tobias rode south out of town to check out the Marker ranch. Three miles out of town, he moved off the main road and worked his way to where he could see the ranch. Tobias hid his horse before moving closer to the buildings to find out how many men were working the ranch. There was a lot of activity going on. He counted four men working in the yard. He did not see Burt and wondered if he was at the right ranch. He was still watching the ranch when a buggy drove in. When the door opened at the house, he saw a young blond woman come out, and the man who followed her he recognized as one of the men who arrested him.

Tobias watched as the man and woman got out of the buggy and went into the house. After they were in the house, he returned to his horse and rode to the cabin to inform Ike.

Ike asked, "Did you find out where he lives?"

"He doesn't live in the area, but he is staying at a ranch three miles south of El More," said Tobias.

"How did you find out where he is?" asked Archie.

"The waitress at the café told me where the ranch was located," said Tobias. "I rode out there and saw Burt is at the ranch."

"Did you find out how many men they have working the ranch?" asked Ike.

"Four men were working around the ranch. I believe there could be as many as three more," Tobias said.

"Tobias, I want you to watch the ranch tomorrow and see if any other men are there," said Ike.

The next day Tobias rode to the Marker ranch and took his position where he could watch. By late afternoon Tobias decided to return to the cabin after not seeing any new people. Even the buggy from the day before was gone. Returning to the cabin, he reported to Ike.

Thursday morning, the party of Hannah, Milo, Rosie, Cody, Nate, and James left for El More. They brought along three tents in a wagon with supplies. Nate drove the wagon while everyone else rode horses. It was late in the afternoon when they arrived at the Marker ranch.

Riding into the Marker ranch, Ned Davis, the foreman, met them. He went to Milo and said, "You must be Milo and Mrs. Ryder. Welcome to the Marker ranch."

Milo got down, shook Ned's hand, and introduced the rest of the party. When he was done, Milo asked, "Where would you like us to put up our tents?"

"We cleared an area behind the house where you can put your tents," said Ned. "First, I think Albert will want to welcome you."

"Nate, you and James move the wagon behind the house, and we will come to help you get the tents set up," said Milo. "We will go in and say hello to Wanda and Albert."

While they were talking, the front door opened, and Shellie and Burt came out. Shellie went down to Hannah and said, "We are so glad you could make it."

"We are looking forward to the wedding," said Hannah. "Let me introduce you to Rosie. Cody's wife. Rosie, I want you to meet Shellie Marker, soon to be Shellie Ward."

"Hi, Shellie," said Rosie. "I have heard a lot about you and have been looking forward to meeting you."

"Hi, Rosie," said Shellie. "I, too, have been looking forward to meeting you. But, ladies, please come into the house. Ma has some lemonade."

They all went into the house to see Wanda and Albert. Albert met them as they came into the front room. "Milo, Hannah, how are you?" asked Albert. "Cody, this must be your wife."

"Hi, Albert, said Cody. "This is my wife, Rosie. Rosie, I want you to meet Albert Marker."

"Hello, Mr. Marker," said Rosie.

"Please call me Albert. Come into the kitchen and meet my wife, Wanda."

Once they got into the kitchen, Albert said, "Wanda, I want you to meet Rosie, Cody's wife."

"Welcome to our home," said Wanda. "I was starting supper, so you must excuse me."

"Can we help with anything?" asked Hannah. "We brought supplies with us."

"Thanks, but I think I have enough for all of us," said Wanda. "I know that you have to set up your tents. I will call when supper is ready."

Burt went out with the rest to help them set up camp. He went over and shook hands with Nate and James. "How are you guys doing?" asked Burt.

"We're still single," joked Nate.

By the time the three tents were set up and their gear inside, supper was ready.

Everyone got caught up on what everyone had been doing since the last time they were together. After supper, the women helped Wanda clean up and do the dishes while the men went to the porch for a drink and talked about what they needed to do the next day.

CHAPTER 23

Ike decided they would go to the Marker ranch and take care of Burt. So, getting their horses, they rode out. It was late in the morning when they were close to the Marker ranch. Tobias was surprised to see three tents behind the house after stopping where they could see the buildings.

"Ike," said Tobias, "those are new tents behind the house that were not there yesterday, and it looks like a lot more people are there."

Ike took out his field glasses and started looking for the men Tobias had told him about. He was looking at the barn when Milo came out. Surprised to see the marshal, he said, "The man who came out of the barn is that marshal we ran into in San Luis de la Culebra. I wonder how many men he has with him now?"

"He wasn't here yesterday," said Tobias.

"Do you think they are here for the wedding?" asked Frank.

While they were watching, the rest of the men who came with Milo and the ranch hands came into view, and they saw that there were ten men at the ranch.

Frank asked, "What do you want to do?"

"There are too many men for us. That marshal has four men with him that he had in San Luis de la Culebra," said Ike. "I need to devise a plan with them and the four ranch hands. We may have to wait until after the wedding."

Tobias said, "I think we have been spotted."

"Let's get out of here before they decide to come check us out," said Ike.

Ned was coming out of the barn when something caught his eye on the hill south of the ranch, where he thought he saw movement. Taking a closer look, he saw dust rising. Knowing that no wind would cause the dust, Ned headed toward the corral to get his horse. Albert asked, "Where are you going?"

"I thought I saw some movement on that hill," said Ned. "I am going to take a look."

Milo, hearing Ned, said, "Let me get my horse, and I will go with you."

The two men rode to the top of the hill. Ned and Milo got down and looked at the ground. Ned said, "It looks like there were four horses here. It looks like one of the horses has a chip missing from its shoe."

"It looks like they left in a hurry," said Milo. "They rode north back the way it looks like they came here. Have you been having any trouble lately?"

"No, everything has been quiet," said Ned. "I hope this isn't a sign of trouble with the wedding on Saturday."

"We will have to keep watching for them to return," said Milo. "If they think you saw them, they may try to return to a different spot."

"Do you think it has anything to do with the time when Shellie was kidnapped?" asked Ned.

"It could," said Milo. "I think we took care of them, but I cannot think of anything else that would bring attention to the ranch here."

"We can talk to Albert and see if he knows of anything going on," said Ned.

When they returned to the ranch, Cody asked, "What did you find?"

"There were four men up there," said Milo. "One of the horses has a chip missing from one of its shoes."

"I wonder what they were after," said Cody.

"We are going to talk to Albert and see if he knows about anything going on," said Ned.

"Why don't we have James and Nate follow their trail and see if we can find out who was up there," said Cody. "I will tell them to look at the track you saw, so they know what horse to follow."

"Go get them and have them follow the trail," said Milo. "Have them go as deputy marshals in case they run into trouble."

Cody found James and Nate by the tents and told them about the four men watching the ranch. "Milo wants you to try and trail them to find out who they are," said Cody. "Take a look at the tracks; one of them has a chip missing from its shoe."

James and Nate got their horses and found the trail the four men left. The trail led them north toward El More. Nate studied the trail and found a rear hoofprint with a missing chip inside the shoe. Nate said, "James, did you see this print?"

"I did," said James. "We will have to keep looking for it."

They continued to follow the trail into town. But, now, Nate and James had a problem, as the prints they were following were ridden over by several wagons and horses. So, while they rode into town, they kept looking for the unique print.

Not knowing the people of the area and the horses they rode, Nate kept looking for the print with the missing chip. As they rode past the saloon, James spotted the print and saw it belonged to a white quarter horse tied to the hitching post. Riding up the street further, he told James to stop.

"What did you see?" asked James.

"See that white quarter horse tied to the hitching post by the saloon?" asked Nate. "It is the horse we have been following. Let's find a spot where we can watch it and see who it belongs to."

Finding a couple of chairs in front of the mercantile, they sat down and waited. Two hours later, Ike and his men came out of the saloon. Nate didn't know Tobias, but he recognized Ike. Seeing who it was, Nate grabbed James and said, "Quick, go into the mercantile."

Once inside, Nate said, "That is Ike Evens and his men."

James looked out the window and said, "You're right. We need to let Milo know that he is in the area. The question is, what were they doing at the Marker ranch?"

They continued to watch the four men until they rode out of town.

Once they were out of town, James and Nate got their horses and followed them. They stayed far enough back to see their dust but could not see them. So they continued to follow them to a cabin where it looked like they were staying. Nate concluded that there were only four men without seeing more than the four horses.

James said, "I wonder if there are more who are not here at this time. After Ike lost so many men, I think he would try to get more men to help him."

"We need to let Milo know and see what he wants to do," said Nate. "Let's wait a bit and see if more men show up."

After watching the cabin for a while, they started back to the ranch.

After Tobias noticed that they were spotted, they rode to town. They stopped at the saloon and went in. Ike felt confident that they were not known in El More. Finding a table, they sat down near the back of the room, away from the windows.

The barkeep came over and asked, "What will you have?"

"Bring us a bottle and four glasses," said Ike.

While waiting for the bottle to arrive, a large black man walked into the saloon and went to the bar. Frank heard the barkeep say, "Deputy Wagner, what can I get you?"

"I'll have a beer," said Deputy Wagner.

"Let me take this bottle to that table, and I will get your beer," said the barkeep.

While the barkeep was taking the bottle, Deputy Wagner looked at the four men sitting at the table. Noticing that they were all strangers to El More, he decided to keep an eye on them.

After the bottle arrived, Frank asked, "What do you want to do about that marshal?"

"Right now, there are too many men at the ranch," said Ike. "Frank, you said there was going to be a wedding on Saturday. If they are preparing for a wedding, there is going to be more people showing up. We need to watch the ranch after the wedding and find out when the marshal and his men leave."

"We will have to be careful," said Tobias. "Since we were spotted, they will be looking for us."

Frank was looking at the window when Nate and James rode by the saloon. "I think I saw two of the marshal's men ride into town."

"Do you think they followed us?" asked Archie.

"Let's wait and see what they do," said Ike. "They might be in town for supplies. It looked like they stopped at the mercantile."

Ike and his men finished the bottle and got up to leave. Getting their horses, they rode north, leaving town. As they rode past the mercantile, Frank said, "I saw them in the mercantile. Maybe they are after supplies."

While riding back to the cabin, Tobias and Frank kept looking behind them to see if they were being followed. However, when they reached the cabin, they had not noticed that Nate and James were still following them.

Deputy Wagner remained in the saloon until they left. When he walked outside, he saw them riding out of town. Thinking no more about it, he went to the office.

While James and Nate rode out, Milo and Ned went in to talk to Albert. They found Albert in his office. When they walked in, Albert asked, "Do you need something?"

"I saw some movement on the hill south of the ranch. When Milo and I went and checked on it, we found where four horses stood. Do you know of any problems around here?" asked Ned.

"No, I have not heard of any trouble," said Albert.

"We sent James and Nate to follow their trail. Hopefully, they will be able to find out who they are," said Milo.

"Which way did they head?" asked Albert.

"They rode north toward town," said Ned. "If they went into El More, James and Nate could lose their trail."

"Do you think it could have something to do with what happened at the T Bar Ranch?" asked Albert.

"The last I heard was that Ike and the men he still has were near Durango," said Milo. "Ike and most of his men were wounded. So I figured they would have to get more men if they were going to try anything."

"We will wait and see what Nate and James find out," said Albert.

It was later in the afternoon when Nate and James returned. Milo and Albert met them as they rode in. Once they got down, Albert said, "Let's go in the house, where we can talk."

Going into the office where the women couldn't hear what they were saying, Milo asked, "Were you able to find out who was watching the ranch?"

Nate said, "We followed them into town, where they stopped at the saloon. When they came out, we recognized Ike Evens."

"Ike Evens," said Milo. "Why would he be here, and why would he be watching your ranch, Albert?"

"I don't know," said Albert. "I had nothing to do with what happened to him at your new place."

"How many men did Ike have with him?" asked Milo.

"He had three men with him," said James. "We followed them and found where they were staying, in a cabin north of El More. We waited and watched the cabin for a while, and no others showed up."

"Do you want us to go back and watch their place?" asked Nate.

"Seeing how we know who and where they are," said Milo, "I think we need to keep watch here until after the wedding. If they show up, maybe we can arrest them before the wedding. If not, we will go after them after the wedding."

"Tomorrow is the wedding, and there will be a lot of people here," said Albert. "I don't think they would try anything during the wedding if there are only four of them."

"We will have to watch the guests as they arrive to make sure that you know who they are," said Milo.

"Your men know Ike and his men," said Albert.

"We don't know if he has more men that were not at the cabin," said Milo.

While they were talking, Burt came into the office and asked, "What is going on? I thought I heard you mention Ike."

"James and Nate followed the four men watching the ranch," said Milo. "They found out that it is Ike Evens and his men."

"I thought he was west of here," said Burt. "Do you know where they are now?"

"James said they followed them to a cabin where they are staying," said Milo.

"Do you want to go after them since they did escape from the jail?" asked Burt.

"We will wait until after the wedding," said Milo. "If we find out that there are only four of them, we can handle them, and you can return to the T Bar Ranch after the wedding."

"You don't have to worry about them for now," said Albert. "We have enough men here to ensure that nothing happens during the wedding. So, for now, I would not tell Shellie about what we found out. There is no reason for the women to worry about anything but the wedding."

"We still have some things to finish for tomorrow," said Ned. "I'll get the men working on them. They finished digging the pit to roast the steer. I think we will have enough tables and benches for everyone to eat at. I will go check on things."

All the men got busy getting chores done. Then, at suppertime, everyone gathered around the table. Burt and Shellie sat beside each other, and Shellie could hardly eat.

Hannah looked at Shellie and said, "Are you nervous about tomorrow?"

"I have butterflies in my stomach," said Shellie. "I hope I don't fall when I walk to the minister."

"I am sure you will be fine," said Wanda.

"Are we sure we have done everything we needed?" asked Shellie.

"Look at Burt," said Ned. "He is eating like it's his last meal."

Everyone sitting at the table began to laugh. Burt didn't say anything but kept on eating.

Rosie said, "When Cody and I got married, I was so nervous that I couldn't sleep. I think I was up all night, and then I was afraid that I would fall asleep during the ceremony. You will be fine."

"Well, I am glad you all have the confidence in me to make it through tomorrow," said Shellie.

"Burt, you need to sleep in the bunkhouse tonight," Wanda said. "Tomorrow, you are to stay away from Shellie until after the wedding. Shellie has a lot to do to prepare, and you are not to be with her while she is getting ready. You can see her at breakfast but not after that."

When everyone finished eating, the women got busy cleaning up the dishes while the men took Burt to the bunkhouse. Before going there, Ned said, "Milo, you and your men are invited to join us as we send Burt off. There they had prepared to celebrate and took out a couple of bottles. Some of the men took out cigars and started smoking them and having a drink.

Milo raised his glass and said, "To Burt, may you have a long and happy life with Shellie."

The men raised their glasses and cheered Burt.

It was getting late before Milo, James, Nate, and Cody left and went to their tents. Albert returned to the house, where the women had already gone to bed.

When Milo entered their tent, Hannah asked, "How is Burt doing?"

"He will be fine if the boys don't give him too much to drink so he would be hungover for the wedding."

"I think Burt knows enough not to get drunk," said Hannah, laughing.

"This is the first time he is getting married," said Milo. Being young, he may overdo it and have that hangover in the morning."

"We will see," said Hannah.

It wasn't long, and they were both asleep.

CHAPTER 24

THE MORNING STARTED BUSY. ALL the last-minute preparations had to be finished and made ready. Ned sent Boone and Porter to check the area to ensure the four men had not returned. When Cody heard Ned instructing Boone and Porter, he said, "I will send James and Nate with them just in case they come across the four men.

The four men rode out together while everyone else continued to get ready for the wedding.

Josh and Rebecca, with their two children, arrived early to help. Rebecca went into the house where all the cooking was going on and started to help the other women. The children ran around the yard, chasing each other and playing. Josh went looking for Burt to spend some time with him. With Burt about to become his brother-in-law, he wanted to get to know him better.

Burt was talking to Cody when Josh found him. When Josh walked up to them, Burt said, "Cody, I want you to meet Shellie's brother, Josh Marker. Josh, I want you to meet Cody Paxton, the Lazy S Ranch operator."

Cody and Josh shook hands, and Josh asked, "Have you known each other for some time?"

"Burt hired on to the Rocking R Ranch when I was the foreman there," said Cody. "When Milo put me in charge of the Lazy S, Burt became the foreman. Now he owns half of the T Bar."

"I was going to ask you if you would buy into the Lazy S Ranch with Milo," said Burt.

"Milo talked to all of us about doing that if we wanted to," said Cody. "Rosie thinks it is a good idea. So when we get back, I will talk to Milo."

"How can a cowhand and foreman afford a ranch?" asked Josh.

"Milo is a US Marshal," said Burt. "He will deputize us when we go after outlaws, and if there is a reward, he shares it with whoever is with him. I saved a sum of money that allowed me to go in as a partner with Milo."

"There are a few of us that have been with Milo on several hunts," said Cody. "Most of the time, there is a reward."

"Was there a reward when you brought Shellie home?" asked Josh.

"We were not looking for a reward," said Burt. "We were doing it because Wanda and Albert asked us if we would help."

"You might say Burt is getting his reward for that today," said Cody, laughing.

"Josh, what do you think about me marrying Shellie?" asked Burt.

"Mom and Dad have talked much about you and Milo," said Josh. "As long as Shellie and they think it's a good idea, I'll go along with it. Shellie was lost when she first returned, and she kept talking about Burt, and I wondered who Burt was. Shellie would have nothing to do with any of the men around here, stayed alone, and only left the ranch when someone was with her."

"Your sister has a good man here," said Cody. "You will find that the men that work for the Ryders are all good, honest men. When you work for them, you become one of the family and are treated as one."

"I heard Ned talking about some excitement yesterday," said Josh. "What was it?"

"Four men were watching the ranch," said Burt.

"Do you know who they are?" asked Josh.

"They are four men we arrested in San Luis de la Culebra," said Cody.

"What did they want?" asked Josh.

"We don't know, but we think it could be related to driving them off the T Bar Ranch out there," said Burt.

"What are you going to do?" asked Josh.

"That is up to Milo," said Cody. "Two men who work for us followed them to a cabin where they are staying. Milo didn't want to do anything with the wedding today. I think he may want to go after them after the wedding."

"Who would go after them?" asked Josh.

"It would be Milo, Nate, James, and myself," said Cody. "Burt has to return to San Luis de la Culebra and the ranch, seeing that it is still new."

"I would not want to leave Shellie right after we get married," said Burt. "As Cody said, I need to get back to the ranch and ensure it runs smoothly. All the hands have been there for several years, but they have only known me for a few weeks."

While they were talking, they heard three buggies coming up the driveway. Josh said, "It looks like the guests are starting to arrive. I should go greet them."

By one o'clock, all the guests had arrived. The food was cooked and ready to be served. Shellie was in the house getting ready with the help of Rebecca and Wanda. With Shellie dressed, Rebecca got dressed. Hannah and Rosie coordinated the work in the kitchen, and Albert oversaw the steer roasting.

Cody and Burt were in the bunkhouse getting ready and waiting to come out after all the guests were seated. Three men from town brought their instruments and were set up, ready to play.

After Wanda was seated, Ned got Cody and Burt. Once Burt and Cody were standing by the minister, the music started. Rebecca made her way to the front of the aisle and stood to the minister's right. The music changed, telling Shellie and Albert it was time for them to walk down the aisle. All the guests stood until the bride and Albert were in front of the minister.

After everyone took their seats, the minister began. The ceremony lasted a half hour, and when the minister finished, he told Burt to kiss the bride. Everybody cheered when they kissed. When they finished, Shellie and Burt walked down the aisle to where they could greet all the guests.

Wanda stood up and said, "After you greet the newlyweds, go to the tables and eat."

Once everyone had finished eating, the music started, and people began to dance. Then, early that evening, people started to leave for home.

Before some of the women left, they helped Wanda, Hannah, and Mabel clean up.

Before the wedding, Burt and Shellie had talked about when they would leave for the T Bar Ranch. Knowing that Burt wanted to return to the ranch, Shellie had packed the items she wanted to take with her and had them ready to go.

With the wedding over, Burt wanted to leave for the T Bar the next morning. When Burt was alone with Shellie, he said, "I would like to leave for our home in the morning, if that is all right with you."

"I can be ready," replied Shellie. "I am looking forward to us being in our home. That way, I know I will be with you."

"We will have a lot to do when we get home," said Burt.

"Home," said Shellie. "It seems strange to be calling someplace other than here home. I am sure that working with Loretta, we will have the house the way we want it."

It wasn't long after they had gone to bed that they were sound asleep. When Burt woke, Shellie was still sleeping. Gently he woke her. When Shellie was awake, she said, "I have not slept that well in a long time. Getting married to you is the best thing I have done."

They got dressed and went to the kitchen. When Shellie and Burt entered the kitchen, everyone was already there eating. Those sitting at the table started to clap, embarrassing Shellie and Burt. Wanda said, "We were wondering if you would get up today or not," causing everyone to laugh.

"What are your plans?" asked Albert.

"We are going to start for home this morning," said Shellie.

"We are getting ready to head back to the Lazy S and Rocking R today," said Milo. "You can travel with us."

"How soon are you going to leave?" asked Burt.

"We are almost packed now," said Milo. "We could leave within the hour."

"We are packed except for some last-minute items," said Shellie. "Burt had said that he wanted to leave the day after the wedding, so we have loaded the buggy."

"When you are ready, let us know," said Hannah.

After breakfast, those leaving finished loading their gear and got ready to leave. Rebecca, Josh, Lori, and Abraham hugged Shellie. Rebecca said, "I will miss you, and so will the children."

Shellie said, "You must visit the T Bar Ranch."

Getting into the buggy, Shellie turned, looked at the only home she had known, and waved.

Wanda, Albert, Rebecca, Josh, the children, and the men from the ranch watched as they rode away.

Frank was on a hill overlooking the ranch when the eight people rode out of the ranch. Even with those eight gone, Frank didn't think it would be safe to attack the ranch or go after the cattle. He did not remember seeing the man with the woman and kids before. He would have to go back and let Ike know.

CHAPTER 25

By late afternoon they reached the Rocking R Ranch. Cody, Rosie, and James had left the rest and gone to the Lazy S, where Sadie was surprised to see them and got busy fixing food for them.

Hannah invited Burt and Shellie to stay the night at the Rocking R. Then, they would be back at the T Bar Ranch the next day.

Maria heard them and went to greet them. Seeing Hannah, Maria said, "I will get busy and make some supper for you. You must be hungry."

"Thank you," said Hannah. "I will help you."

Maria went up to Shellie, hugged her, congratulated her on her wedding, and said, "It is great to see you again."

"Thank you," said Shellie. "It is good seeing you as well, and I can help you get food ready."

While the women were preparing food, the rest of the ranch hands greeted Burt and congratulated him.

While eating, Burt asked Milo, "What are you going to do about Ike and his men?"

"I think I will go after him. Nate and James know where they are hanging out, so it shouldn't be too hard to capture them," said Milo.

"How many men will you take with you?" asked Shellie.

"I will take four men with me," said Milo. "Nate said they only saw Ike and three of his men."

"What do you think he is doing near El More?" asked Hannah.

"There are some mines there," said Milo. "Maybe they are going to rob one of them. From the report we got from Sheriff Drew, they didn't get any money when they tried to rob the bank in Durango. So they may think that a mine might be easier to rob."

"When will you go after them?" asked Maria.

"The day after tomorrow," said Milo. "I have some things I need to do here before we go."

"Do you need me to go with you?" asked Burt.

"No," said Milo. "I will use the men here on the ranch to go after them. I know you want to return to our other ranch, and I don't want to take you away from Shellie since you were just married."

When they finished eating, the women helped to clear the table and clean the dishes. The men went into the living room and had a drink.

Burt asked Milo, "Is there anything you saw at the ranch that needed care?"

"The only thing I can think of is getting that fence up in that valley on the north side," said Milo. "You should be able to get the feed you will need this winter from there. The money you found will pay for the fencing material and other things."

"I believe that Richard is having the men work on it and may have it completed by the time Shellie and I get home," said Burt. "Are you going to get me one or two of those Aberdeen bulls for the ranch from the one you have here?"

"You will have to do with what you have for now," said Milo. "We won't see any new bulls until next summer, and they will have to grow some before they can breed. Cody and I will be swapping bulls from the young ones between the two ranches here. I am sure we can come up with a couple of bulls for you."

They continued to talk until the ladies had completed cleaning the kitchen and came into the living room. Burt stood, took Shellie's hand, and led her to the couch, where they sat down. When it was late, Burt said, "I think we should go to bed. I want to get an early start in the morning."

Maria said, "I will have breakfast ready by six."

The next day everyone was up early, and Maria had breakfast ready when they entered the kitchen. Hannah told Shellie to sit down, and she helped Maria serve the food.

While eating, the hands congratulated Shellie and welcomed her to the Ryder family. Billy said, "Now that you are officially one of us, we look forward to seeing you and Burt often."

"Billy, you are always welcome to come and visit us at the T Bar Ranch," said Shellie. "And bring Maria with you. I am sure that she would like to see the new place."

Maria smiled and said, "Thank you, Shellie. I will look forward to visiting."

After eating, Shellie and Burt left for San Luis de la Culebra. They arrived late that afternoon and were greeted by Loretta and the rest of the men and women.

After Shellie and Burt rode out, Milo said, "I want to ride into town and see if Tom has heard anything about Ike and his men. I will inform him that we know where he has been staying."

I want to go to town with you," said Hannah. "Maria said that we could use some supplies in the house."

"I will check with Billy and see if there is anything needed for the ranch," said Milo. "We should be able to leave in an hour."

Two days after the wedding, Ike wanted to check the Marker ranch where he had seen Burt and Milo. Unfortunately, they didn't arrive in position to watch the ranch until the middle of the morning. They first found that the three tents behind the house were gone.

"It looks like the marshal has left," said Ike. "I wonder if Burt is still here?"

They continued to watch the ranch the rest of the morning without seeing any sign of Burt. Finally, Archie said, "I don't think he is still here. Do you know where he lives?"

"The marshal lives near Stonewall," said Ike. "I think that Burt works for him. So he must live there as well."

"What do you want to do about this place?" asked Frank.

"I don't see anything that will do us any good," said Ike. "We need to check out the bank in El More. We are running short on money and will need supplies to go after those men."

Leaving, they rode into town. Stopping at the saloon, Ike and his men sat at a table near the window. The barkeep came over and asked, "What will you have?"

"Bring us a bottle and four glasses," said Ike.

While they waited for the bottle, Ike kept looking at the street, trying to figure out how many people were usually out there. Not seeing many, he turned his attention to the bank. Unfortunately, the bank sat near the end of the street where Ike could not see the front door. There were only a couple of people moving near the bank. The rest of the street was empty.

The barkeep returned with their bottle and four glasses. "Can I get you anything else?"

"No, thank you," said Ike.

After the barkeep left, Tobias asked, "What are you thinking?"

"There ain't much activity in town," said Ike. "I think we can take the bank."

"When do you want to do it?" asked Frank.

"Now that the barkeep saw us in here, we need to stay away from here for a couple of days before we go after it," said Ike. "I need to figure out where we will head after hitting the bank. I don't want to head for Stonewall right away. We need to see who comes after us before we go after that marshal once we get the money from the bank."

When they finished the bottle, Ike ordered another bottle to take with them before he and his men got up and left the saloon. As they rode out of town, they slowly passed the bank, trying to get a better look at it. The door opened, and Ike saw that it was small on the inside. He would have to consider that when they robbed it.

Back at the cabin, Ike laid out his plan for the bank. "We will wait until tomorrow and hit the bank on Wednesday. We will pack up here in the morning and head toward Chicosa after we rob the bank. Once people see us heading north, we will circle back and go to Stonewall to locate his ranch."

"What about the marshal?" asked Frank. "Don't you think he will be coming after us?"

"Once the word gets out that we robbed the bank, he will come looking for us," said Ike.

"I thought you wanted to get him at his ranch," said Tobias.

"While he and his men are looking for us, we will raid his ranch," said Ike. "He won't take his wife with him coming after us. We will be able to get to her and take her hostage. When he comes looking for her, we will kill them both."

"What if he doesn't come after us?" asked Archie.

"We will get him at his ranch," said Ike.

Ike and his men spent the next day preparing to rob the bank.

———

Monday morning, Milo called Billy and Nate to the office. "I want to ride over to El More in the morning and look at the cabin where Ike and his men are staying."

"Do you think they are still there?" asked Billy.

"I think they feel safe for the time being and will hole up for a while longer," said Milo. "The three of us will leave and stay in El More tomorrow night. I want to talk to the sheriff in El More and see if he wants to join us in capturing Ike. He may have some information about the cabin and the area around it."

"How long do you think we will be gone?" asked Nate. "I will need to know to put together supplies."

"We should not be gone any longer than a week," said Milo. "We will spend some time in El More unless Ike and his men are not there and we have to follow them."

"We should be able to take what we need on our horses and not need a packhorse," said Nate.

"We will be able to move faster without the packhorse if we have to," said Billy. "Do you want us to take an extra rifle with us?"

"I think if we each take our six guns and one rifle with extra ammunition, we will be all right," said Milo.

After the meeting ended, Milo and Hannah drove into town. The first stop was at the marshal's office. Tom met them as they entered the office.

"Milo, Hannah, it is good to see you. What brings you to town?" asked Tom.

"Hi, Tom," said Hannah. "Milo wanted to talk to you."

"What do you need?" asked Tom.

"Have you heard anything about Ike Evens and his men?" asked Milo.

"I got a wire sometime back from Sheriff Drew saying they had escaped from his jail," said Tom.

"They tried to rob the bank in Durango," said Milo. "From what I heard, they were shot up pretty bad and didn't get any of the money."

"I heard that they wounded some of the men in Durango when they were trying to escape," said Tom.

"Did anyone from town get killed?" asked Milo.

"One of the tellers in the bank died," said Tom.

"Do you happen to know the sheriff in El More?" asked Milo.

"The sheriff's name is Michael Spangler," said Tom. "He has a deputy, but I don't know his name."

"I wonder if he had any posters on Ike," said Milo.

"Now that you mention it, I did receive some posters on Ike and three other men," said Tom. "Just a minute, let me look."

Opening a drawer, he pulled out a stack of wanted posters and started going through them. "Here they are," said Tom. "There is one on Ike Evens, Frank Logan, Tobias Brown, and Archie Garrett. What do you know about them?"

"Burt got married last Saturday over by El More to Shellie Marker. While we were there, we spotted them, and we are going to go after them," said Milo. "Do you mind if we take these posters with us?"

"No, here they are," said Tom. "Aren't these some of the same men you had trouble with in San Luis de la Culebra?"

"Yes, we had them in jail until they escaped," said Milo. "We hope to recapture them and put them in the El More jail. We were surprised when we found out that they were in El More."

"I hope you can recapture them," said Tom. "If there is anything I can do, let me know."

"Thanks, Tom," said Milo.

"It is always a pleasure to see you, Hannah," said Tom. "If you need anything while Milo is gone, don't hesitate to let me know."

"Thank you, Tom," said Hannah.

Hannah and Milo left Tom and went to the mercantile. Esther was finishing with a customer when they entered the store. "Just let me finish up with Ednah, and I will be with you," said Esther. "Thank you, Ednah. You have a good day."

"How did the wedding go?" asked Esther.

"It went fine," said Hannah. "Shellie made a stunning bride. I think between the two of them, Burt was the nervous one."

"Where are they now?" asked Esther.

"They left this morning for San Luis de la Culebra," said Hannah.

"What can I do for you?" asked Esther.

I need a few things," said Hannah, handing Esther a list.

While Hannah was talking to Esther, Milo talked to Arron.

"Is there anything you need, Milo?" asked Arron.

"I am going to need six boxes of .44 cartridges," said Milo.

"Are you going on a hunt?" asked Arron.

"Ike Evens and his men escaped jail and were seen in El More," said Milo. "I am going to take a couple of my men, and we are going to go after them."

"Have you been after them before?" asked Arron.

"They are the ones I ran off the T Bar Ranch that Burt and I bought," said Milo. "I want to ensure he doesn't try to return."

"I heard that Burt got married," said Arron.

"Yes, he did," said Milo. "He was married last Saturday."

"Who did he marry?" asked Arron.

"Shellie Marker," said Milo. "She is the girl that Burt and I rescued in Silverton. They are on their way to the ranch we bought."

"Do you need anything other than the cartridges?" asked Arron.

"I think Hannah has the rest on her list for Esther," said Milo.

Milo paid for the supplies when they were ready. After loading the supplies into the buggy, they started for home.

"Esther said that she and some of the women were putting together a gift for Shellie and Burt," said Hannah.

"When did they think they would be able to get it to them?" asked Milo.

"They were hoping they would be around for a few days, but I told Esther they were on their way home," said Hannah. "She said she would let me know when it is ready."

"Did she say what it was?" asked Milo.

"I believe they are making a special quilt for them," said Hannah. "Once it is done, we can ensure that Shellie gets it."

When they returned to the Rocking R Ranch, Billy and Nate had checked all the gear for the horses, making sure that none of the straps were worn. They checked the horses they were going to ride to El More.

Milo helped Hannah take the supplies into the house and then went to see what Billy and Nate were doing.

"Hi, boss," said Nate as Milo walked up. "We are just about ready."

"How does everything look?" asked Milo.

"The horses are in good shape," said Billy. "We replaced some of the worn shoes on your buckskin. The rest of the gear is ready to go."

"I picked up some more cartridges while we were in town," said Milo. "We stopped and talked to Tom, and he gave me new posters on Ike. It looks like they have increased the reward since they escaped."

"Do we know who the law is in El More?" asked Nate.

"Tom said the sheriff's name is Michael Spangler, and he has a deputy but did not know his name," said Milo.

"Maybe he will want to go after Ike with us," said Billy.

"We can ask him when we get there," said Milo.

"What time do you want to start in the morning?" asked Billy.

"We can leave after breakfast," said Milo.

CHAPTER 26

THE EVENING BEFORE THEY WERE leaving Nate and Bill finished preparing the horses. When the dinner bell rang, they headed to the house. During supper, no one talked about what Milo, Nate, and Billy would do. Those who had gone with Milo in the past knew what would happen.

After supper, Billy waited for Maria to finish in the kitchen. Once she was done, Billy said, "Would you like to go for a walk with me?"

"Yes, I would," said Maria, with a smile.

Walking out back, they walked to the stream and sat down. Once seated, Maria said, "I worry about you when you go off with Milo chasing outlaws."

"Milo knows what he is doing, and he does not take any chances," said Billy. "We have the advantage of knowing where they are hiding out."

"I just don't want to see you get shot," said Maria.

"I don't want to see me get shot either," said Billy, grinning.

Maria reached over, putting her hands on each side of Billy's face, and kissed him. Billy, at first, didn't know what to do. Then he kissed her back. When he had settled down, Billy said, "If we keep doing this, we will have to get married."

Maria grinned and said, "Are you asking me to marry you?"

"I guess in a way I am," said Billy. "I don't know how I will be able to afford to support us."

Jumping up, Maria grabbed Billy and hugged and kissed him.

Maria said, "We can both work here at the ranch. Maybe we could build a small house where we could live. I know we can make it work."

Billy knew that he had money saved from the reward money Milo had given him, but he did not know that Maria also had money from when she sold her property.

"I will have to talk to Milo to see if he would allow us to do that," said Billy.

"When will you do that?" asked Maria.

"I will wait until we get back from El More," said Billy. "He has too much on his mind right now."

They continued to sit, talking about their future. When it got dark, Billy said, "Let me walk you back to the house. Tomorrow will come early."

Maria kissed Billy before she returned to the house, and Billy went to the bunkhouse.

The following morning Milo, Nate, and Billy were in the kitchen before sunrise. Hannah and Maria had made donuts along with fresh bread, eggs, steak, potatoes, and coffee. When they finished eating, Hannah gave Milo a bag with supplies. Maria had put together supplies for Nate and Billy. Nate took the supplies and headed for the barn to get the horses while Milo and Billy said goodbye to the women.

When Milo and Billy came out, Nate met them at the house with the horses. Hannah and Maria stood on the porch and watched as they mounted. When the three men started to ride out, the two women waved and watched until they were out of sight.

Milo, Nate, and Billy rode easy, not wanting to tire their horses. At noon they stopped and built a fire and made coffee. Maria had packed them jerky and donuts. After eating, they rode on and arrived in El More around three in the afternoon. Milo spotted the sheriff's office as they rode through the main street. They stopped and tied their horses and went in.

Sheriff Michael Spangler was sitting at his desk when they entered. Looking up, he asked, "What can I do for you?"

"Sheriff Spangler?" asked Milo.

"Yes, I am Sheriff Spangler."

"My name is US Marshal Milo Ryder, and these are deputies Billy Jenkins and Nate Mayfield," said Milo. "We are here to arrest Ike Evens and the three men he has with him."

"How do you know he is here?" asked Sheriff Spangler.

"We were at the Marker ranch for a wedding this past week, and Nate spotted him and followed them to where they are hiding out," said Milo.

"What are you after them for?" asked Sheriff Spangler.

Milo took out the posters and handed them to the sheriff.

Sheriff Spangler looked the posters over and said, "I think I have seen these men in town. It has to have been two days ago."

"They haven't been back since?" asked Nate.

About that time, the door opened, and a black man walked in. " Emmett, come here," said the sheriff.

"What ya need, Sheriff?" asked Emmett.

"Emmett, I want you to meet US Marshal Milo Ryder and his two deputies," said the sheriff. "Milo, I want you to meet my deputy, Emmett Wagner."

"Deputy Wagner, this is Deputies Nate Mayfield and Billy Jenkins," said Milo, shaking Emmett's hand.

" Emmett," said Sheriff Spangler, "take a look at these posters. Have you seen these men in town recently?"

"No, I have not," said Emmett. "Are you looking for them?"

"We believe they are hiding near here," said Milo. "Nate followed them to their hideout a few days ago."

"Why didn't you arrest them then?" asked Emmett.

"We were here for a wedding and ran into them by accident," said Milo. "We arrested them when I bought a ranch outside San Luis de la Culebra over two months ago," said Milo. "Since then, they have escaped jail and tried to rob a bank in Durango."

After looking at the posters, Deputy Wagner said, "I remember seeing them in the saloon last Friday. They were sitting by the window until they finished a bottle. Then, the man called Ike got a second bottle and took it with them."

"Did they go someplace else in town?" asked Billy.

"No, they got their horses and rode out of town," said Deputy Wagner. "I haven't seen them back in town since then."

"When do you plan on going after them?" asked Sheriff Spangler.

"We will stay in El More tonight and go after them in the morning," said Milo. "You can come with us. There are four of them."

"They haven't done anything in my jurisdiction that I can arrest them for," said Sheriff Spangler. "If you capture them, I will hold them for you."

"Thank you," said Milo.

"Thank you for letting me know what you are doing here," said Sheriff Spangler.

"If I see them in town, where can I find you?" asked Deputy Wagner.

"We will be at the hotel," said Milo.

They left the sheriff's office to go to the livery and put up their horses. The three men took their saddlebags and rifles. They went to the hotel. Milo got rooms for each of them and said, "Put your gear in the rooms, and we will go to the café and get supper."

When Milo got to the hotel lobby, Nate and Billy were waiting for him. Walking across the street, they entered the café. Ruth Meyer, the café waitress, met them. "Help yourselves to one of the tables, and I will be right with you."

They found a table on the side of the room where they could see out the window and sat down. When Ruth returned, she had a coffee pot and three cups. "Would you like coffee?" she asked.

"Yes, thank you," said Milo. "What is the special tonight?"

"Charle is making steak, german potatoes, gravy, and fresh rolls," said Ruth. "You are new. What brings you to El More?"

"We were here over the weekend for a wedding," said Nate. "I came by here but did not stop."

"We are looking for some men," said Milo.

"Were you at Shellie Marker's wedding? That is the only wedding I knew about last weekend," asked Ruth. "She is my friend, but I could not attend the wedding."

"Yes, we were there," said Milo. "She married a partner of mine."

"I met him," said Ruth. "He seemed like a nice man. Now, what can I get you?"

"I believe we will all have the special," said Milo.

While eating, Billy looked out the window and saw Frank ride into town and stop at the mercantile. "Milo, that is one of Ike's men who just went into the mercantile," said Billy. "What do you want to do?"

"If he went into the mercantile, they must need supplies," said Milo. "That means that they are still in the area, and we should be able to arrest them tomorrow."

"You want to let him go for today?" asked Nate.

"If we do anything with him tonight, it will spook the others, and we may not be able to get to them in the morning," said Milo.

While they ate, Billy kept his eyes on the mercantile. When Frank came out, he had a couple of packages in his arms. "It looks like he did get supplies," said Billy. "He has two packages with him."

They all looked out the window and watched as Frank rode out of town.

Milo said, "If he only got a small number of supplies, I wonder what they are up to."

"In the morning, we can ride out to the cabin," said Nate. "If they are planning on leaving, we will want to get there early before they leave."

"How far is the cabin from here?" asked Milo.

"It is about four miles," said Nate.

"Yes, we will want to get an early start," said Milo.

Milo called Ruth over and asked, "What time do you open in the morning?"

"We are open by six," said Ruth.

"We will be here at six," said Milo.

When they finished eating, Milo paid and went to the hotel. Each went to their rooms and said they would meet in the lobby before sunrise.

The following morning at six, the three men were at the door of the café when Ruth unlocked the door. "You said you would be here at six, and here you are," said Ruth. "Please come in, and I will get you coffee."

While they were eating, Sheriff Spangler came in. Seeing Milo, Nate, and Billy, he went to join them. "Do you mind if I join you?"

"No, please take a seat," said Milo.

"Thank you," said Sheriff Spangler. "Are you going after Ike and his men this morning?"

"As soon as we finish eating," said Milo.

"We saw one of his men in town yesterday getting supplies," said Nate.

"We don't know what they are planning, so we want to try and get them before they leave."

Milo and his men finished eating and got up to leave. "Sorry, Sheriff," said Milo. "We need to be going. Hopefully, we will be back with some prisoners for you later today."

"Good luck," said Sheriff Spangle.

Milo, Nate, and Billy went to the livery and got their horses. Then, riding out of town, Nate led the way, knowing where the cabin was.

It was an hour later when they neared the cabin. Nate stopped them and said, "We need to go on foot from here and ensure they are still there."

Tying their horses and taking their rifles, they started through the trees toward the cabin. When they got to the far side of the trees where they could see the cabin, it looked empty.

Nate said, "Wait here, and I will take a look."

Staying low, Nate made his way to the cabin. As he got close, he could smell that bacon had been cooked that morning. Nate made his way to a window, careful not to make any noise. Taking a look, he saw that it was empty. Turning, he motioned for Milo and Billy to come to the cabin. Nate made his way around the side of the cabin and saw that the corral was also empty.

By now, Milo and Billy had walked to the cabin door and opened it. Billy checked the stove and found it still warm. "They were here this morning," said Billy. "Maybe Nate found their tracks, and we can follow."

Nate entered the house and said, "They rode out about half an hour ago. It looks like they are heading toward El More."

"If they are going to El More, I am surprised that we didn't run into them on our way here," said Milo. "Billy, get the horses, and we will follow to make sure that they are going to El More."

Following their trail, they realized that they had ridden over their tracks coming to the cabin, and their trail was leading to El More. So they followed Ike's tracks, saw where they had gone off the road, and waited. Once they knew that Ike and his men were going to El More, they increased their pace.

CHAPTER 27

TUESDAY MORNING, IKE SAT DOWN with Frank, Tobias, and Archie to lay out his plan to rob the bank in El More. "In the morning, we will ride into El More. Frank will stay with the horses while Archie, Tobias, and I rob the bank. This afternoon, Frank, I need you to go and get supplies. While you are there, I want you to check for strangers in town.

After Ike finished, everyone got busy checking their horses and gear, making sure that they would be ready in the morning. Later Frank rode to El More. Ike had given him a list of the supplies they would need.

Riding down the main street, Frank didn't see any activity that drew his attention. He stopped in front of the mercantile and went inside. Handing the list to the clerk, he asked, "Have you seen any strangers in town today?"

"You are the only one I have seen that is new around here," said the clerk.

The clerk filled Frank's order, and after Frank paid, he took two packages to his horse and rode out of town. Back at the cabin, Tobias had supper made when he arrived. Ike asked, "What did you find out in town?"

"Nothing has changed," said Frank. "The clerk at the mercantile has not seen anyone new except for me."

"That's good," said Ike. "All we have to worry about is the sheriff and his deputy. We will eat in the morning and ride into El More."

The following morning Ike, Frank, Tobias, and Archie ate a hurried breakfast and gathered their gear, knowing they would not be coming back to the cabin.

After saddling their horses, they rode out. They had only gone a mile from the cabin when they heard horses coming toward them. Not wanting to be seen on the road, they left, moving into a grove of trees. Where they stopped, they could not see the road but could hear the horses as they went by. Once they could no longer hear the horses, they returned to the road and continued to town.

At the edge of town, Ike stopped the men, taking time to look at the main street and see what activity was happening before entering. Then, not seeing many people on the street, they rode into town.

Ruth was out front of the café when she saw the four men riding up the street. She didn't think much of it until she recognized Frank and wondered who was with him. After they rode by, they stopped at the bank before she turned and went back into the café. Ruth thought it was strange that they stopped at the bank.

Deputy Wagoner was finishing his breakfast as Ruth returned. Ruth went over to him and said, "Four men just rode into town and stopped by the bank."

"Do you know them?" asked Deputy Wagoner.

"I have seen the one, but I have not seen the other three before," said Ruth.

"I better take a look," said Deputy Wagoner, getting up.

Going to the front door, Deputy Emmett Wagoner looked out before opening the door. Emmett saw one man outside the bank holding three other horses. Knowing something was wrong, he opened the café door as the three men came out of the bank wearing masks and holding their guns.

When Ike saw Emmett coming out of the café, he fired at him. But, lucky for Emmett, he missed.

Emmett drew his Colt and returned fire, missing Ike.

By now, the two men who came out with Ike were in the saddle and started to fire at Emmett. Emmett was forced to take cover as they continued to fire as they rode away. Finally, with no more shooting, Emmett ran to the bank to find out what had happened. Emmett found no one was hurt inside the bank, but the money was gone. Going back out, he saw three men riding hard coming in from the north. When they got closer, he recognized Marshal Ryder. They stopped by Emmett, and Milo said, "We heard shooting. What happened?"

"The bank was robbed, and they rode out of town going south," said Emmett, pointing to the direction Ike had gone.

"How many men?" asked Billy.

"Four," said Emmett. "I will get Sheriff Spangler, and we will follow you."

Milo said, "Let's go."

Milo, Billy, and Nate started after them. On the edge of town, they picked up their tracks. Milo saw they were riding hard, leaving an easy trail to follow. "If they keep pushing their horses this hard, they won't get far," said Milo.

Milo and his men put their horses in an easy canter that ate up ground, saving the horses as they continued to follow Ike.

Ike and his men continued to ride hard for the first mile. When Ike looked back, he saw they were not being pursued, so they slowed down. Now that Ike had money, he wanted to go after Marshal Milo Ryder. Leaving the trail, he turned west, heading for Trinidad.

After riding for an hour, Ike wanted to stop and rest the horses. They had not seen anyone trailing them, so he felt they were safe.

"Do you think they will come after us?" asked Frank, after they had stopped.

"They will as soon as they can get a posse together," said Ike. "We covered our trail when we turned off the road. They will have a hard time following it."

Milo, Billy, and Nate came to where Ike and his men had slowed down and lost the trail. Backtracking to where they first lost it, they spread out on each side of the road, searching for a track. Nate was the first one to find where they had left the road. "I found where they turned off," called out Nate. "They are heading west, but not on a trail."

Milo and Billy caught up to Nate, and they slowly started following the faint trail that Ike had left. At times Nate would get down to take a close look to make sure they were still following the right trail.

"I wonder where they are going?" said Billy. "They are headed in the direction of Trinidad."

The three men continued to follow Ike. The horses were getting played out, so Milo had them stop. Nate got busy getting a fire going so they could make coffee. Billy took out some jerky that they could eat with their coffee. An hour after they had stopped, they tightened their cinches and started following Ike's trail again. Two miles further, they found where Ike and his men had stopped.

Looking at the tracks, Milo said, "I don't think they know we are following them. If you look at their tracks leaving here, they are not in a hurry."

They continued to take it easy following the trail. Milo had them stop and make camp when it was getting late in the afternoon.

"We can't be that far behind them," said Nate.

"We don't want to come upon them in the dark," said Milo. "If they hear us coming, they could set up an ambush, and we would fall into it without seeing them. We will get an early start in the morning, and with luck, we will still catch them in their camp."

Milo was up the next day while it was still dark. After getting the fire going, he woke Nate and Billy. "Coffee is about done. We can make some breakfast and be ready to leave by sunrise."

While eating, Nate asked, "Do you think we can capture them without a gunfight?"

"If we can get the drop on them while they are still in their camp, we might be able to," said Milo.

"The last time we put them in jail, they were able to escape," said Billy. "Where do you want to take them after we arrest them?"

"We are close enough to Trinidad," said Milo. "We can take them there and turn them over to Marshal Bullion before we return the bank money to El More. But, first, we have to arrest them."

They were saddling their horses just as the sun started rising in the east.

Billy looked at the sky and said, "It looks like it is going to be clear and hot today."

Billy took the lead when they rode out following Ike's trail. Half an hour after they left, Billy smelled smoke. Stopping the others, he whispered to Milo, "I think they are just ahead of us. I can smell the smoke of a campfire."

Leaving their horses there, the three men made their way on foot toward the smoke. Nate was the first one to see one of Ike's men. When he saw him, he stepped on a branch, alerting the man that he was there.

The man turned and ran back to the camp.

Ike, Frank, Tobias, and Archie continued riding until late afternoon. Then, when Ike found a good spot to camp, he pointed to it and said, "We will camp here tonight."

Frank started making supper while Tobias and Archie took care of the horses. Ike looked in the bag they took from the bank and found that there was more money than he thought they had gotten. But for now Ike wanted to find Marshal Ryder's ranch and kill him. After that, he would work on another plan to get more money and find the rest of the men that put him in the San Luis de la Culebra jail and took the ranch.

After supper, Frank said, "Do we want to keep a guard on the camp in case a posse did follow us?"

"I have not seen any sign of anyone following us since we left El More," said Ike. "I think we lost them, and Sheriff Spangler can only follow us so far, and we are out of his jurisdiction."

As soon as they had finished eating and cleaning up, they rolled out their bedrolls and lay down. It wasn't long before they were all asleep except for Frank. Frank kept having an uneasy feeling that they were not alone. Finally, getting up, he decided to walk out of camp and look around to see if he could hear or see anything that would change his mind about not being alone. Frank walked back the way they had ridden in, hoping to hear if someone was following them. Finding a spot off the trail, he stopped and waited where it was quiet. After an hour and the moon came out, he had not heard or seen anyone. Feeling that Ike was right, that they were not followed, Frank returned to camp and lay down. It wasn't long before he was asleep as well.

Shortly before sunrise, Frank woke up and found that the rest of the men were still sleeping. So getting up, he stoked the fire and started coffee. The smell of coffee cooking woke the others. Ike got up and helped Frank with breakfast while Tobias and Archie went to tend to the horses. Breakfast was ready by the time Tobias and Archie returned.

"Are we going to stop in Trinidad?" asked Tobias.

"I think we will go around Trinidad and head to Stonewall," said Ike. "Sheriff Spangler has probably sent telegrams to the closest towns to be watching for us. If we go on to Stonewall, that is near where Marshal Ryder has a ranch."

They finished eating and cleaned up. Frank walked out to relieve himself when he heard a branch snap. He quickly returned to camp and warned the rest, "I think someone is out there. We need to get out of here now."

Everyone got on their horses and hurried out of there as Milo, Billy, and Nate hurried into their camp only to see them riding off in the distance.

"Who is that?" asked Archie.

"I don't know. All I saw was one man, but it sounded like more were there," said Frank.

"Maybe we need to try and find some help," said Tobias. "Didn't you know a man in Trinidad?"

"Cyrus Slade used to be there, but he got caught for murder and was hung," said Ike. "I know where his Lazy C Ranch is located. Maybe we can hide out there. Some of his men who might help us could still be there."

They continued to ride hard, putting a good distance between them and Milo. When they came to the land that was rock, they slowed down, walking and leading their horses across the rock and changing direction. Not leaving a trail, they moved further across the rock until they came to a stream. Going into the stream, they headed south until they found a place where they could leave the stream and not leave a trail.

Milo, seeing them ride off, said, "We need to get back to our horses and go after them."

Once they got their horses, they followed Ike and his men. By now, they had gotten a mile head start and were out of sight. Their trail was easy to follow, as they were running their horses.

When they reached the rock Ike and his men had crossed, they halted. Getting down, Billy tried to find which way they were heading. Walking and leading his horse, Billy kept his eyes on the surface, looking for any mark the horses could leave from their shoes. After an hour, they still had no clue which direction the men had gone.

"It is like they vanished," said Billy. "What do you want to do?"

"We know that they were heading toward Trinidad," said Milo. "Let's head to Trinidad and see if we can pick up their trail. Maybe Marshal Bullion has seen them."

Now not following a trial, Milo led the way to Trinidad. But unfortunately, it was late when they rode into town. Stopping by the marshal's office, they found out that the marshal wasn't there, so they went to the livery to take care of their horses. With the horses taken care of, they went to the café. Inside the café, Milo spotted Marshal Bullion sitting at a table by himself.

When Marshal Henry Bullion saw Milo, he waved him to the table. "I take it these are your men? Why don't you all take a seat?" said Henry.

"Thank you, we will," replied Milo. "Henry, I want you to meet Billy Jenkins and Nate Mayfield. They work for me and are my deputies."

"Gentlemen, I am glad to meet you. What brings you to Trinidad?"

"We were following Ike Evens and lost him crossing the rocky land east of here. We believe that he is heading to Trinidad, and we are hoping to meet him here."

"I received a telegram from Sheriff Spangler about a bank robbery," said Henry. "He mentioned Ike Evens."

"Do you know what he looks like?" asked Billy.

"No, I have never seen him or a description of him," said Henry. "Do you have any information on him?"

Milo took out the posters he was carrying and showed them to Henry. After Henry looked at them, he said, "I have not seen him or any of these men in Trinidad. Have you been after him long?"

"I bought a ranch in San Luis de la Culebra and had to run him off the ranch. As you can see, he and his men are on posters for several crimes, including bank robbing," said Milo.

"Since you took care of Cyrus Slade and his men, everything has remained quiet in Trinidad," said Henry. "We have had a few minor incidents but nothing major."

"If he had been in town, it would have been late this afternoon," said Milo.

"Do you know if he knows anyone around here?" asked Henry. "He could be holed up anywhere."

"Who is running Cyrus's ranch?" asked Milo.

"Milt Skinner is running the ranch," said Henry. "He took over about a year ago."

"Has he caused any trouble around here?" asked Nate.

"No," said Henry. "He sticks mainly to the ranch and sends someone in to get supplies."

"Do you know if he was with Cyrus?" asked Milo.

"I believe he was," said Henry.

"I wonder if Ike knew Cyrus?" questioned Nate.

"What do you mean?" asked Henry.

"If Ike knew Cyrus, he might think he could hide out at the ranch," said Nate.

"We could ride out there and watch the ranch," said Billy.

"Why don't you spend the night in Trinidad and go out there in the morning," suggested Henry. "I could ride out with you."

"That would be good," said Milo. "You could check on the ranch, and Ike wouldn't know you."

"Why don't we meet here by seven in the morning for breakfast," said Henry.

"We will meet you here then," said Milo.

After eating, Milo, Billy, and Nate went to the livery to get their gear before going to the hotel and getting rooms. The following day they met Henry at the café.

While they were eating, Henry said, "When we get close to the ranch, if you hold back, I will talk to Milt. He may tell me if Ike has been there."

After eating, they all went and got their horses and headed for the ranch.

That same morning while Ike, Frank, Tobias, and Archie were eating at Cyrus's ranch, Milt asked, "What are you going to do?"

"I want to hole up for a few days. When we first left El More, we didn't think we were being followed, but we found out that we were followed," said Ike.

"What did you do in El More?" asked Milt.

"We robbed the bank," said Ike.

"Did they follow you here?" asked Milt.

"We lost them crossing some rock. Since then, we have not seen them," said Ike.

"Well, as long as you are sure that you weren't followed here, you can stay for a few days," said Milt. "If someone shows up looking for you, you will have to stay out of sight," said Milt. "We have remained clean in the area ever since Cyrus was arrested. However, the marshal does show up here sometimes. Usually, after we have done a job out of the area."

"Has he ever tried to arrest you?" asked Frank.

"He has not had any evidence that we did the job," Milt said. "With no evidence, he had to leave us alone."

"If he shows up, we will stay hidden until you tell us it is clear," said Ike. "Do you think he could come by now?"

"If he found out that you were heading this way, he could show up," said Milt. "If you stay out of sight, there is nothing he can do."

Early morning after breakfast, James Alvord came in the house and said, "The marshal is heading this way. I don't think he is alone."

"Ike, you and your men, go to the barn and stay there until I tell you it is clear," said Milt.

Ike and his men quickly went to the barn. Ike got to a place where he could see who rode in but would be out of sight. It wasn't long when Marshal Bullion, along with Marshal Ryder and his men, rode into the yard. Ike recognized Milo and ducked back into the shadows of the barn.

Frank asked, "Isn't that the marshal who arrested us in San Luis de la Culebra?"

"That is him," said Ike. "It must have been them that were following us."

Milt came out of the house and greeted Marshal Bullion, saying, "What brings you here?"

"We're looking for four men," said Marshal Bullion. "Have you been anywhere in the past five days?"

"No, I have been here at the ranch," Milt said.

"What about your men?" asked Marshal Bullion.

"They have been here with me," said Milt.

"Have you seen any strangers around here in the past day?" asked Marshal Bullion.

"I can't say I have," said Milt, glancing toward the barn. "What did they do?"

"They robbed a bank in El More," said Marshal Bullion.

"Isn't that a little out of your jurisdiction?" asked Milt.

"This is US Marshal Milo Ryder," said Marshal Bullion. "These two men are US deputy marshals with Marshal Ryder."

"As I said, I have not seen anyone other than the men working here," Milt said. "Who are the men you are looking for, Marshal Ryder?"

"Ike Evens, Archie Garrett, Frank Logan, and Tobias Averill," said Marshal Ryder. "They are wanted for several things. The last was robbing the El More Bank."

"I can't say I know any of the names," Milt said.

"Thank you," said Marshal Bullion, indicating to Milo and the others that they should leave.

Turning their horses around, they rode out. Once they were out of sight of the ranch, Billy said, "Did you see Milt glance at the barn when Henry asked about seeing any strangers?"

"I saw that," said Milo. "I wonder if Ike and his men are in the barn."

"I think we need to watch the ranch for a while," said Nate. "If they were in the barn, they will have to come out sometime."

"We know what they look like," said Milo. "Nate, you and Billy stay here and watch the ranch. Then, I will ride back to town, get some supplies, and return. But first let's find a spot where you can watch the ranch and stay hidden, so I know where to find you."

It wasn't long before they found a high spot where they could see the ranch and not be seen. Leaving Nate and Billy, Milo rode to town with Henry. After gathering some supplies, he rode back to Nate and Billy.

CHAPTER 28

After Marshal Bullion, Milo, and his men left the ranch, Ike went to see Milt. "That was Marshal Milo Ryder with the local marshal," said Ike. "He is a US marshal, and the two men with him are US deputy marshals."

"Marshal Bullion introduced them to me," said Milt. "They are looking for you."

"I wonder if they will hang around," said Ike.

Milt called Solomon over. "I want you to follow them and see what they do. Make sure that they do not see you."

Solomon got his horse and followed them off the main road. When he saw them standing and talking, he hid and waited. Solomon watched as Marshal Bullion and Marshal Ryder rode off, leaving the two deputies behind. Solomon continued to watch them as Nate and Billy settled into a place to watch the ranch.

Once Nate and Billy had settled, Solomon circled the ranch, staying out of sight. Then, when he was on the back side of the buildings, Solomon rode into the ranch. Leaving his horse at the barn, Solomon walked to the house. He found Ike, Tobias, Frank, and Archie inside the house with Tobias.

"What did you find out?" asked Milt.

"They left two men watching the ranch," said James. "They are just out of sight but can still see into the yard. If I were you, I would stay in the house until dark."

"Is there a way we could get to them without them seeing us leave?" asked Frank.

"They would see us before we got close to them," Solomon said.

"What do you want to do?" asked Milt. "I think we wait until dark and leave," said Ike. "If they are going to stay and watch, we can get away from here before they realize that we are not here."

At dark, Ike and his men, wanting to stay out of sight, saddled their horses in the barn. With the horses saddled, they rode through the field, keeping the buildings between them and where Milo and his men were watching. Once they were far enough away, they headed toward Stonewall.

Before reaching Stonewall, they found an empty rancher line shack. Taking care of the horses, they went inside. The inside of the shack had a stove table with two chairs and two bunks. "It is not much," said Ike. "We can stay here tonight and look for a better place to hole up in the morning."

Billy and Nate were unaware of Solomon watching them. They placed themselves where they could see movement in the yard of the ranch. They watched while Solomon rode in from the back of the ranch and put up his horse. They saw him go to the house. They thought he was just out working the cattle, so they didn't think any more about it.

Milo returned shortly after noon. "What has been going on?" he asked.

"Not much activity at the ranch," said Billy. "It looks like it is just the hands working around the ranch. One man came in from what looked like he had been with their cattle."

"If Ike is there, he is not showing himself," said Nate. "We know he has three men with him, and they have not shown themselves either."

"We will continue to watch the ranch until tomorrow," said Milo. "If we don't see them by tomorrow, we will go home. I hate to say this, but it looks like we lost them."

The rest of the day ended with no results of finding Ike and his men.

Milo decided that they would camp out and check the ranch in the morning. They would have to come out sometime if they were in the house.

The following morning Billy went to watch the ranch while Milo and Nate took care of the horses and made breakfast. After Milo and Nate ate, Nate went to relieve Billy so he could eat. When Billy returned to camp, Milo asked, "What is going on at the ranch?"

"Nothing unusual," said Billy. "Milt came out of the house and went to the barn. He talked to one of the men, who got two other men and headed for town. None of them were Ike or any of his men."

"What did Milt do after that?" asked Milo.

"He stopped and talked to some of the other people working at one of the corrals before returning to the house," said Billy. "I don't think Ike is there."

When Billy finished eating, Milo and Billy went to check on Nate. Nate told Milo that he had not seen Ike or any of his men.

Milo decided to go home. He would wait until he heard about Ike again and then go after him.

Riding back to Trinidad, they stopped and talked to Marshal Bullion.

"I am surprised to see you," said Henry. "What did you find out?"

"We watched the ranch yesterday and this morning," said Milo. "We did not see Ike or any of his men. I think we have lost them."

"What are you going to do now?" asked Henry.

"We are going back to Stonewall and my ranch," said Milo. "If you see or hear of them, send me a telegram and we will come back.

"Now that I know what Ike looks like, I will watch for him," said Henry. "I will send a telegram if he shows up."

"Thanks," said Milo. "Let's head for home, boys."

They arrived at the Rocking R Ranch right before suppertime. Hannah was coming out of the barn after putting her horse up from taking a ride. Looking up, she was surprised to see Milo, Billy, and Nate coming up to the ranch. She called out to Maria.

When Maria heard Hannah, she thought that there was a problem. She got excited when she came outside and saw Billy coming home. She ran over to Hannah, and they both waited for the men to reach them.

When the men got close, Billy jumped down, grabbed Maria, and hugged her. Hannah waited until Milo got down before she hugged him.

"How did it go?" asked Hannah.

"We thought we had Ike, but we lost him," said Milo.

"Where did you lose him?" asked Hannah.

"Over by Trinidad," said Milo.

"Hey, boss, how did it go?" asked Cord Martin, as he walked up.

"Hi, Cord," said Milo. "We lost our man by Trinidad. I have Marshal Bullion keeping an eye on the town, and he will let me know if he sees him."

"Do you think he could show up here?" asked Porter, who had joined them.

"I don't know," said Milo. "We will have to wait and see when we hear about him again."

"Milo, Billy, let me take your horses and put them up for you," said Porter, taking their reins and starting for the barn.

"You better hurry, Porter. Supper is almost ready," said Maria.

Nate said, "Let me put up my horse, and I will meet you in the house. I am ready for a good home-cooked meal again."

Both Maria and Hannah laughed. Then, Maria said, "Didn't Milo cook that well for you?"

Billy went and put his gear away before returning to the house. By the time the rest of the men had arrived, supper was on the table.

Cord asked, "Didn't things go well this trip?"

"No, we lost Ike and his men on the other side of Trinidad," said Milo. "We thought they were holing up at a ranch where Cyrus Slade lived before he was hung. We watched it but never saw them. They must have left during the night when we couldn't see them if they were there."

Hick asked, "What are you going to do now?"

"The only thing I can do is go back to ranching until I hear where he is," said Milo. "If he is in the area, we should hear about him soon."

"For now, I am glad he is home and safe again," said Hannah.

"I have to go along with Hannah," said Maria.

"When are you two going to get married?" asked Hick.

Maria's face turned red as she began to blush.

"Now, Hick," said Hannah. "That is up to them to decide when they are ready."

Over the next few days, things returned to normal at the ranch.

The day after leaving Cyrus's ranch, Ike sent Tobias and Archie to find a better place to hide out. They went north of Stonewall and found a deserted house that had not been lived in for some time. After checking around, they did not see any sign of movement in the area except deer or elk. Returning, they reported to Ike what they found.

"Let's move," said Ike. "If no one has been living there, we could stay and find out where the marshal lives."

After they moved into the house, Ike said, "I wonder what happened to the people who lived here?"

"We found some graves on the hill," said Tobias. "It looks like something happened to the family that wiped them out."

"We will have to keep watch for anyone coming around the area just in case there is still someone taking care of the place," said Ike.

For the next two days, all four of the men stayed near the house. Ike wanted them to be out of sight from everyone, giving the law a chance to quiet down and forget about them. However, he still needed to find where the marshal had his ranch. He knew that the ranch in San Louis de la Culebra was not the ranch where the marshal lived.

Finally, after a week of remaining out of the public eye, Ike decided to send Frank into town. "I want you to go and see if you can find out any information about the marshal who drove us out of the ranch in San Luis de la Culebra," said Ike.

"Do we need any supplies while I am in town?" asked Frank. "Sometimes the mercantile is a good place to pick up information."

Frank saddled his horse and put a packsaddle on the packhorse, with two panniers to hold the supplies. Once he was ready, Frank rode to Stonewall. His first stop was at the mercantile. Inside he was met by Arron Salavan, the owner. "What can I do for you?" asked Arron.

"I am going to need some supplies," replied Frank, handing Arron a list.

Arron looked the list over and said, "I should have all of this. It will take me a little if you want to wait."

"That's fine," said Frank. "Nice little town you have here."

"We enjoy it," said Arron.

"How long have you lived here?" asked Frank.

"My wife and I have been here most of our life," said Arron.

"Has the town always been this peaceful?" asked Frank.

"No, we have had our troubles," said Arron.

"Oh, what kind of trouble?" asked Frank.

"A while back, our bank was robbed," said Arron. "Thanks to Marshal Ryder, he and his deputies recovered the money and arrested the ones who robbed the bank."

"This marshal, does he live around here, or was he passing through?" asked Frank.

"Marshal Ryder has a ranch in the Purgatoire Valley," said Arron. "He and his wife come in for supplies. He has been doing quite well for himself. I understand he bought a third ranch near San Luis de la Culebra."

"How does a marshal afford so many ranches?" asked Frank.

"He retired on his ranch in the Purgatoire Valley first," said Arron. "When he is needed, they ask him to go after outlaws, and he invests his money in ranches. I understand that one of his hands went in as a partner in his latest ranch."

"How far is his ranch?" asked Frank.

"His main ranch is about five miles northeast from here," said Arron. "Are you looking for work? I understand he is a great man to work for, and I heard he is looking for another hand at the ranch."

"I have an offer for some work near Denver, and I am heading there," said Frank. "If that doesn't work out, I will remember this Milo Ryder and check him out."

Frank paid when Arron finished gathering his supplies, and Arron helped him load them in the panniers on the packhorse. Arron noticed that he was riding a white horse and his packhorse was a black and white paint.

Frank left the mercantile and went to the Red Dog Saloon. Inside at the bar, Frank ordered a beer. While drinking his beer, the barkeep asked, "Are you looking for work?'

"No, I am passing through," said Frank.

"Too bad," said the barkeep. "I understand that Milo Ryder at the Rocking R Ranch might be looking for another hand."

"I was in the mercantile, and the man there was telling me about this Milo Ryder," said Frank. "It sounds like he has done well for himself. I believe that the man said he has three ranches."

"That is what the rumor is," said the barkeep. "I know that the men that work for him are happy with their job. His foreman said they are all treated like family and would do anything for the former marshal."

"He is a former marshal?" asked Frank.

"He was," said the barkeep. "I understand that he was reinstated as a marshal but only takes on certain jobs as marshal."

Frank finished his beer and said, "You need to give me a bottle to take with me."

After getting the bottle and putting it with the other supplies, Frank returned to the house where the others were waiting.

"What did you find out?" asked Ike.

"Marshal Milo Ryder has a ranch in the Purgatoire Valley about five miles northeast of Stonewall," said Frank.

"Do you think you can find it?" asked Ike.

"We should be able to find it," said Frank. "I can take Tobias with me tomorrow, and we should be able to locate it."

Frank and Tobias saddled their horses the following day and headed for the Purgatoire Valley. Unfortunately, the way they traveled put them north of the ranch. When they realized it, they started south and came across the Lazy S. Thinking they had found the right ranch, they found a place where they could observe it.

While watching, Cody came out of the house and went to the barn. Frank said, "That is one of the men who run us off the ranch in San Luis de la Culebra. This has to be the marshal's ranch."

"Now, what do you want to do?" asked Tobias.

"Let's see if the marshal is here," said Frank.

"He could be gone," said Tobias. "You know that he was in El More."

"That was for that wedding," said Frank.

"Remember Milt said it was US Marshal Ryder who was with the marshal from Trinidad," said Tobias. "It must have been him and his men following us."

"If it was, they could still be looking for us," said Frank. "If we don't see him by this afternoon, we will tell Ike we found his ranch and see what Ike wants to do."

They continued to watch the ranch. When James came out of the house at noon, Frank said, "I believe he is one of the men that arrested us. This has to be his ranch."

"Let's ride back to the house and let Ike know," said Tobias.

They returned to the house they were using as a hideout. Going in to see Ike, Frank said. "We found the marshal's ranch. He wasn't there, but we saw two of the men that were with him."

"Where do you think he is?" asked Ike.

"He is still looking for us," said Tobias. "We know he was in El More for the wedding, and we were spotted spying on the ranch where the wedding was. He was with the marshal from Trinidad who came to Milt's ranch."

"How many men did you see at his ranch?" asked Ike.

"We only saw three or four men there," said Frank.

"Did you see his wife?" asked Ike.

"We saw two women at the ranch," said Tobias. "The one looked to be the housekeeper. I had not seen the other woman before."

"How big is the ranch?" asked Ike.

"We didn't get a chance to look it over," said Frank. "If they only have four or five men working it, it cannot be that big."

"Are you sure you found the right ranch?" asked Ike. "If he can afford to buy more ranches, where is he getting his money if his main ranch is that small?"

"We saw a couple of the men that arrested us," said Frank. "If that ain't his ranch, I don't know where it is."

"I think we need to do more investigating and make sure we have the right ranch," said Ike. "Tomorrow, we will all ride over there and take a look."

The next day after breakfast, Ike, Frank, Tobias, and Archie rode over to the Lazy S Ranch. Before going to where they could watch the buildings, they looked at the cattle. Seeing that several could be sold, Ike began to think about taking the cows. But before he would do that, he wanted to know where the marshal was.

Reaching a spot where they could see the buildings, they stopped and waited. Ike recognized Cody when he came out of the house. When a woman came out and kissed him, he knew something wasn't right. If that was the marshal's wife, why would she be kissing him?

"Who is she?" asked Ike.

"I thought she was the housekeeper," said Frank. "There is another woman in the house."

Closer to noon, Sadie came out of the house and went to the barn. Ike began to think that she could be the marshal's wife. Now he needed to know how many men were working the ranch. With the activity going on at the ranch, Ike counted six men. While watching, two more men rode onto the ranch and went to the house. So that meant there could be eight men working the ranch.

Now he had to figure out if he could get one of the women and draw the marshal out where he could kill him. But first, he would have to get the one he last saw. The man they had seen kissing the other woman had to be the housekeeper.

CHAPTER 29

Several days had passed, and Milo still had not heard anything about Ike and where he was. However, he knew that Ike must have been close to Trinidad when they lost him. He was sure that Ike was at Cyrus's old ranch, but they never saw him or his men.

While he was thinking, Hannah came in and said, "I need to go to town for supplies."

"Let me get the buggy, and we can go," said Milo. "I want to talk to Tom and see if he has heard anything about Ike."

When they got to town, their first stop was at the mercantile. Arron greeted them when they entered. "I see you are back," said Arron.

"We got back the other day," said Milo. "How has business been?"

"Some days it's slow," said Arron. "Say, the other day I had a guy come in, said he was passing through but got to asking questions about you and where you live."

"Did he tell you his name?" asked Milo.

"No, he stood about six feet with dark hair. His full beard looked like it covered a scar on his right cheek. I thought he might be looking for work, but after he got his supplies, he went to the saloon," said Arron.

"Did he have a wagon?" asked Milo.

"No, he was riding a white quarter horse and had a black and white paint as a packhorse," said Arron.

"Was he alone?" asked Milo.

"As far as I could tell, he was alone," said Arron. "Do you know him?"

"He fits the description of one of the men that robbed the bank in El More," said Milo. "What day was he in here?"

"The day before yesterday," said Arron. "He went to the Red Dog Saloon from here. You might want to go over and see if you can find out more about him."

"Thanks, I will," said Milo. "Hannah, I will be right back. I need to check on a man who was in here the other day."

Milo walked over to the Red Dog Saloon. Inside, Hank asked him, "What will you have, Mr. Ryder?"

"Just some information," said Milo. "I understand that the other day a man about six feet tall, with dark hair and a full beard that looked like it was covering a scar on his right cheek, was in here. Did you talk to him?"

"Yeah, I remember the fella," said Hank. "He had a beer and bought a bottle before he left."

"Did he happen to mention his name?" asked Milo.

"No," said Hank. "I asked him if he was looking for work, and he said he was passing through. We do get several men who are passing through. Is there something I should know about him?"

"I believe he is one of the men who robbed the bank in El More," said Milo. "If he is here, three other men are with him."

"He has not been back since that day," said Hank.

"Thanks," said Milo. "If he comes back by chance, try and get word to Tom."

"I will," said Hank.

Milo returned to the mercantile, where Hannah finished her order. After loading the supplies into the buggy, Milo said, "I need to stop and talk to Tom."

When Hannah and Milo entered the marshal's office, Tom stood up and said, "Hannah, Milo, what brings you here?"

"Hi, Tom," said Milo.

"Hannah, please have a seat," said Tom.

"Did you hear about the bank being robbed in El More?" asked Milo.

"Yes, I did," said Tom.

"A couple of my men and I followed them till we lost them north of Trinidad," said Milo. "Today, when I was talking to Arron, he described one of the men we were following who had been in the mercantile. I believe they are in the area."

"Do you know who they are?" asked Tom.

"It is Ike Evens and his men," said Milo. "The one in the mercantile stands about six feet tall, with dark hair and a full beard covering a scar on his right cheek. He rides a white quarter horse."

"I remember seeing that horse in town the other day," said Tom. "I believe he had a paint horse with him."

"That is the man," said Milo. "I talked to Hank at the Red Dog and told him if the man comes back in to get word to you."

"You are sure he is one of the robbers?" asked Tom.

"He was one of the men we arrested in San Luis de la Culebra with Ike Evens," said Milo. "I believe his name is Frank Logan. You might have a poster on him."

"I will watch for him," said Tom. "You think three other men are with him, including Ike Evens?"

"They were the ones who got away from the bank robbery in Durango," said Milo. "I have been waiting to find out any information about them. Now it sounds like they are in our area."

"I will let you know if I find anything," Tom said.

"Thanks," said Milo.

When they got ready to leave, Tom said, "It is always a pleasure to see you, Hannah. Try and keep your husband out of trouble."

"That is harder than you think," said Hannah, laughing. "It is good seeing you again as well."

When they returned to the ranch, Milo called Nate to the house. "While we were in town, I found out that Ike is in the area," said Milo. "I don't know where they are, but Arron said that Frank Logan was in the mercantile and bought supplies. "If anyone leaves the ranch, I want at least two men together. We need to get word to Cody, so I want you to send someone there and let Cody know."

Nate went to the yard where Billy was working with one of the young horses. "Billy, I need you to go and inform Cody that Ike Evens and his men are in the area," said Nate. "Milo found out from Arron in the mercantile that one of his men had been there. He wants at least two men together when leaving the ranch, so get one of the men, and you both ride over to the Lazy S Ranch and let Cody know."

Billy put up the horse he was working on and found Emmett. "Emmett, we need to ride over to Cody's place," said Billy.

While saddling their horses, Emmett asked, "What is going on that you need me to ride over there with you?"

"Milo found out that Ike Evens is in the area, and he doesn't want anyone riding alone," said Billy.

While riding up to the Lazy S Ranch, Emmett caught a flash of light from some trees off to their right. Without looking at it, Emmett said, "Did you see that flash of light?"

"Yes," said Billy. "When we see Cody, we will ask him if he has men up there."

Stopping in front of the house, they tied their horses and went and knocked on the door. Rosie opened the door and saw Billy and Emmett. She invited them in. "Cody went to the barn, but he will see your horses and come in," said Rosie. "Would you like some coffee?"

"Thanks, that would be good," said Billy.

They had sat down when Cody came in. "What brings you over here?" asked Cody.

"Milo found out when he was in town this morning that Ike Evens is in the area," said Billy. "He is concerned about not knowing where. He wants everyone to travel in pairs."

"Do you have men on the hill overlooking the ranch?" asked Emmett.

"No," said Cody. "Why are you asking?"

"When we rode up, we saw a flash of light, like the sun reflecting off metal," said Emmett. "If you don't have men up there, you might want to find out who is there."

"Why would Ike be in the area?" asked Cody.

"We followed them toward Trinidad but lost them before getting there," said Billy. "They had robbed the bank in El More before we could arrest them."

"How did Milo find out he was in the area?" asked Cody.

"When he was talking to Arron," said Billy. "Nate told me that one of Ike's men had been there getting supplies."

While they were talking, Luke came in. Billy said, "Hi, Luke."

"Hello, Billy," replied Luke. "What brings you over here?"

"Milo found out that Ike Evens and his men are in the area, and he wanted me to warn Cody," said Billy.

"Luke, did you send anyone to the top of the hill overlooking the ranch today?" asked Cody.

"No," said Luke. "Why are you asking?"

"Emmett said they saw a flash of light like a reflection of the sun on some metal," said Cody.

"Do you want me to send someone up there to check?" asked Luke.

"Have Sam and Jose check it out," said Cody. "Tell them to try and get there without being seen."

Luke left, going to the barn, where Sam and Jose were working on shoeing some of the horses. Walking over to them, Luke said, "Cody wants you two to work your way around that hill to the east that overlooks the ranch. Emmett said he saw a flash of light come from there. They think there could be someone watching the ranch. Be careful not to be seen getting there."

Getting their horses, they rode north before circling to get to the back side of the hill. Once they started moving toward the hill, Sam spotted two of the men. Stopping Jose, Sam said, "I can see two men, but I think there are more."

"Let's leave the horses and see if we can get closer," said Jose.

They found four men watching the ranch as they worked their way up the hill. Jose said, "We need to let Cody know."

As they started to return to their horses, Sam stepped on a branch that alerted Ike and his men.

When Tobias heard the branch break, he saw Sam and Jose rushing to their horses. Tobias said, "The two we saw ride out found us."

Drawing his Colt, he fired, hitting Sam. Sam stumbled, but Jose caught him and helped him to his horse. Tobias fired a second time but missed.

Ike heard Tobias and said, "Let's get out of here before more come."

Cody and the others heard the gunshot and ran outside. Knowing where the men were, Billy and Emmett got on their horses and rode hard toward the hill. As they approached, they saw the four men ride off. Not knowing that Sam was wounded, they followed the four men. Billy regionalized the white quarter horse and said, "Emmett, that is Ike and his men. We need to find out where they are hiding."

While Emmett and Billy were following Ike and Tobias, Cody and Luke rode up and found Jose helping Sam. They took Sam back to the house. Rosie took off his shirt and found the bullet had passed through his side, hitting one of his ribs. Cleaning the wound, she put salve on the openings and wrapped a rag around him to hold the patch in place.

While Rosie was working on Sam, Jose told Cody that there were four men and Billy and Emmett were following them.

"Luke, get my horse," said Cody. "We are going to help Billy and Emmett. Tell James to saddle a horse as well."

Ike, Frank, Tobias, and Archie rode hard for a mile before slowing down. Archie was the last one and kept looking back to see if they were being followed. Not seeing anyone, they began to relax.

"What do you want to do, Ike?" asked Frank.

"We need to get back to the house and let things quiet down," said Ike. "Why did you shoot at those men? Now we will have the marshal after us."

"They don't know who we are," said Frank.

"That isn't going to stop that marshal," said Ike. "Tobias wounded one of his men."

"By tomorrow, they won't be able to follow us," said Tobias. "Archie said that we are not being followed now."

While following Ike, Billy noticed the mark left by one of the horses was the same mark they had followed from El More. "Emmett, see that marked shoe?" asked Billy. "That is the same print we followed from El More. I know for sure that it is Ike Evens and his men. Milo will want to know where they are staying."

Billy and Emmett continued to follow Ike staying far enough back that they would not be seen.

When Ike reached the house, they took care of their horses and went in the house. Tobias started to make supper while Ike tried to figure out what he would do. Now that they had been seen at the ranch, Ike knew Marshal Ryder would be looking for them to return. Ike needed to figure out a way to get the marshal away from the ranch.

While they were in the house, Billy and Emmett found the house. Not getting too close, Billy left his horse with Emmett and went where he could see the horses. When he saw the white quarter horse, he knew Ike and the others were there.

Returning to Emmett, he said, "We need to let Milo know where they are staying."

Getting their horses, they started to return to the Rocking R Ranch.

They had ridden about an hour when Billy heard horses coming toward them. Not knowing who it was, they stopped and waited. He relaxed when he saw that it was Cody and some of his hands.

When Cody saw them, he stopped when he got to them. Cody asked, "Did you lose them?"

"No," said Billy. "We found the place where they are holed up. We will get Milo and see what he wants to do."

"Could we get them now?" asked Cody.

"They are in a house, and I don't see a way we can get them out," said Billy. "We need to look at the place during the day."

Turning around, they started for the Lazy S Ranch.

"Was anybody hurt?" asked Emmett.

"Sam was hit," said Jose. "Rosie took care of him, and he will be all right."

When they reached the Lazy S, it was past suppertime. Rosie and Sadie had food waiting for them. While they were eating, they heard horses come into the yard. Cody went to see who was coming to the ranch this late. When he got to the front door, he saw that it was Milo with Nate.

Opening the door, Cody said, "Come in. Rosie has coffee."

"We came to see what happened to Billy and Emmett," said Milo.

"They are inside," said Cody. "I will let them tell you what happened."

When they entered the kitchen, Rosie said, "Milo, please have a seat, and Sadie and I will get you and Nate some coffee."

"Thanks," said Nate.

"We came looking for Billy and Emmett," said Milo. "When you didn't return, we thought something happened to you. From what Cody said when we came in, what did happen?"

"When we got here, Emmett saw a flash of light from the hill east of the ranch," said Billy. "Cody sent Sam and Jose to check it out. There were four men, and one of them shot Sam. Emmett and I followed them and discovered that it was Ike and his men. They are staying in a house about ten miles from here."

"How bad was Sam shot?" asked Milo.

"I took care of him," said Rosie. "He will be all right in a few days."

"We missed our chance to get him in El More," said Billy. "I thought we could get him here."

"Did you get a good look at where they are staying?" asked Milo.

"It looks like a deserted farm," said Emmett. "The house could be hard to get them out of. We may have to wait until they decide to leave before we can arrest them."

"What do you want to do?" asked Cody.

"I think, in the morning, we need to ride over there and check it out," said Milo.

"We can meet here and ride over there," said Cody. "How many men do you want to take?"

"Billy and Emmett will go, as they know where they are," said Milo. "I would say if you, Cody, and James go with us, that will be five."

"We will be ready when you get here," said Cody.

Milo, Billy, Nate, and Emmett got up to leave. Outside they got their horses and said goodbye to Cody, saying they would see them in the morning.

It was late when they rode into the yard at the Rocking R Ranch. Hannah and Maria were waiting to find out what had happened. Maria was happy when she saw Billy and he wasn't hurt. Going to him, she asked, "Are you all right?"

"I am fine," said Billy. "We found Ike Evens. He and his men were at the Lazy S watching it."

After putting up their horses, Billy went into the house with Milo. Hannah asked, "What do you mean Ike Evens was watching the ranch?"

"Emmett spotted them when we rode into the ranch," said Billy.

"Billy and Emmett found where they are staying," said Milo. "We are going to go after them in the morning. We will meet Cody and James."

"I don't understand why they would be watching Cody's ranch," said Hannah.

"I don't know either," said Milo. "I thought they would have left the area by now."

"We will want to get an early start in the morning," said Billy. "I think I will go to bed."

Maria walked Billy outside. After kissing him, she said, "You need to be careful tomorrow. I get afraid every time you go after someone with Milo."

"We are always careful," said Billy. "Milo knows how to get the outlaws."

"I will see you in the morning," said Maria, kissing Billy again and going back inside.

CHAPTER 30

Early the next morning, Billy and Emmett met Milo in the house, where Hannah and Maria had breakfast waiting for them.

Hannah asked, "How long will you be gone?"

"We should be back no later than tomorrow," said Milo.

"We will pack you some supplies for a couple of days," said Maria.

"Who is going with you?" asked Hannah.

"We are meeting Cody and James at the Lazy S Ranch," said Milo. "They will be going with us."

When they finished breakfast, it was still dark. Putting supplies in the saddlebags, the three men mounted after Milo and Billy said their goodbyes to Hannah and Maria. They arrived at the Lazy S Ranch as the sun was coming up. Cody and James were waiting as they rode up.

"I told Rosie we would be gone about two days," said Cody. "She has packed supplies for us."

"That is what we told Hannah and Maria," said Milo.

With everyone mounted, Billy led the way. They took their time not to tire the horses in case they ended up chasing Ike and his men. By midmorning, they arrived at the house. Staying out of sight, they tied their horses and moved in closer to better look at the house and what was around it.

Activity at the house was quiet. Then, one of the horses in the corral started to act up. While watching, one man came out to see what was causing the horse to act up. The horse quieted down when he got near. Not seeing anything, he returned to the house.

Milo said, "That looks like Frank Logan. I wonder if the rest are still in the house."

"Do you think we could take them while they are in the house?" asked Cody.

"If we attack the house, I think we will be in trouble," said Milo. "If we can get them out of the house, we will be better off. Cody, you and James, see if you can get to the back of the house. That way, if any of them try to escape, you will be there to arrest them."

Cody and James left. Getting their horses, they rode back to where they could ride around the ranch and approach it from the back. Once they had tied their horses, Cody went to the right while James went to the left. They found a spot where they could see each other and the back of the house. Now they had to wait.

Billy made his way to the west side, where he could see the corral. Counting the horses, he found that two of them were missing. Returning to Milo, he said, "I think two of the horses are missing. There are only three horses in the corral, and I believe one is the packhorse."

"That could mean that there are only two still in the house," said Milo. "I wonder where the other two could have gone?"

That morning Ike got up with a feeling that something wasn't right. Ike went to check on the horses and found them standing and not alerted to anything in the area. Feeling that he was worried for nothing, he returned to the house.

Tobias was making breakfast when Ike came in. "What were you checking outside?" asked Tobias.

"I had this feeling in my gut that someone was near here," said Ike. "The horses were not alerted to anyone in the area. Maybe it's just me."

"After we eat, I will go out and check the area," said Frank. "We did not see anyone following us when we returned yesterday. But, if there had been anyone here, I am sure the horses would be alerted to them."

"Tobias, I want you to ride over to their ranch and watch what they are doing," said Ike. "Make sure you stay out of sight."

"Maybe one of us should go with Tobias," said Archie.

"You can go with him, Archie," said Ike.

Tobias and Archie went out and got their horses and rode out.

"Why don't you check the area while Tobias is gone," Ike said to Frank.

Once they finished eating, Frank got his horse and rode around the ranch, looking for any sign that someone had been watching the house. Finally, he found a place where there looked like fresh prints. Taking a closer look, Frank determined that whoever it was must have been riding by. He kept looking without finding any other tracks.

When Frank returned to the corral, Ike was there and asked, "Did you see anything?"

"Naw," said Frank. "There were tracks where someone had ridden by, but I didn't see that anyone was watching the place."

"You didn't see anything other than that?" asked Ike.

"I didn't find any tracks except ours from yesterday," said Frank.

After reporting his findings to Ike, they went back into the house. "What do you want to do about the marshal?" asked Frank.

"We need to wait a day and then go back and see if we can find the marshal," said Ike. "Maybe we can get one of those women at the ranch and use them for bait to get the marshal."

"From what I saw, they seem to stay near the house or in the house," said Frank. "The other problem is that the men seem to stay at the ranch. I saw when they rode out, and they rode in pairs."

One of the horses started acting up in the middle of the morning, so Frank got up and went to see what was going on. Walking out to the corral, Frank looked around but couldn't see anything that would disturb the horse. When he got to the corral, the horse came over to him and settled down. "What's the matter?" said Frank to the horse. "You miss your friend?"

After petting the horse, Frank returned to the house. "What was up with the horse?" asked Ike.

"I think he was looking for the paint that Tobias took," said Frank. "I didn't see anything out there. He seems to have settled down."

"We will have to wait and see what he finds out," said Ike. "I don't want to stay here longer than we have to. Someone could come to check on the place."

"Well, maybe Tobias and Archie will have news for us when they get back," said Frank.

"With two possibly gone, what do you want to do?" asked Billy.

"We need to find out where they went," said Milo. "Go find Cody and James and bring them back. We need to move away from here and wait for those two to return."

Billy made his way to the back of the house and found Cody. When he got there, Cody asked, "What is happening?"

"Milo wants you and James to return to where he is," said Billy. "It seems that two of the men are not here."

"What do you mean two are not here?" asked James.

"When I checked the horses in the corral, two are missing," said Billy.

When they were again with Milo, he said, "We need to move away from the house and wait for the two men to return. As far as we know, there are only two in the house, and one we know is Frank Logan. We don't know who the other one is. I want to ensure we get Ike, and he could get away if he is not in the house."

"You want to wait until the two missing return?" asked Cody.

"Yes," said Milo. "If we keep watching, we can arrest them before they reach the ranch, then we would only have the two there to deal with."

Moving back, they found a place where they could make coffee while Billy and Emmett stayed and watched the road. They would be relieved later.

After the men ate breakfast, Hannah said, "Maria, let's go over to the Lazy S and visit with Rosie and Sadie. I am sure that they would like some company."

"I would like to see them," said Maria. "We have not gotten together for some time. Maybe it will help the time go by faster with the men gone."

Hannah called Nate to the house. When he arrived, he asked, "What do you need?"

"Maria and I are going to go visit Rosie and Sadie. We will need a couple of horses."

"Do you want to take a buggy?" asked Nate.

"No," said Hannah. "We will go on horses."

"I will have a couple of men ride with you," said Nate.

"We should be all right without them," said Hannah.

"Milo gave orders that no one is to leave the ranch alone, and he would not forgive me if I let the two of you go by yourselves," said Nate. "I will have Hick and Porter ride with you. They can check on how the bull is doing."

Nate went out and found Hick and Porter. Hick asked, "What's going on, boss?"

"I need the two of you to ride with Hannah and Maria to the Lazy S," said Nate.

"Is something going on over there?" asked Porter.

"The women want to visit with Rosie and Sadie," said Nate. "Milo doesn't want anyone going alone, and I think the two women should have an escort. When you get your horses ready, get horses for the women. I am sure Hannah will want to ride Buttercup."

"Is there anything you want us to do while we are over there?" asked Hick.

"No, I can't think of anything," said Nate. "Just make sure the women are safe."

When the women had cleaned up the kitchen and got ready to ride over to the Lazy S Ranch, Hick and Porter had their horses ready and were waiting for them by the house. When the women came out, they helped them on their horses and left for the Lazy S.

As they rode into the yard, they were unaware that two men were watching them from the trees. Tobias and Archie had arrived at the ranch and were again sitting in the trees overlooking the yard when Hannah, Maria, Hick, and Porter arrived. "I wonder who they are?" said Tobias.

"Do you suppose they are neighbors who came to visit?" asked Archie.

They continued to watch as Rosie and Sadie came out of the house. Both women were carrying rifles when the four rode into the yard. When they saw who was coming, they put their rifles down.

Rosie and Sadie, glad to see Hannah and Maria, met them and hugged them. "We are happy to see you," said Rosie. "Come in the house so we can talk."

"Whoever they are," said Tobias. "They look to be good friends or family."

"Maybe we should follow them when they leave and see where they live," said Archie. "Ike may want to go after them to draw the marshal out."

Hick and Porter took the four horses to water and loosened their saddles. While taking care of the horses, Luke and Rufus walked over to them. "What brings you here?" asked Luke.

"Hannah and Maria wanted to visit with Rosie and Sadie," said Hick. "Milo doesn't want anyone riding alone as long as Ike is in the area."

"I thought Cody and James went with Milo to arrest Ike," said Rufus.

"They did," said Hick. "Billy and Emmett said they knew where they were staying. If they are there, I am sure that they will arrest them."

"I heard Sam was wounded the other day," said Porter. "How is he doing?"

"Rosie has kept him in the house," said Luke. "He is recovering, but Rosie is afraid he might get an infection."

"Maybe before we leave, we can stop in and say hi to him," said Porter.

"I am sure that Rosie will let you," said Luke. "When one of us gets hurt, she is like a mother hen taking care of her chicks," said Rufus, laughing.

"Did Jose go with them?" asked Hick.

"No," said Luke. "He is out back working with one of the young horses."

"Did he ever breed his stallion to one of your mares?" asked Hick.

"He bred two of the mares," said Luke. "They are due any time now. We are all waiting to see how they come out. I know Milo bred the paint. How did that work out?"

"The one mare dropped twin colts," said Hick. "They are hard to tell apart, but they look like they will be as good as their father."

They turned the horses loose in the corral and went behind the barn to talk to Jose.

Tobias said, "I don't see that many men at the ranch today, like we did yesterday. I wonder where they are?"

"I only saw the three hands before these two showed up," said Archie.

By now, it was getting close to noon. Maria came out and rang the dinner bell. Hearing the bell, the men washed up and went to the house.

Tobias said, "There are only the five men and the four women at the ranch now."

"What are you thinking?" asked Archie.

"Maybe after those four who came to visit leave, we can get one of the women and take her to Ike," said Tobias.

"I don't know about that," said Archie. "You saw when they came out of the house and had rifles. I am sure they know how to use them."

"With the three men and those two, we would up against five guns," said Tobias. "We will have to let Ike know that the women are armed as well as the men."

They were talking when the men went into the house for dinner.

Inside, Sam was sitting at the table. Hick said, "Sam, you don't look too bad for being shot. How are you feeling?"

"Rosie is taking good care of me," said Sam. "I wanted to move back into the bunkhouse, but she won't let me. She thinks I might get an infection."

"Now, Sam, you behave yourself," said Rosie. "If you got infected and died, I would have to face Cody as to why I let you get the infection."

"Milo wants all of you healthy," said Hannah.

Rufus asked, "Maria, when are you and Bill going to get hitched?"

Maria's face turned red, saying, "We have not made any plans for that."

"What are you waiting for?" asked Hick. "We could all get together and build you a house at the Rocking R."

"That would up to Hannah and Milo if that would happen," said Maria. "I don't think Billy has asked. But I know if we get married, we both want to keep working for Hannah and Milo."

"I am sure Milo would go along with building a second house on the ranch for you and Billy," said Hannah. "I wouldn't want you to leave if you want to stay."

"Thanks," said Maria.

After eating dinner, the women helped clean up the kitchen.

Hannah said, "I think we need to get back home."

"We are glad you came to visit," said Rosie. "Do you think the men will be home tonight?"

"That I don't know," said Hannah. "Milo thought it could take two days. If they are not back by tomorrow night, we will have the men go look for them."

Hick and Porter got the horses ready and were waiting for Hannah and Maria. When they came out, they said their goodbyes and rode out.

Tobias and Archie were still watching the ranch when they left. No one looked to be in a hurry.

Tobias said, "We should follow them and see where they go."

Getting their horses, they followed far enough back to see the dust the four horses were raising. When they reached the Rocking R Ranch, they stopped. They watched as a couple of hands came out and helped take care of the horses the women were riding. The women entered the house, and the men went to the barn.

Once they got to the barn, Hick said, "I think I saw a couple of riders trying to stay hidden. Cord, let's take these horses and see who they are."

Porter said, "Let's go out the back, so they don't see us, and try to get behind them."

The four men rode out the back and stayed between the buildings after the two men. They hurried their horses after the men when they reached the open space behind the ranch.

"Well, we know where they live," said Tobias. "I have been thinking that one woman looks familiar. I can't figure out where I have seen her."

"Well, let's go tell Ike," said Archie.

They started to return to their hideout. Tobias and Archie were walking their horses when Archie saw someone coming after them. Archie said, "We're being followed. We need to get out of here."

Spurring their horses, they headed for higher ground and cover. Once they reached the trees, they hid and waited. It wasn't long, and the men following them rode past their hiding place. As those pursuing them went by, they stayed under cover until they could again get on the road to the hideout. It was late afternoon when Tobias and Archie got close to the house.

When Hick, Porter, Cord, and Nate returned to the ranch, Nate went to the house. Inside he found Hannah and said, "Did you know that you were followed?"

"No," said Hannah. "Do you know who was following us?"

"We tried to catch them, but we lost them," said Nate. "We have to be more careful. If it was part of Ike's people, we could be in danger."

"When Milo gets home, we will have to let him know," said Hannah. "Maybe he will have arrested them."

———

Milo and Cody were watching the road when they saw Tobias and Archie. They remained hidden until Tobias and Archie were close to them. Stepping out with their Colts drawn, Milo said, "Raise your hands. You are under arrest."

Tobias drew his gun, but Cody shot him, hitting him in the shoulder and knocking Tobias off his horse. Archie raised his hands.

When Tobias was hit, he dropped his gun.

Cody went over and picked up Tobias's gun before seeing how badly he was hit.

Milo said to Archie, "Take your gun out of your holster and drop it."

Archie dropped his gun.

Then Milo said, "Get off your horse."

Bill, Emmett, and James heard the gunshot and went to see what had happened. Seeing that one man was wounded and Milo had the other one under control, Billy went to help Milo while James and Emmett went to help Cody.

"What happened?" asked Emmett.

"When we told them to raise their hands, this one went for his gun," said Cody. "I wonder if they heard the shot at the house?"

Billy tied Archie's hands and made him sit down.

"We need to check the house and see if they heard the gunshot," said Milo. "Cody, you and James watch these two. Emmett, you and Billy, come with me."

The three men made their way to where they could see the house. But when they got there, they couldn't tell if the other two were still inside.

Ike and Frank were sitting at the table when they thought they heard a gunshot. Frank went out to see if he could find out for sure. Outside it was quiet. Still, Frank could swear that he had heard a gunshot. Not taking any chances, he went to check the horses. He found the horses moving around and looking toward the south, where the road was. He thought to himself, *If they are looking that way, that has to be where the shot came from.*

Frank returned to the house. "There had to be a gunshot. The horses were moving around and looking south up the road."

"Maybe we need to get out of here," said Ike.

They left the house and moved into the woods, where they could watch the house. It wasn't long before they heard movement coming toward them. Waiting to see what it was, it didn't take long when they saw three men working their way toward the house. Ike recognized Marshal Milo Ryder.

"That's the marshal," said Ike.

Ike aimed at Milo and fired. His shot missed but hit a tree next to Milo, spraying splinters into Milo's face.

Billy, seeing where the shot came from, started shooting into that area. Hearing someone yell, he knew that he had hit someone.

Emmett also was shooting at the spot where Ike had shot from.

Milo dropped to the ground, trying to get the splinters off his face. He wasn't hurt badly, but it interfered with his sight, causing him to be unable to return fire.

When Ike shot, Frank also started shooting. He had not seen anyone as clearly as Ike had, so he was taking wild shots. While shooting, a bullet hit him, knocking him back into a cactus and causing him to yell out.

Ike, seeing Frank get hit, decided he wanted to get out of there. Unfortunately, a bullet hit him when he started to move, causing him to lose his gun.

Emmett saw Ike starting to move and shot and wounded Ike. Seeing Ike go down, Emmett said, "Billy, I think we got the two waiting for us."

"Let's make sure before we look for them," said Billy.

They waited, not hearing anything coming from where Ike fell. Then, finally, Emmett started making his way toward Ike.

While waiting, Billy checked on Milo before he and Emmett went to check on Ike and Frank. They found Ike lying on the ground, not moving. Checking him, they found that he was still alive. Emmett's bullet had hit Ike on the side of his head. Emmett stayed with him while Billy went to check on Frank, who was still yelling in pain.

Billy found Frank wounded from a bullet that hit him in the shoulder, but he was also wounded from the cactus he fell in. "Drop your gun," said Billy.

Frank dropped his gun, seeing Billy's gun pointed at him. Billy went over, kicked his gun out of the way, and helped Frank out of the cactus. With Frank out of the cactus, Billy picked up Frank's gun before leading him back to Milo's location.

By now, Milo had gotten the splinters out of his face and was seeing clearly again.

Billy saw the blood on Milo's face and asked, "Are you all right? Were you hit?"

"I will be fine," said Milo. "I wasn't hit but got the spray from the tree where a bullet hit."

"Can you watch Frank while I help Emmett?" asked Billy. "I think he has Ike. I don't know if Ike is alive."

Cody and James, hearing the shooting, secured the two men they had and went to see if Milo and the others needed help. Finding Milo with a bloody face, Cody asked, "Were you shot?"

"No," said Milo. "I got hit with slivers from the tree. James, go see if Emmett and Billy need help with Ike."

With the help of Billy and James, Emmett got Ike up. Looking at Ike's wound, it looked like the bullet had just grazed his head. With Ike standing again, they led him back to where the others were waiting.

"Let's get some bandages on the wounded and take them to town," said Cody.

CHAPTER 31

AFTER CARING FOR THE WOUNDS, Milo said, "We need to check the house and see if the money from the El More bank is there. So they moved the prisoners closer to the house and made them sit on the ground while they searched the house.

When they got to the house, Milo said, "Billy, you and Emmett see if you can get a couple of horses for Ike and Frank. While Billy and Emmett were getting the horses, James watched the prisoners, and Cody and Milo searched the house.

Cody found saddlebags inside the house in one of the rooms. He opened the saddlebags and found them full of money from the El More Bank. Cody called Milo and said, "I believe this is the money they took from the El More bank."

Milo came into the room where Cody was and looked in the saddlebag. Milo said, " I believe this is the El More Bank money. From what I can see, this looks like most of the money is still here. We will take it in with Ike and his men. I am sure that Tom will make sure it gets back to the bank."

They took the money with them and went outside as Billy and Emmett brought the horses up. After getting the wounded tied on their horses, they started for Stonewall.

It was dark when they rode into town. There were lanterns lit in the two saloons. It looked like the café was still open, but the marshal's office looked dark. When Milo and his men stopped in front of the marshal's office, they looked inside and found it empty.

Milo lit a lantern while Cody and the others got the prisoners and brought them in.

Milo went back out to see if he could find the marshal. Outside he found a young boy walking up the street. Milo stopped him and asked, "Son, do you know Marshal Sieke and where the doctor's office is?"

"Yes, sir, I do," said the boy.

Milo said, handing the boy fifty cents, "Go tell the doctor to come to the jail, then go find the marshal and tell him that Milo Ryder has prisoners for him. Can you do that?"

"Yes, sir," said the boy. "I will get them right away."

While Milo was busy talking to the boy, Cody and the others put the prisoners in cells. They separated the wounded ones from Archie.

It wasn't long before Dr. Selman arrived. Looking at Milo's face, he asked, "Did you get in a fight with a cat? A little ointment will fix you up."

"No, I need you to look at some of the prisoners," said Milo. "Three of them have been shot. I was hit with splinters from a tree."

While the doctor was working on the prisoners, Marshal Sieke came in. "Are you taking over my office?" he asked Milo.

Milo laughed and said, "No, I have four prisoners for you and the money from the El More Bank here."

"Who have you got in my jail?" asked Tom.

"Ike Evens, Frank Logan, Tobias Averill, and Archie Garrett," said Milo. "There are posters on all four. Dr. Selman is in with them, taking care of the wounded."

"How many are wounded?" asked Tom.

"Three were shot," said Milo. "I don't think any are in danger of dying."

"I will send a telegram to the El More bank and tell them that you recovered their money," said Tom. "I will check the posters and get your money for you. That will take a few days. The bank may offer a reward for returning the money. If they do, I will let you know."

"Thanks, Tom," said Milo.

"Milo, I hate to ask, but what happened to your face?" asked Tom. "It looks like you got in a fight with a cat."

"A bullet hit a tree next to my face, and I got the splinters," said Milo. "I am sure Hannah will also be wondering about them."

"For the record, let's go over what happened," said Tom.

When Milo finished telling Tom what happened, Tom said, "I have what I need. I am sure you and your men will have to come in when it goes to court."

"We will be there," said Milo. "We will head home if you don't need anything else from us."

"No, you are free to leave," said Tom. "Say hello to Hannah and Maria for me."

Milo got the men together, and they started for home. When they got close to the Rocking R Ranch, Cody said, "James and I will leave you and see you later. You can let me know when we have to go to court."

Milo, Billy, and Emmett continued to the Rocking R. All was dark when they rode into the yard.

Nate heard riders coming in and woke the other men. "Some riders are coming in," said Nate. "We need to find out who they are."

They all got up and garbed their rifles. Nate went out as Milo, Billy, and Emmett rode in. When they got close, Nate saw that it was Milo. Calling back to the others, Nate said, "It's Milo and the others. They must have gotten Ike."

The noise going on in the yard woke Hannah and Maria. They got up and lit lanterns. Nate lit a lantern and walked up to where the men had stopped. "I see you made it back," said Nate. "How did it go?"

"We got Ike and his men," said Milo. "Tom has them in the jail."

While they were talking, the front door opened. Hannah and Maria came out, seeing it was Milo and Billy. They went to make sure they were all right. When Hannah saw Milo's face, she said, "Come to the house. I need to take care of those cuts. What happened?"

Nate said, "I will take care of your horse. You go let Hannah take care of your face."

Maria asked, "Are you hungry? Let me heat some food for you. I will have it ready by the time you take care of your horses and clean up."

When Billy and Emmett came into the house, Maria had food on the table, and Hannah had taken care of Milo's cuts. Sitting down, Hannah said, "Tell us what happened."

Milo explained that when they got to the hideout, only two of the outlaws were there, so they had to wait for the other two to return. When Milo finished telling what happened, Hannah and Maria were glad that Milo was the only one injured, with minor cuts.

"We had some excitement while you were gone," said Hannah.

"What happened?" asked Milo.

"Maria and I decided to see Rosie and Sadie," Hannah said.

"You didn't go over there by yourselves, did you?" asked Milo.

"Hick and Porter rode over there with us," said Hannah.

"So what happened?" asked Billy.

"When we returned to the ranch, Hick saw that there were two men following us," said Hannah. "Nate, Hick, Porter, and Cord went after them."

"Did they find out who they are?" asked Billy.

"No," said Hannah. "They lost them in the hills."

"When did you come home?" asked Emmett.

"After dinner," said Maria. "Rosie and Sadie insisted that we eat with them before returning home."

"Those could have been the two men we were waiting for," said Emmett. "The time would be about right for when they showed up where we were waiting."

"You said that they followed you from the Lazy S Ranch," said Milo. "That must have been some of Ike's men. Billy, you and Emmett trailed Ike from the Lazy S Ranch to the house where we arrested them. They must have gone back to watch the ranch."

"If that is true, then we don't have to worry about them anymore," said Maria.

"It is getting late," said Hannah. "We can all talk more in the morning."

Maria walked out with Billy. While standing on the front porch, Maria said, "When we were with Rosie, I was asked when we would get married."

"What did you tell them?" asked Billy.

"I said that we did not want to leave the ranch. You and I both like working here," said Maria. "Hannah thought we could have a house built on the ranch to live in and continue to work on the ranch."

"I have been saving some money," said Billy. "When we go after outlaws, if there is a reward, Milo shares it with those who were with him. "I am sure we could find our own place if we couldn't stay here."

"Are you asking me to marry you?" asked Maria.

"I guess I am," said Billy. "Will you marry me?"

"Yes, I will," said Maria, letting out a scream.

Hannah and Milo heard Maria scream and rushed to the porch to find out what was wrong. When they got there, they found Maria and Billy wrapped in each other's arms, kissing.

"What happened?" asked Hannah.

"Billy asked me to marry him," said Maria.

"It's about time," said Milo. "I heard rumors you are afraid you would not be able to stay on the ranch and keep working for us. So, knowing you don't want to leave, Hannah said we should build you a house here on the ranch. That way, Maria can work in the main house, and you can still work on the ranch and train horses."

"Maria, we have a lot of work to do, but it is late, and we can start planning tomorrow," said Hannah. "I know that Rosie and Sadie will want to help."

"I will talk to Nate in the morning and see what we can do about getting a place built for you and Maria," said Milo.

That night Maria didn't sleep much. She had all kinds of things going through her mind now that Billy had asked her to marry him.

CHAPTER 32

Maria was up in the kitchen before anyone was awake. When Hannah heard a noise coming from the kitchen, she got up. Finding Maria making donuts and bread, Hannah asked, "Did you have trouble sleeping last night?"

"I couldn't sleep," said Maria. "I am so nervous I don't know what to do."

"You will be fine," said Hannah. "Remember, we went through Cody and Rosie's wedding. We will get through your wedding as well. We will get word to Rosie, and I am sure that Sadie and Rosie will come right over. First, we must go to town and get you a wedding dress."

"What about a place to live?" asked Maria.

"You let Milo worry about that. I am sure that between our men and Cody's men, they can have you a place in no time," said Hannah. "Now let's get breakfast made. The men will be coming in soon."

When Nate came in, he said, "What did you do to Billy last night? He kept most of the men up all night."

"I didn't do anything to Billy," said Maria. "It's what Billy did to me."

"Now, just what did Billy do to you? If he hurt you, I will take care of him," said Nate.

"He asked me to marry him," said Maria.

"Well, it is about time," said Nate. "When are we going to have the party?"

"We have a lot to do before they can get married," said Hannah. "We are going to build them a place to live so they can stay here."

"I will get the boys working on it," said Nate.

While he was saying that, the rest of the men came in. Porter asked, "You will get us working on what?"

"A house," said Milo, as he sat down.

"A house for who?" asked Porter.

"Billy and Maria," said Hannah. "They will need a place to live where they will be alone."

"Are you and Billy getting married?" asked Hick. "Is that why you need a place to live?"

"Well, I cannot stay in the bunkhouse with all you men," said Maria.

Billy was the last one to come in. He looked like he was still half asleep. "What is the matter with you?" asked Cord. "You already having second thoughts about getting married? If you don't go through with marrying Maria, you will have to answer to all of us."

All the men started laughing and giving Billy a hard time.

By the time breakfast was finished, they had started planning to build a house.

Milo said, "Cord, I want you to ride over and tell Cody I need to talk to him."

"He doesn't have to go," said Hannah. "Maria and I need to talk to Rosie and Sadie. I can tell him. Cord, if you wouldn't mind, would you saddle our horses when you get done eating?"

"Yes, ma'am. I will have them ready when you are ready to leave," said Cord.

When Hannah and Maria arrived at the Lazy S Ranch, Cody came out of the house. "This is a surprise," said Cody. "Are we starting daily visits?"

"No, but Milo would like you to come over. He wants to talk to you," said Hannah. "Seems we will need some additional labor to build a house."

"What is going on?" asked Cody.

"I will let Milo explain what he wants," said Hannah. "Is Rosie in the house?"

"She and Sadie are in there," said Cody. "Tell her I am going to your place to talk to Milo."

Hannah and Maria found Rosie and Sadie in the kitchen. Rosie, seeing Hannah, said, "Is something wrong?" with a surprised look.

"We have a problem," said Hannah. "We have to get Maria a wedding dress, get a house built, and have a wedding."

"Maria, you and Billy are going to get married?" asked Sadie.

"He asked me last night," said Maria. "Milo wants to build us a house on the ranch so Billy and I can stay there and still work for them."

"Well, we have a lot of work to do," said Rosie. "We need to go to town and get some material to make your wedding dress. Have you picked a bridesmaid?"

"No," said Maria. "I don't know that many people. Sadie, would you be my bridesmaid?"

"I would love to," said Sadie. "That is a good reason for me to get a new dress."

"I will have Cody get us a buggy," said Rosie.

"Oh, I forgot," said Hannah. "Cody is on his way to talk to Milo. Milo wants to use some men to help build a house for Maria and Billy."

"Luke can get it for us," said Rosie, going out to find Luke.

When Rosie returned to the house, she said, "Luke will have a buggy ready in a few minutes. Then, while in town, we can have dinner at Millie's café. Do you remember the wedding cake she made for Cody and me? I am sure she would be happy to make one for you."

The women were ready to go when Luke brought the buggy to the house. Rosie and Sadie were in the buggy, and Hannah and Maria followed on horseback. The first stop was at the mercantile. Esther was surprised to see the four women come into the store at the same time. "This is a surprise," said Esther. "Is there something going on that I need to know about?"

"We need material," said Hannah.

"What kind of material do you need?" asked Esther.

"We need material for a wedding dress and a bridesmaid dress," said Hannah.

"Who is getting married?" asked Esther.

"Maria and Billy are getting married," said Hannah. "Now, let's see what you have."

After going through the material, Maria found what she would like as a wedding dress. Then they looked for material for Sadie, the bridesmaid.

While Hannah was paying for the material, Esther said, "Hannah, you are becoming quite the matchmaker. First, Cody and Rosie. Now, Maria and Billy."

"You forgot this is the third wedding with the ranch hands," said Hannah. "Burt and Shellie were married earlier."

"How are they doing?" asked Esther.

"We haven't heard much from them, but what we have heard sounds good," said Hannah.

After putting the material in the buggy, the four women went to Millie's café.

Betty saw them come in and had a table ready for them. "What brings the four of you to town?"

"We are on a mission," said Sadie.

"What is the mission?" asked Betty.

"We have another wedding to plan," said Rosie.

"A wedding?" said Betty.

"Maria and Billy are going to get married," said Hannah.

"Just a minute," said Betty. "Millie, you need to come out here."

When Millie arrived, she asked, "What do you need?"

"We have another wedding to plan," said Betty. "Maria and Billy are going to get married."

"What can I do to help?" asked Millie.

"I hate to impose on you," said Maria. "But would you mind making a wedding cake for us?"

"I would be happy to," said Millie. "When is the wedding going to happen?"

"We haven't set a date yet," said Maria. "Milo is going to build us a house at the ranch so Billy and I can continue to work there."

"Well, let me know when you need it, and it will be ready," said Millie. "Who is going to be your bridesmaid?"

"Maria has asked me to be her bridesmaid," said Sadie.

After eating dinner, the women headed home. Rosie and Sadie went to the Lazy S Ranch, taking the material so they could work on the dresses.

Hannah and Maria went to the Rocking R to find out what Milo had done about the house.

When Hannah and Maria arrived, they saw the men staking out where the house would be built. That night at supper, the talk was about the house. Nate said, "Cody will bring a couple of his men over, and we will get started as soon as we can get the lumber delivered. In the meantime, we will prepare the ground."

Hannah asked, "Do you know how long it will take to build?"

"Once we get the lumber, we could have it built in three weeks," said Milo. "I will go into town tomorrow and order the lumber."

CHAPTER 33

Three weeks after the lumber arrived, the house was built. The wedding was scheduled for the following Saturday. Rosie and Sadie had completed the dresses, and all the guests were notified.

Shellie and Burt were coming, and so were Shellie's parents, Wanda and Albert, and her brother, Josh, and Rebecca with their son and daughter. They all arrived the day before the wedding.

When Wanda and Albert arrived with Shellie's brother and his family, she hit the family with a surprise. Shellie said, "Maria, I don't want to take away from your day, but Burt and I are expecting a baby."

"That is great," said Maria.

Wanda was excited about having another grandchild. Rebecca hugged Shellie and said, "That is great news."

Everyone was busy preparing for the wedding. Millie came out the night before to make the cake. Rosie and Sadie brought the wedding dress and Sadie's bridesmaid dress so they could dress at the ranch.

With the house finished, Maria moved into the house while Billy remained in the bunkhouse. However, that would change after the wedding.

Billy had asked Nate to be his best man, and Nate had accepted, so on the day of the wedding, with everything set, Marshal Tom Sieke came with the news that the reward money would be arriving in two days, and Ike and his men were on their way to Denver and prison.

It seemed that the good news was giving people even more of a reason to celebrate. The guests included Dr. John Selman and his wife, Martha; Arron and Esther Salavan from the mercantile; Millie and Betty from the café; and several of the townspeople. In addition, of course, all the men from the Lazy S and Rocking R ranches were there.

It was eleven o'clock when the wedding started. Billy and Nate were standing with the minister, and the guests were seated with an open aisle between them. Some of the men from the town had brought instruments and were playing music.

Sadie was the first one to walk down the aisle. She moved off to the minister's right when she reached the front. Everyone got quiet when Milo came out with Maria on his arm. As they approached the aisle, everyone stood while they walked to the front. When Milo handed Maria to Billy, he took his seat next to Hannah, and everyone sat down.

The service was focused on Maria and Billy. When the minister said, "I now pronounce you husband and wife," everyone cheered.

With the ceremony over, the women put out the food, and everyone started to eat after congratulating Maria and Billy. When Maria tried to help Hannah, she told her to sit with Billy. "This is your wedding, and we will take care of everything," said Hannah.

With the food on the table, everyone kept looking at Maria and Billy, who looked lost but happy.

Tom asked, "Billy, what is wrong? You look like you just lost your best friend."

"I have never been married before," said Billy. "I guess I am nervous."

Maria wrapped her arms around Billy's arm and said, "You have nothing to worry about. I have never been married before either, but we will learn and be great together."

"Maybe Billy needs a drink," said Emmett. "Getting married can be harder than going after outlaws."

Those who heard Emmett started laughing as Billy's face turned red. Even Maria laughed and said, "I think he is going to find out that being married is easier and not dangerous."

After everyone finished eating, the music started, and people started to dance. While the dancing was going on, Rosie found Shellie and said,

"I heard that you are going to have a baby. Congratulations! I haven't told anyone yet, but Cody and I will also have a baby."

"Congratulations to you and Cody!" said Shellie. "When is your baby due?"

"From what I can tell, I am only two months along," said Rosie.

"I believe you and I will be having our babies about the same time," said Shellie. "I think we should tell Hannah."

Shellie and Rosie found Hannah talking to Esther, Betty, and Millie. When Hannah saw the look on Shellie and Rosie's faces, she asked, "What are you two up to?"

"You know I am going to have a baby," said Shellie. "Well, it looks like Rosie is going to have a baby about the same time as me."

The four women looked at Rosie and together hugged her. "We will have to plan baby showers for both of you," said Esther. "Since Hannah and Milo have moved to Purgatoire Valley, it is starting to grow in a nice way."

"I think we should let all the people know," said Betty. "This is better than just a wedding."

They walked over in front of the band, and Hannah said, "Can I have your attention? I have just discovered that this will be a great day to remember. Not only do we have this great wedding of Maria and Billy to remember, but I have also received word that two additional people will be added to our family in the near future. Most of you have heard that Shellie and Burt will have a baby, but I have just learned that Rosie and Cody will have a baby at about the same time."

Maria got up and said, "That is exciting news. We will always have something special to remember on our anniversary about the announcement of the addition to our family of the Ryder ranch."

As the afternoon went on, the women helped Hannah clean up the dishes and food before they left. It was late when Rosie, Cody, and the men from the Lazy S Ranch left to return home.

With everyone gone, Maria and Billy went to their new home. There they relaxed and got to know each other better.

Milo and Hannah went to their bedroom while getting ready for bed. Hannah said, "We were never able to have children of our own, but I feel that the family we have created is better than if we'd had our own children. I feel that the babies that Shellie and Rosie will have will be like our grandchildren."

Made in the USA
Middletown, DE
09 April 2023